Praise for Mary Wine's Scottish romance

"A wonderful, sensuous, highly charged romance. Cleverly written, totally believable, and nearly impossible to put down."

—*RT Book Reviews,* 4.5 Stars

"One gripping plot twist follows another: dastardly English trickery, complex Scottish alliances, and kilt-tossing, sheet-incinerating lovemaking."

—*Publishers Weekly*

"Whenever I pick up a book by Mary Wine I know I'm going to be engrossed in the story for hours."

—*Night Owl Romance Reviewer* Top Pick

"Love in the Scottish Highlands has never looked so good... Great characters, thrilling drama, and smoldering passion make this a 'must read' novel."

—*Romance Reviews*

"Not to be missed."

—Lora Leigh, *New York Times* #1 bestselling author

"Mary Wine brings history to life with major sizzle factor."

—Lucy Monroe, *USA Today* bestselling author of *For Duty's Sake*

Also by Mary Wine

To Conquer a Highlander

Highland Hellcat

Highland Heat

The Highlander's Prize

A Lady Can Never Be Too Curious

The Trouble with Highlanders

A Captain and a Corset

how to
HANDLE
a HIGHLANDER

MARY WINE

sourcebooks
casablanca

Published by Sourcebooks Casablanca, an imprint of Sourcebooks,
Inc.
P.O. Box 4410, Naperville, Illinois 60567-4410
(630) 961-3900
Fax: (630) 961-2168
www.sourcebooks.com

Printed and bound in the United States of America.
VP 10 9 8 7 6 5 4 3 2 1

This book is for the amazing Kimberly Rocha. She's got the heart of a saint and the spirit of an adventurer. Thanks for all the pep talks and the unwavering belief in my ability to entertain readers. If you haven't met this wonderful gal, go check her out at Book Obsessed Chicks.

One

"Bari Fraser is up to no good," Gahan Sutherland insisted.

His father, Lytge Sutherland, peered at him through narrowed eyes. He was gripping the stem of a silver goblet, turning it slowly as he pondered.

"Now that the snow is melting, Bari will be on the move," Gahan added. He spoke softly, not wanting to sound impatient, although he was.

"That might be so," the earl said, "but you cannae convict a man before he acts. Thinking a thing does nae make a man guilty."

"His sister tried to kill ye," Norris interrupted from where he sat on the other side of his father. "I agree with Gahan—Bari Fraser will use the spring to try and cause trouble."

Gahan locked stares with his brother. Norris was his opposite, with blond hair and green eyes. He kept his chin scraped clean and stood six feet. Gahan's own hair was dark as midnight and his eyes even blacker. They shared a father, though Gahan's mother hadn't had the blessing of the Church. Gahan was a few inches taller than his sibling, and more than one old woman had been heard muttering it was God's way of making sure Lytge Sutherland knew his sins would not be hidden from the sight of the righteous.

Gahan had chuckled at their judgment. His father welcomed him as warmly as he had his legitimate son. That fact was his greatest gift, because it would have been less trouble for the earl to leave Gahan in the village, the way many a nobleman did with his bastards.

There was no hint of jealousy in his sibling's eyes, which was something Gahan treasured. It wasn't often that the legitimate son welcomed a bastard son at his father's table. Even if their sire invited his by-blow to join the family at the high table, the heir often made it clear that competition for their noble parent's good favor wasn't welcome. But the Sutherlands were strong because they were united. In this case, against the young Fraser laird.

"Father, it's imperative that we move our retainers closer to the border," Gahan continued.

"I agree," Norris said. "Even with the hawks to warn us, the snow melts later here than on Fraser land."

The mood in the great hall was subdued. Conversation wasn't flowing along the long trestle tables filling the large space in front of the dais where the high table sat. The Sutherland retainers were doing their best to listen in. The earl frowned and leaned forward to scowl at his clansmen. He thumped his goblet on the table and stood up. The young boy assigned to his cup leaned around him to snatch it up now that it was no longer in his laird's grasp. Gahan found himself watching the drinking vessel to make sure it wasn't unattended. His gut tightened, just a fraction, as he waited for the lad's fingers to close around the silver stem. One careless moment of inattention could—and nearly had—cost his father his life.

Someone moved near the front of the dais, drawing Gahan's attention. His sister-by-marriage climbed the three steps and lowered herself before Lytge. Daphne MacLeod waited only a moment before offering Norris, her husband, a smile, and moving to join him. Her dark eyes sparkled with merriment, and her belly was large and round.

"Agreeing or nae does nae matter," Lytge said firmly. The earl raised his voice so it would carry. "We've had enough of assumptions clouding the thinking of the men inside this hall."

Gahan ground his teeth with frustration but had to agree. Daphne frowned, looking between them as she sat down. Silence hung over the table as she tried to catch the earl's eye and then Gahan's. Gahan reached for his own goblet to avoid her scrutiny. She tapped a single fingernail on the surface of the table impatiently, and Lytge broke.

"'Tis naught to concern yerself with, lass," the earl said.

"If it involves trouble with the Frasers, it concerns me. I find marriage agrees with me, and I am in no hurry to be a widow," Daphne argued. She reached for Norris's hand and clasped it. Gahan stared at the touch, because he was almost certain Daphne had reached for his brother's hand out of instinct.

There was a bond between the pair that intrigued him. Norris was the heir, the legitimate son of the Earl of Sutherland. Daphne was the daughter of a laird. Their match was logical and brought a great deal of gain to the clan. Yet they loved each other. It was evident in every look his brother cast toward his bride. Norris could have had any daughter of any Highland laird, and more than one had tried her luck at snaring his affection.

But they had all been disappointed. And then fate had brought Daphne into his path.

Gahan stood up. He tugged on the corner of his bonnet in respect before leaving the high table. There was a line of maids waiting to serve the table; two of them leaned over to offer him a view of their cleavage. He passed them by without a second glance. Sandra Fraser's face flashed across his memory every time a woman flirted with him now. He saw the calculating gleam in her eyes as she had tried to convince him to turn traitor against his brother. The maids were no different, he thought bitterly; their goal was to use him to better their lot. Most of them wouldn't hesitate to pray for a babe, simply to make sure they had a reason to expect support from him. None of them understood what it was like to be the bastard son. True, his sire had always provided for him, but the gossips had always made sure he knew that support might be ended at any moment. The Church would consider it his lot to endure on his own, since he was born in sin.

"Ye're stewing in dark thoughts again."

"And ye're forgetting that being me man is nae the same as being me brother," Gahan growled at his half-brother Cam. Their common blood came from their mother. Cam was legitimate.

"It's pretty much the same, only our mother is nae here to smack ye on the top of yer hairy head when you growl."

Gahan grinned in spite of his dark mood. "She wielded a spoon like a sword, sure enough." He reached up and rubbed the top of his head. "I was sure I'd have lumps for life."

"Maybe ye do, beneath all that devil-dark hair," Cam suggested playfully. "It's spread to yer face again." He pulled a dirk from the top of his boot. "I can remedy that."

Gahan rubbed the short beard decorating his face. It was groomed to perfection. "It will have grown back in before morning, so save yer effort." To be smooth-faced, he'd have to shave it twice a day. His duties didn't often allow him so much time to devote to vanity.

Dunrobin was a large castle. As Gahan climbed the stairs, he enjoyed stretching his legs on his way to his chamber. On the fourth floor of the second keep, the chamber was spacious, but he still wasn't at ease inside it. As head of Norris's retainers, his duty had been to guard his brother's back. It was something Gahan had never expected to change, but their father had decreed differently. He could not legitimize him, because his mother had died before Norris's, but the earl had recognized Gahan in the Church, in front of the clan. In the Highlands, that was as good as Lytge marrying Gahan's mother posthumously, and that secured Gahan's place in the same instant. Gahan had his own retainers now, and Cam was his captain.

"Ye might at least wipe that scowl off yer face," Cam scolded as he helped Gahan remove his sword. "There are surely more than a few bastards who would like to have their father give them a position that includes fine chambers."

"Aye, I am nae blind to the blessings given to me, but tell me ye are nae feeling stifled inside these walls," Gahan said.

Cam opened his mouth but shut it again without answering. Gahan chuckled and let his brother take his doublet away. Neither of them had been raised to expect more than enough to survive. Lytge's lady wife had not been fond of their common-born mother—or of her sons. While the lady had lived, neither of them had set foot inside Dunrobin.

"Ye seem to have ideas about getting out into the spring weather," Cam stated suggestively. "I believe me duties do include anticipating what ye'd enjoy."

Gahan grinned. "There are times I like hearing that brotherly tone in yer voice."

"Even if it means I know ye too well?"

Gahan rolled his shoulders and popped his neck. "Since ye know me so well, do nae disappoint me by nae being ready at first light."

Cam eyed him suspiciously. "Yer father was very clear."

"Me father is nae finished discussing the topic. He's done only with the part he's willing to let his men hear."

Gahan didn't say any more. He moved to one of the large arched windows. It was set with shutters of glass panes that opened outward. Behind him, he heard Cam leave the chamber and close the door. The sound was still a bit jarring. Outside that door there would be two retainers. As the acknowledged son of the earl, he was never alone. Sandra Fraser had proven just how necessary protection was. Even Cam would not spend the night alone. He'd retire with the other men. Growing up in the village had not prepared Gahan for such a life. His father had seen to his training and moved Gahan into Dunrobin the day after the earl's noble wife had died.

He drew in a deep breath to dispel his discontentment. His life was a fine one. No man went through his days without feeling the weight of his responsibilities on his back. At least no man worthy of respect. He had a place at Dunrobin, and Bari would not find it simple to strike against them.

That was something he was going to make very sure of.

There was a hint of spring in the night breeze. Somewhere there was newly turned earth and trees budding. The moonlight sparkled off snow, but the river was roaring in the distance, proof that the ice was melting and spring was on its way. Behind him the fire in the hearth was burning low. There was plenty of firewood stacked nearby, but he let the flames die. It was not so cold that he needed a fire for warmth, and he enjoyed the darkness.

Morning would come early, but he remained in the window frame, waiting to see if his instincts were right. He heard the scraping of the stone against the floor before turning around to see a section of the wall pushing inward. A figure loomed in the darkness before stepping into the chamber.

"What does Father say?" Gahan asked Norris.

"I'll tell ye meself." His father's voice came from inside the passageway. "As soon as me knees stop complaining about climbing a few stairs."

Lytge Sutherland made his way through the opening in the wall. "I am going to enjoy the spring warmth." He stopped for a moment and considered Gahan. "But I cannae be enjoying the new season if we're feuding."

Gahan grinned. "As I said, I will be happy to address the situation."

"Nae without me, will ye," Norris insisted.

Lytge sat down in a large chair near the hearth. The coals cast a red glow over him. "I did nae always spend so many hours in thought. There was a time when I was young enough to follow me passions." The earl looked at Gahan, and his lips rose into a satisfied grin. "Yer mother was one of those times. If she'd lived longer than me wife, I'd have wed her. Ye should nae have to suffer for me sins. Yet ye are bastard-born because I was young and unruly."

His father was lost in thought for a moment. At last he drew in a stiff breath and focused.

"I've heard rumor that Bari Fraser is making visits to the Matheson. Faolan Chisholms sent word of it. Achaius is bitter over the defeat at Sauchieburn, and his sons are being kept at Court by Lord Home to make sure the Matheson clan is loyal to the new king."

Gahan snarled, but his father raised his hand.

"I am as suspicious as ye are, most likely more so, for I've known Achaius Matheson longer than ye. He is nae a man to be trusted, but he will say the same of me, for I supported the young prince over his father."

"James III was nae worthy of the crown," Gahan growled.

"Highlanders do nae follow blindly," Lytge agreed, "which is what makes Achaius a dangerous man. If he thinks Bari Fraser has a just cause, the man might just be willing to meet his end on one last, glorious charge into battle. He'll nae stop to consider the lads who will die along with him, or that those who survive will carry on a feud in his name."

"We'll ride out at first light," Norris decided.

"Ye'll be staying here," the earl countered. "If ye ride out, the rest of the Highlands will hear we're feuding, and the fact that we have nae said a word about it will nae matter. Some will think to join us while the rest take advantage of our being distracted. I need ye here to maintain order. As heir, it's yer place to see to Sutherland land first. Gahan will ride for Chisholms land."

"At first light," Gahan confirmed.

Lytge pointed at him. "Carefully, lad. Sutherland was nae built on bursts of passion but on careful thinking. I may nae have cared for the number of times me own father jerked me back into line, but I see the wisdom of it. Ye'll go because it will give the gossips something else to ponder besides whom we may or may nae have a reason to feud with."

There was a hint of something in his father's tone that challenged Gahan to think on just what else his sire had in mind. A laird had to be sharp-witted if he wanted to be victorious.

"They'll wonder if ye've sent me off because Daphne is making ready to present Norris with an heir, and ye no longer need me to safeguard the family line."

The earl slapped his leg. "Ye're sharp as a whip." He chuckled. "Aye, they will be thinking I am making ready to be done with ye since the bloodline is now secure. Ye'll have to play the part of being unsure of yer future."

"Which just might gain me a welcome from Achaius Matheson," Gahan added.

"Brilliant," Norris agreed.

"Make sure ye take four hawks, and never let yer guard down. Bari wants vengeance, and that's a fact."

"He's nae the only one," Gahan muttered.

Lytge stood. He paused in front of Gahan and reached up to clasp his shoulder. The earl was not a small man, but Gahan still looked down on him. Gahan was grateful for the low light in the chamber, because for just a moment, his eyes glistened as his sire's strong grip sent a surge of emotion through him.

"I'll do ye proud, Father."

"Ye'll do Sutherland proud," Lytge told him in a rough voice. "Ye are more than me son. Ye are a laird of Sutherland. Do nae listen to the gossips. Ye have a place here now and always. So kindly do nae let that bastard Bari Fraser slit yer throat. The man no doubt thinks it his right. I'm right glad Norris did nae wed any of that blood. It's tainted with insanity."

Seabhac Tower, Fraser land

The snow was melting.

Moira felt the sun chasing the chill from her nose

for the first time in weeks. Seabhac was set against the shadow of the mountains. The stone of the three keeps was dark, and when the days were short, it sometimes felt like night lasted too long. But the mews were built facing the valley. The hawks needed the light. The long building that housed the raptors was constructed on the ground, but she didn't mind the number of stone steps needed to reach them. Among the perches, she might at last be free from her half brother's attention.

She smiled, amused by her thoughts. Freedom was not something she had ever enjoyed. Her half brother, Bari, was laird, and he'd always kept her on a short leash. Even a half sister was expected to learn how to run the castle, in case he ever wanted to use her to secure an alliance through marriage. A laird negotiated for a bride who could keep the estate books and run his home. The skills were many and often frustrating to learn, but she admitted to enjoying the challenge. She doubted her laird and half sibling would like it if she ever confessed that to him. Bari did enjoy thinking he was pressing her into submission.

At least Sandra was gone. No matter how unchristian it was, more than one Fraser was relieved to be rid of the spiteful redhead. Sandra had been a demanding mistress, quick to remind one and all that she was the full-blooded sibling of the laird and she would someday wed well. Moira had served the high table as a reminder that she had common blood in her veins, even if she was legitimate. Sandra's mother had been a blue-blood, and she made sure everyone knew it. She expected to hook herself a noble husband, preferably one with a title and enough gold to ensure Sandra never had to do anything more than enjoy herself. There had been no challenging moments of ensuring the castle was running smoothly for Sandra. She had never concerned herself with making sure every inhabitant was provided for as the traditions of the Highlands demanded. Instead, there had been intrigue and schemes. Sandra enjoyed Court, often demanding money from the household accounts to fund her newest gowns. Moira's own clothing was worn and tattered from Sandra's excesses because there had been little coin left after Sandra was satisfied.

Sandra's ambition had been the end of her.

For a moment, Moira was caught in the grip of lament, but it wasn't truly sadness over Sandra's death. It was more of a feeling of pity for the way Sandra had wasted her life. She had left nothing but scandal and hardship behind. Moira found herself happy to wear her worn dress, because at least she'd come by the tattered hem honestly. No one would speak ill of her when fate decided her days were over.

There were more than a dozen hawks waiting for her attention in the mews. They flexed their wings and twisted their heads, using their sharp beaks to tend to their feathers. Each wore a hawk's hood, but they could sense the sunlight. They heard her steps, and several cried out, eager to be chosen for the first hunt of the day. Moira stopped in front of a hawk and stroked its back. She removed its hood. She cooed softly to it as she cleaned around its perch. The raptor watched her with keen eyes, and she kept her motions slow to avoid startling it.

"There ye are," said a familiar voice.

The raptor let out a shrill cry and flapped angrily. Bari's head of house froze instantly, her eyes rounding.

Moira cooed to the bird. The hawk kept its head turned, one eye on the housekeeper.

"Ye have an amazing way with the birds," Alba observed.

Moira shot her a grin. No matter how much of a sin pride was, she was proud of her feathered babies. "I raised Athena from a hatchling after her mother died."

"Aye, ye did, and I recall more than one man saying it was best to just give her a quick end." Alba twisted part of her skirt, her expression one of contemplation. At last she nodded. "I've come to fetch ye up to the keep. The laird is asking for ye."

There was the firm ring of duty in Alba's voice, and her expression was guarded. She looked away when Moira tried to catch her eye.

Moira's belly twisted, which irritated her. Her half brother, Laird Bari Fraser, was not going to frighten her. He wielded the authority of the lairdship like a whip over every person wearing the Fraser colors, but she had decided long ago that she would not be afraid of him.

Apprehensive, perhaps, she admitted.

She made her hands stop shaking. The hawks' perch was on the far side of the tower. Moira tried not to let her belly twist again because Alba was following her. There was only one reason the head of house would be walking behind her, and that was because Bari had ordered the woman to make sure Moira made an appearance.

Whatever her brother wanted to say to her, it wasn't going to be pleasing.

Seabhac Tower was comprised of three keeps. There was only a small courtyard between them, so it took her little time to make it to the steps of the newest keep. The stone was dark and still cold from the night. The keep rose three full stories into the sky, but only the top story was being kissed by the morning light. The rest would be in the shadow of the mountains for another few hours.

The air was chilly inside, and the scent of smoke tickled her nose. Bari was in the hall, sitting at the high table. The hall wasn't really big enough for the raised platform, but her brother had insisted on it being built. The dais for only the laird's table now took up a quarter of the hall's floor space.

Her father had never seen the need for such a display. Her half brother, on the other hand, sat smugly at his high table while she made her way down the center aisle. She stopped and lowered herself. A tingle traveled along her skin when she noticed there were more than a few retainers standing nearby. They watched her intently, as if they expected her to bolt.

"Rise," Bari instructed.

Straightening up allowed her to see more. Moira's throat felt like it was closing up, but she swallowed and looked her brother straight in the eye. Better to face him with courage.

"Are you suffering yer woman's curse?" he asked bluntly.

Her cheeks heated, and she looked away out of surprise. To have any male ask such a question was intrusive. Only a husband had the right to know such a thing.

Husband…Bari had been threatening to find her one for a while. She stiffened and looked back at her brother, her teeth grinding as her temper flared.

"I am yer laird. Answer me."

She slowly shook her head.

"Pack her things. We leave within the hour."

Bari stood up, and his men shifted. Alba had lowered herself in deference to the command from her laird. Moira turned one way and then the other, watching everyone moving as though they understood perfectly what was happening, while she was left in bewilderment.

"Where am I going?"

Bari had already reached the edge of the platform. He looked back at her, his lips twisted with displeasure.

"Ye know yer place, Moira, and I promise ye that Laird Matheson will expect ye to remember to keep yer mouth shut unless ye are asked a question."

Her brother's voice echoed between the stone walls of the hall. Alba grabbed her arm and tried to pull her away, but Moira resisted.

"Ye haven't told me my purpose." Her brother always had something in mind when he made decisions. She'd learned long ago how to pry information from his lips. All she needed to do was allow him to think she wanted to do her duty.

Bari paused and played right into her hands.

"Yer purpose is to wed Achaius Matheson. I need the Matheson clan to help me win vengeance for Sandra." Bari descended from the platform and walked toward her. He studied her face for a long moment. She honestly couldn't recall the last time he'd looked at her so directly. "Ye're no beauty, but ye'll do. Ye will be his fourth bride. The last one died in child-birth. The man may be old, but he seems to still have a taste for a warm bed."

Moira gasped, and Bari laughed at her horror. "Aye, ye heard me right. 'Tis old Laird Matheson ye're set to wed. Both of his sons have been called to Court. It seems the young king wants to make sure of their loyalty. It's left Achaius alone, and he does nae like having his family questioned by those in Edinburgh."

"The Sutherlands are in good standing with the king," she warned.

Bari's face darkened. He lifted his hand but didn't deliver the blow. "Ye're lucky Achaius wants to enjoy ye as soon as possible. He's paid off the Church to allow him to wed ye before the week's end. Otherwise, I'd darken yer cheek."

Alba was tugging on her arm again, but Moira wasn't willing to give up. Desperation was clawing at her. "The Sutherlands are nae weak. Even with the Mathesons with ye, it will nae go well."

"I told ye to make ready. Me word is given on the match, and that's nae just the word of yer brother, it's the promise of yer laird. Ye will wed Achaius Matheson." He looked at the men lingering in the hall. "Make sure she's ready."

She heard their steps on the floor and felt them closing in on her. Alba's grip became painful, and Moira stopped resisting. There was no point. Bari ruled absolutely on Fraser land.

But the thought that Highland lairds usually did brought her little consolation or made forgiving Bari any easier.

❧

"Hurry…Hurry…We must…"

Alba paused and cleared her throat as several maids scrambled to stuff Moira's meager belongings into leather bags. Two retainers had delivered one of Sandra's old trunks, but after another man had snapped that the laird would be riding fast, it was only half-full and sat abandoned with its lid open. There would be no cart for the trunk.

"'Tis such a shame ye'll nae be able to take all this finery." Alba still sounded as though she might begin weeping.

"It was nae mine and should stay," Moira assured her.

Alba looked up at her. "Laird Matheson will be expecting ye to arrive with a suitable wardrobe."

"It seems me laird is nae very worried about what I shall be taking with me," Moira said softly. "All that pile of silk does is remind me of how many are in need of winter boots because of the coin paid for those Court fashions." Her own toes felt like they were still frozen, because she had on only a pair of shoes. But the stable boys needed boots before she did.

"That is a solid truth," Alba agreed. "A shameful one at that. Yer father would nae have allowed it. He was a man of honor. A true Highlander."

Moira gave her hair a final pass with a comb, then began braiding it. She made the plait tight, because she had no idea how long it would be before she might attend to her grooming again. Her chamber was on the ground floor, and she could hear the horses being brought out into the yard. Above her chamber, she could hear the hawks, and the sound of her babies screeching threatened to make her weep. "Bari is concerned only about how quickly I shall be ready to depart."

She spoke firmly, trying to steady herself. She had never been off Fraser land but had to accept that she was leaving. Only children cried over such unchangeable facts of life.

"Aye, and that is a shame. He should have given thought to making sure ye'd arrive as a bride should. A thought for how the Fraser name will be spoken when ye arrive in rags like a servant. There should be a trousseau, or at the least a wedding dress."

Alba brought her a cap made of fine linen. It was made to cover her hair and keep the wind from tearing at it. Once tied beneath her chin, only a thin line of her blond hair peeked out. Alba returned to the trunk and searched through it. With a soft grunt, she tugged a bundle free from near the bottom.

"Yer sister would never have worn this." The older woman spoke with a tone rich in reprimand. "It is far too practical, since it is wool, but it is a pretty color. Green befits a bride."

There was no way to tell what shape the dress was because it was bundled and tied with a ribbon. Alba pushed it into the single sack Moira was allowed to take.

"At least ye shall nae have to be a wife for long. Laird Matheson is very old."

There was kindness in Alba's voice. When Moira

looked at the woman, she saw a wealth of experience in her eyes. "It's nae as though ye ever thought to have any say in who ye wed."

"Nay," Moira agreed. Of course not. That would have been foolish and guaranteed to bring her nothing but grief. Even a half sister of the laird knew her place was to secure alliances for her clan.

"How old are ye?" Alba asked, slightly embarrassed by her lack of knowledge. Sandra's birthdays had seen lavish suppers, with jugglers and musicians brought in especially for the event, but there had never been any fuss over Moira.

"Twenty-two, and before ye ask, I understand what me duties will be as a wife."

Alba nodded, her relief obvious. She glanced at the half-full trunk and surprised Moira by smiling approvingly.

"All of that fine cloth never made a bit of difference on how rotten the woman wearing it was."

Never once had Moira heard any member of the house staff speak against their mistress. Now the chamber was heavy with emotion as the maids all froze, their attention on their head of house.

"Even in death, she's still bringing trouble." Alba reached for Moira's hand and clasped it firmly. "Perhaps yer brother has never treated ye as the mistress, but ye are the daughter of the laird I served faithfully. Ye have put the members of this household above yer own comfort. We are yer clanswomen, and I'm asking ye, one woman to another, to do yer best to keep peace. For our sake."

There was pleading in the older woman's voice, and the other maids reached for her too. She'd never felt so much responsibility before, never seen so many looking to her for assistance.

"I do nae know what I can do."

"A man who has a bride happy to welcome him often finds reasons to delay leaving his keep," Alba suggested in a low tone. "He'll have ye either way, but if ye make him think ye enjoy his company, he may nae be so willing to join yer brother in battle."

Alba's eyes were bright with unshed tears, and all around her, the other women began to nod. Moira's life had never been full of unkindness, but she realized that she had never had the opportunity to help others. Not in such a large way.

The desire to make such a difference for her friends and kin grew quickly. It burned away the reluctance that had been fueling her anger.

"I will try. I promise ye I will try very hard."

Alba smiled. Moira's hands trembled, then Alba patted the top of Moira's hand. The tension in the room broke, and Moira smiled.

Aye, she would indeed do her duty and give her marriage her best effort.

Bari just might not get the feud he was hoping for.

❧

"Ye did nae ask permission to take that hawk."

Moira walked toward Bari as she left Seabhac Keep for the last time. Athena was perched on her wrist, a thick leather gauntlet protecting her skin. There was a small perch attached to the front of her saddle for the hawk. Once the raptor was more at ease with being on the horse, she would rest her arm.

"I raised Athena."

"Yer duty was to look after the hawks. That one is no different than the others."

Moira stroked Athena's feathers gently. "She is different, for her mother died, and she would have too if I had nae taken pity on her."

Her brother scowled at her. "I recognize no difference. Yer time belongs to me."

"Yet there are differences that ye have no control over." A retainer held the mare waiting for her, and she took the hand offered to her to mount. Athena shifted, raising her wings and crying in warning, then settled down as Moira gained the saddle.

"What do ye mean by that?" Bari demanded.

Moira surprised him by smiling. "Ye might order me to wed and have yer retainers ensure that I arrive on Matheson land, but when the wedding chamber doors are closed, only I will have the power to control me actions." She fluttered her eyelashes. "I wonder how pleased Laird Matheson will be with a weeping bride?"

Bari's complexion darkened. "Ye'll do no such thing."

Moira stroked Athena's back again. Her laird and half brother snorted.

"Take the bird. At least Matheson will nae be able to claim I sent ye with naught."

Her brother urged his stallion forward, leaving her behind. Alba stood at the top of the keep's steps, watching her with a gleam in her eyes that looked something like approval. It was a small thing, and yet, a victory for Moira.

"We've land to cross!" Bari ordered. "And a wedding to witness."

He never looked back at her. The lack of any sort of compassion from her sibling made it easy to ride through the gate and away from Seabhac Tower. She wouldn't call it home; no, she would not. She had friends there but no family, and it was family that made a place a home.

Maybe she'd find it on Matheson land.

Her confidence wasn't strong enough to shield her from doubting it. She searched her memories, trying to think of any tales she'd heard of Achaius Matheson, but there were none. If he was a monster, there would be rumors. At least that was what she tried to convince herself of.

But she'd be lying if she said she was completely at ease.

❦

"Well now, it seems the Frasers are out to enjoy the spring weather," Cam muttered.

Gahan held up his hand to shade his eyes and watched the column of Fraser retainers. One man carried a pole with the Fraser laird's pennant fluttering atop it. "Bari is with them as well."

Temptation was toying with him. It took all of Gahan's control not to order his men to sweep down into the valley and claim the vengeance he craved. His hands tightened on his reins until his stallion snorted because he was pulling so hard on the bit. He eased his grip and scanned the Frasers once more. Something caught his eye, and he focused on it.

"They're riding with a woman," Gahan said.

Cam lowered his spyglass and looked at Gahan. "That might be bad news."

"Or the evidence we need to prove Bari is making trouble," Gahan replied. "The man has a half sister, and he's heading toward Matheson land."

"Did nae Matheson's wife die during the winter?"

Gahan nodded. "I believe it would only be fitting to make sure a member of the Sutherland family is present at the wedding of a vassal laird."

"I'm sure the earl would agree," Cam offered. "But ye cannae stop Bari from contracting his sister."

Gahan put his spyglass back into the pocket on his saddle. It was a costly item not easily replaced. He made sure the pouch was tied closed, but the time needed to do so frustrated him. There was a sense of urgency riding him that was hard to control.

But only a lad went off without thinking, or a fool who didn't care if the Frasers ended up with the right to start a feud with his father. The king was a boy, who took a great deal of advice from Lord Home. Home was a man who understood how to manage power, and he'd be happy to see Sutherland weakened by feuding with vassal clans, because it would make the king that much more powerful.

Which left Gahan with the very difficult challenge of trying to find a way to keep Bari Fraser from wedding his half sister to Achaius Matheson and forming an alliance.

He grinned as he leaned over his horse's neck and gave the powerful animal his freedom. There was nothing he loved better than a challenge. Especially if it meant gaining the opportunity to snatch something Bari Fraser wanted from his grasp.

Two

Matheson Tower

TO MOIRA'S EYES, MATHESON TOWER WAS MORE impressive than Seabhac.

There were three main towers with thick curtain walls connecting them. Several cannon were set into the walls, and as they rode closer, the sound of construction drifted on the evening breeze. A bell began ringing up in one of the lookout towers. Soon more joined until all the bells were ringing. Men leaned out of the archer holes along the top of the wall to see who was approaching. There was a groan as the two men posted above the heavy iron gate unlocked it in case they were given the order to lower it.

Bari never slowed. He continued on and rode through the open gate without any resistance. By the time they made it to the inner yard, many of the Mathesons had come out to watch the visitors arriving. The women hung back but watched Moira intently. The Matheson retainers nodded, obviously expecting them.

"Where is she?"

Achaius Matheson still possessed a booming voice. She heard him before the laird made it out of the main keep. His men parted as he made his way to the top step. His hair was gray—at least what there was of it. Deep wrinkles covered his face, and a stringy beard covered his chin and neck.

"Where is me bride?" he demanded. "Get the lass closer, so I can see her."

The Matheson retainers moved instantly. Moira's mare sidestepped nervously as they closed in. For a moment, every muscle in her body tightened. Panic gripped her, and Athena flapped her wings as she felt the unease of her handler. The hawk's hard feathers cut at her face. Moira regained her composure as she soothed the bird. She let the bird climb off the saddle perch and onto her arm. Athena let out a shrill cry before settling down again.

"So ye have a way with hawks?" Achaius said, his voice cracking a little.

"Me sister is an expert in raising and training hawks," Bari said.

Moira ignored the hands offered to her and dismounted. Her skirts fluttered into place, and her feet ached as they took her weight for the first time in hours. Her hips were stiff and her mouth dry as bone because Bari had pushed them hard to make the distance before nightfall.

"I've lads aplenty to see to hawks. I crave a wife who knows how to soothe a man when his blood is up. Now get the lass up here where I can see her."

Her belly twisted with nervous fear, but there was

no refusing. Her only choice was to walk up the steps or be pushed up them by the Matheson retainers. She ordered herself to do it. Alba was relying on her. A retainer moved closer to her, tugging on his cap before offering his arm for Athena. At least it gave her a moment to compose herself as she handed the raptor off.

Achaius waited for her with a grin that displayed his rotten teeth. At least her feet stopped hurting by the time she made it to the top of the steps.

"Closer, lass."

She held her chin steady and moved closer. He chuckled softly, then boldly reached out to cup her breast.

"What are ye doing?" The words were out of her mouth before she could think about it. She jumped back and collided with one of the Matheson men. The man hooked her under her arms and set her back in front of his laird like a supper plate. Shock filled her as Achaius reached for her breast once more. She was trapped, but what bothered her most was the sting of tears in her eyes.

She would not cry. No, she would not.

"Nice and plump…" Achaius cooed. "Turn around."

The retainer behind her didn't wait to see if she'd comply. He hooked her bicep and spun her around for his laird's pleasure. Try as she might, her eyes still widened when Achaius boldly patted her bottom in full view of all. The Matheson retainer in front of her stared right past her, his face set in a bored expression.

Obviously she was not the first bride to be welcomed in such a manner.

A strong voice rang out from below. "Laird Matheson, are ye greeting a bride or inspecting a mare?"

Whoever the newcomer was, the Matheson retainers responded to him. The ones crowding her close to Achaius moved away, suddenly torn between their laird's wishes and whoever had spoken.

Achaius snorted. "A wife is meant to be ridden, is she nae?" He turned and stumbled. His men were quick to right their laird, proving they were accustomed to his lack of balance. "Mind yer tongue, Gahan Sutherland. Being Sutherland's son means ye have the right to witness me wedding, but ye're still bastard-born and have no say over how I welcome me bride. I like to know what I'm getting before I let them inside to sup at me table."

"What in hell is he doing here?" Bari demanded.

Achaius let out a growl. "Ye'll mind yer place as well, Bari Fraser. This is Matheson land—my land—and whoever is on it is here by my say so."

Achaius grumbled as he stumbled back through the open doors. His men followed, granting Moira some relief. It was short-lived though, as Gahan stepped toward Bari. Her brother wasn't small, but Gahan was a huge man. He had devil-dark hair and wide shoulders packed with hard muscle. The man didn't seem to feel the chill in the air; his shirt sleeves were rolled up and tied at the shoulders, the muscles along his arms clearly on display.

She was no stranger to listening to Bari proclaim his position, but this man radiated authority. It surrounded him so thickly she would have sworn she could taste it. Gahan glanced at her, and for a moment she was transfixed. It was the briefest moment, yet she felt as if the man looked straight into her soul. Sensation rippled along her skin in response.

"Ye seem to have forgotten to tell me father that ye had contracted yer sister to Matheson." Gahan's voice was smooth and even, but there was a core of solid steel in it too.

"After ye allowed Sandra to die on yer land?"

Gahan crossed his arms over his chest. "That bitch poisoned me father. Either confess ye knew her plan or condemn her as a murderess."

"I will nae—" Bari shut his mouth so hard his teeth clicked.

"Will nae what?" Gahan pressed. He took another step toward Bari.

"Discuss it with ye."

Gahan and the other Sutherland retainers were not satisfied with his answer. They pressed forward. Bari suddenly reached for Moira, his fingers biting into her bicep as he dragged her up beside him.

"Moira is me half sister, and her mother was common-born. Something ye should know a bit about, bastard."

"I know a thing or two about it," Gahan agreed as he reached out and captured her other bicep. Unlike her brother's grip, his didn't hurt, but it was firm and unbreakable. "And I know what a man looks like when he's hiding behind a woman."

Gahan set her behind him in a swift motion. In the same instant, his other hand captured Bari's wrist and twisted it upward. Moira stumbled into Gahan's men, who parted to allow her through, then closed ranks behind their laird once again. She ended up in the doorway of the keep.

"Nae that I should be surprised. Ye let Sandra stand in front of ye as well."

Bari shouted, "I'm escorting Moira to her groom. It's a good match, better than her common birth deserves."

"And why are ye in a hurry to celebrate this wedding?"

"It's spring," Bari said. "If Matheson made ye welcome, it's his business. But me sister is going to wed him."

Bari stormed through the Sutherland retainers and renewed his grip on her arm. As he pulled her into the keep, she looked back. She really shouldn't have but couldn't seem to control her impulses. Gahan Sutherland was watching her, his black eyes glittering. She stared at him, astounded that she hadn't heard even a hint of rage in his voice. His strength was more than flesh; it was there inside him too. The man didn't need to raise his voice to make sure everyone knew how immovable his opinion was. There was an intensity that radiated off him. Even separated by several feet, she felt it. A curious sensation raced through her, leaving her breathless. When she looked forward again, her cheeks were warm with a blush—which was very bad. Because if there was one thing she didn't need, it was to be blushing over Gahan Sutherland.

She was set to wed another man.

❧

"Ye handled that well," Cam muttered with a good dose of sarcasm.

"I did nae kill him," Gahan replied. "All in all, I agree with ye."

Cam gave him a raised eyebrow in response but Gahan wasn't in the mood to banter with his sibling. "He's up to no good."

"Aye," Cam agreed. "Yer suspicions are proving true. The cook is busy preparing a feast for tonight."

"Tonight?"

"Aye," Cam confirmed. "Bari is a hard man to be sending his sister to such an old man's bed."

"She might be in agreement. Sandra was nae innocent of scheming. As a common-born daughter, she would do well wedding herself to a laird."

But there had still been something about her that seemed out of place, if indeed she was in agreement with her brother's schemes. There had been no bright smile on her face, only a solid look of determination.

Gahan shook off his suspicions. The lass was set to do what her brother wanted, no matter her horror over the groom. He needed to listen to his gut instinct. Moira was kin to Sandra; that made her a master of deceit. She was using Achaius as much as the old man was planning on using her young flesh. It shouldn't sicken him. At least not beyond the pure callous nature of it.

But it did.

❧

"I do nae like him here," Bari complained.

"Well, there is naught ye can do. The man is me overlord. Yers too," Achaius groused. "I do nae know how he learned of the wedding, but it does nae matter.

I cannae tell him to leave unless ye want him to know we plan to unite our clans against his father. He has the right, as me overlord's son, to witness the wedding. The union will be stronger for it too."

"Then let's get the vows spoken."

Achaius shook his head. "Nae until I have the dowry."

"I brought it," Bari snapped.

"Me secretary is still drawing up the contracts. Until ye sign them, the dowry is nae complete because of the land ye promised. Ye cannae claim to have that in yer hand."

Bari slammed his mug down on the table. The door opened as one of the Matheson retainers looked into his laird's private chamber to investigate the sound. Achaius gave the man a wave of his old hand, and the door shut again.

"Do nae make the mistake of thinking me a fool, lad." Achaius was stopped by a coughing fit. It racked his body for several long moments before he cleared his throat. "Every bride I've wed increased the Matheson land. Yer sister will be no exception. Land is better than gold, because when ye have land, it can be farmed and the crops sold. Land is a man's true wealth. I'll see the papers signed and witnessed before there is any visit to the church."

"If that was yer feeling, ye had some nerve handling her so publicly."

"I've got nerve aplenty, lad, which is why ye're sitting here. For all yer words of how worthless yer sister is, she's something I want, and ye know it."

"Half sister," Bari corrected. "Her mother was me father's second wife. A common-born woman."

"Ah, yes. Ye see? Yer father knew the value of wedding, and I bet his second wife brought gold or silver with her since she did nae have a claim to a fine family." Achaius took a swig from his mug and smiled as he swallowed. "Now Sandra was a fine bit of woman. I'd have enjoyed spreading her out in me bed." He reached down and rubbed his crotch. "I'm hard just thinking about it."

Bari snarled, and Achaius chuckled.

"Was she meant for better men than me?" He leaned forward. "Do ye think I do nae know ye would never have offered her to me?"

"Sandra was a rare beauty."

"And a conniving bitch." Achaius pounded a fist on the table. "Better ye understand, lad, I'll be the master here."

Bari set his mug down. "Maybe I should take me offer and go, because ye promised ye'd ride out against the Sutherlands with me in exchange for me sister. It seems all ye are interested in at the moment is fucking and collecting land from me."

"Until I have the contracts signed and sealed, that is all I'm interested in. I agreed to the match and yer terms of riding against the Sutherlands in exchange for the land ye agreed to settle on Moira. Money a man can make, but land, well, that is something they do nae make any more of. That's what set yer sister above the other lasses I might have chosen. Ye are nae the only man who knows me retainers are the best and plentiful."

"Then we're still agreed. Let's get the vows spoken," Bari pressed.

Laird Matheson held up his hand as Bari stood up. "Tomorrow will be soon enough. Yer sister will have less fight in her after a sleepless night."

"She'll do her duty," Bari promised.

"She nearly retched upon me boots when she got a good look at me, lad!" He laughed good and long but dissolved into a coughing fit. "Nae that I care. She'll settle in, and it will be me pleasure to break her to ride. But ye'll mind me, lad, on the matter of Gahan Sutherland. There will be no poisoning beneath me roof. I've enough trouble with the king."

"Does it matter how he dies?"

"Aye, lad, it does. I'm a Highlander, even if age has had her way with me. The Matheson will ride out with ye because it will increase our lands. Until then, me overlord's son is welcome here."

"His bastard, ye mean," Bari grumbled.

"But one the earl acknowledges. That makes all the difference, and ye know it," Achaius insisted. "When ye add in the fact that the earl has only the one legitimate son, well now, his bastard becomes even more important. Especially when there seem to be no others. I hear Norris has no children either. The Sutherland blood is getting thin, it seems. He would nae be the first bastard getting a title in the Highlands. Besides, it will be good to have the union witnessed. The earl will nae argue if his own son was here and did nae stop it from happening."

Bari nodded. "True. Since ye are planning to keep me here, I hope yer maids are friendly."

Achaius waved him toward the door and reached for his mug again. He really was ancient-looking, but

Bari didn't bother concerning himself with that. He was laird of the Matheson, and that was what interested him. Sisters were meant to be used to further the clan's interest.

Even Sandra had known that.

ᵈ⤳

No one seemed to want to deal with her. Moira reluctantly watched the man holding Athena take the bird off to the yard. She had to curtail the impulse to keep the hawk with her. Just because she longed for companionship didn't mean she had the right to deprive Athena of supper.

But no one else came near her. Moira stood in the hallway. Through an arched doorway she could see the Great Hall filled with tables and benches. Women were busy setting out baskets of bread for the evening meal. They stole peeks at her, but no one invited her in. Since she was to wed the laird, she really didn't need an invitation, but it felt wrong to enter where she had not been bidden.

She sighed and chastised herself. Her current lack of courage wouldn't do. Respect was earned. At least true respect was, and she wasn't interested in the false sort that she'd witnessed Sandra getting.

Moira shifted away from the great hall, walking slowly down the hallway to get a look at her new home. To begin with, she'd get a sense of where things were. The light was dim now and the shadows growing deeper. The lamps in the passageways were not yet lit, but the window shutters were still open to let the fresh air in.

"Inspecting yer new possession?"

She recognized Gahan's voice instantly. It was slightly unnerving how swiftly she identified him.

"Yer sister would have found it beneath her," he added.

Gahan parted from the shadow of a doorway. The hall was farther behind her than she'd realized; the setting of the supper table was now only a dim buzz. A strange twist of excitement went through her belly, startling her. But it also left a bitter taste in her mouth, because she realized she preferred Gahan to her groom.

It was knowledge she could have done well without.

"Nae that I'd expect any less of any woman wedding such an old man," Gahan informed her.

His tone was condescending at best, and it irritated her. He was her better. The fine weave of his kilt and the silver buttons running up the sides of his knee-high boots showed off just how much his father gave him. She should have kept her mouth shut, but her pride flared up and she propped her hand onto her hip.

"And will yer father give ye any choice when he contracts a bride for ye?" she questioned boldly. "Or will ye turn yer nose up no matter who is depending upon ye to do yer duty? Like a spoiled child who knows naught of the way alliances keep a clan safe?"

His eyes narrowed. For a moment, it looked like he was considering what she said, almost as if she'd surprised him somehow.

"Nae if me duty includes making sure me kin can start a feud."

"I have no such desire." She shouldn't snap at

him but just couldn't squelch the urge. "A contented man"—she had to stop to swallow the lump lodged in her throat—"is happy to stay at home."

He studied her for a long moment, one that felt far longer than it really could have been. She felt like he was looking at her thoughts, his gaze cutting past her realistic reasons, to see her true feelings.

"So what is it that draws ye to a man old enough to be yer grandfather? The title? I suppose I can believe that. Yer sister was certainly enchanted by titles."

"Half sister." She paused, realizing that what Bari had so often used to insult her was something she prided herself on.

"And I'm bastard-born," he replied softly. "Which changes nothing when it comes to me loyalties. Or, I doubt, yers."

He was trying to intimidate her, but instead, his words somehow impressed her. There was something in his dark eyes that intrigued her, and she stared into the dark orbs, trying to decipher it.

He snorted at her. "Do nae try it."

"Try what?"

He crossed his arms over his chest, and she suddenly realized just how close he was. There was no more than a pace between them now, and she jumped back, colliding with the hard stone of the wall. His lips twitched.

"I admit, ye play the innocent better than Sandra ever did, but ye'll nae find it simple to seduce me."

She straightened up, stepping away from the wall as her temper simmered. "Ye have no right to accuse me of nae being innocent. Or of trying to act like a harlot. Ye were the one waiting in the shadows."

His lips parted to flash his teeth at her. "I knew ye had claws. Ye are a Fraser after all."

There was a ring of triumph in his tone, which irritated her beyond every bit of self-discipline she had.

"What I have is the sense to know when I'm hearing naught but drivel. Son of an earl or nae, ye do nae have the right to insult me for obeying me laird. I do nae need the Matheson thinking I turned up me nose at their laird. Marriage is for forming alliances. I'm nae so selfish as to think an insult to a laird, like refusing his offer, will nae become a festering point of contention."

But her voice lowered as she finished, and she had to push the last sentence past her lips because she just didn't want to believe she was one day away from having to wed Achaius Matheson.

"And I was nae trying to seduce ye," she added.

His grin remained arrogant and large, but he opened his arms, offering her a view of just how wide his chest was. "Ye were looking into me eyes."

"And ye were looking into mine," she countered. He was suddenly too large and the hallway far too compact to suit her. "Enough arrogance. Perhaps ye are accustomed to only the sort of women who like to seduce, but I am nae of that sort. I'm set to wed, and I do nae think it wise to be standing here acting like—"

"Like lovers flirting in the night shadows?"

His voice dipped low and sent a tingle along her limbs. There was a gleam of mischief in his dark eyes.

She shook her head, her tongue feeling frozen with shock.

"Nay, we are nae acting like lovers, or are ye

arguing that we are nae lovers—yet?" He pressed forward another few inches.

Something snapped inside her. She gasped and went to shove him away from her.

"Ye obnoxious lout!"

She flattened her hands against his chest, but he didn't budge. She'd used a fair amount of strength, but Gahan Sutherland only chuckled at her attempt to move him.

"Ye have no right to accuse me of such indecent things. Maybe there are plenty who would remind me that ye're me better and can say what ye will, but I will do me duty."

He closed his hands around hers, but he didn't remove them from his chest. Instead, he trapped her there with her hands upon him.

"What if I told ye I would nae be opposed to becoming yer lover? I promise ye will find me bed more to yer liking."

Her mouth dropped open, and her temper exploded. She never really thought about what she was doing; her body simply refused to remain still. With a snarl, she sent her knee toward his unprotected groin. One moment he was chuckling at her, and the next, she felt her blow connecting. Pain flashed across his face as he whipped into action. She was free in a moment, but his hand rose into position to deliver a strike to her jaw.

"I'm looking into yer eyes sure enough, Gahan Sutherland…"

She realized she'd never really seen his emotions, because his face became a mask of fury now, yet it was mixed with self-loathing. He lowered his fist and sucked in a deep breath.

"I would nae have hit ye. Me hand went up out of reflex. Ye have to expect that when ye deliver such a low blow to a man."

She believed him, which was foolish, because men didn't suffer the sort of thing she'd done to him well. Especially one of noble blood like him. He might have her lashed, but even that knowledge didn't keep her silent.

"Ye should expect such a reaction when ye pin innocents in dark hallways and try to blame them for yer own suspicious nature."

His face tightened. "Yer sister almost killed me father. That is nae suspicion. It is proven."

"Which is why ye should leave. Bari is nae content—"

She was saying too much, letting her thoughts spill past her lips without considering the consequences. She needed to prevent bloodshed, not give Gahan Sutherland solid reason to go looking for Bari's blood. Even if she knew Bari deserved it.

"Is nae…what?"

Gahan's voice was soft, but there was a flame flickering in his dark eyes that terrified her. She hadn't been afraid of him until that moment, because she was certain she was looking at the rage churning inside him over almost losing his father. She felt his pain but was powerless to soothe it.

"I cannae help ye, no more than I can stop me own wedding."

She was saying too much again, her deepest feelings pouring out because she was so frightened. "Ye should just…go." Tears burned her eyes, and her voice was thick with them. "That's all I can do for ye."

Moira grabbed her skirts and ran. She heard him give chase behind her, but she made it to the arched doorway and inside the Great Hall before he caught her. Matheson retainers looked up, catching her in their sights. Gahan jerked back at the last moment, but she felt his dark stare on her.

She was trembling, her entire body shaking like it was bone-chilling cold.

Yet she was hot, and her cheeks burned with a blush.

"Moira, come here." Bari was sitting at the high table, his expression stormy. She forced herself to walk down the aisle, fighting against the urge to run.

Where would she go? There was no sanctuary for her, and Gahan no doubt still lingered in the darkness. Bari tapped the top of the table impatiently. Moira squared her shoulders and moved toward the high table. Better to face what she must and be done with worrying about it.

"Ye'll nae wed until tomorrow." His eyes narrowed, and he leaned forward to get a closer look at her, his gaze lingering on her bright cheeks. "I expect ye more composed by then."

Bari snapped his fingers at one of the maids. She hesitated before moving toward Moira.

"Come, miss." She bit her lip. "Mistress."

The girl sounded as unsure as Moira felt. At least there was someone she might feel something in common with.

Yet it was a beginning to her new future, and that pleased her. Moira followed the girl from the hall with a sense of renewed hope.

～

"The lass is quick," Cam observed.

"I would nae have struck her," Gahan said gruffly.

His half brother didn't respond, but Gahan saw the reprimand in his expression. That was something his father had taught him to take notice of. Just because he was in command, it didn't mean the men following his orders agreed with him. Scotland had a young king because his father had been too arrogant to notice that those around him were growing resentful of his personal excesses.

"I deserved it," he admitted.

"Aye, ye did at that. Ye won't be getting any argument from me." Cam spoke softly to keep their words between them. "Are ye going to take her advice?"

"And leave?" Gahan shook his head. "Maybe Bari will make enough of a mistake and give me the opportunity to break his neck right here."

"That would save a bit of trouble for the rest of us. But I think the earl is going to be displeased about ye looking to start a fight under a vassal laird's roof."

"Publicly, he will be." Gahan flashed his sibling a grin. "But I am a bastard, after all."

He was planning on using the stain of his birth to right the wrong Bari Fraser had done to his family. Some might accuse him of dishonorable conduct, but as far as he was concerned, poison was even lower.

And Moira Fraser knew the truth of the matter. She'd almost spilled the facts. His suspicions were confirmed. Bari had known full well what his sister was planning to do to Lytge, and it seemed that Moira knew too.

For some reason, that knowledge left a bitter taste in his mouth. He didn't have time to wonder why. She was kin to Sandra and Bari. No doubt she'd learned to use her blue eyes to beguile men the same way Sandra had. Her impending marriage was a fine example of using the union of matrimony for gain. He shouldn't be surprised or even overly interested in the matter.

But the bitterness remained.

❧

"The laird's last wife used this chamber."

The maid froze two steps into the room when she looked at the bed. A bundle of rosemary, withered and brown, still decorated the headboard. Someone had brought it to Matheson's last wife in the hope it would cleanse the chamber and help her have a safe delivery. The dry leaves had fallen onto the pillow now, a blunt reminder of how dangerous childbirth was. No one had cleared it away, because no one wanted bad luck plaguing them.

"We should try another place."

The girl made the sign of the cross over herself as she hurried from the room. Moira lingered, looking around the chamber for clues as to what her new life would be like. It was a modest room, the furniture sturdy but not lavish. A thick comforter was kicked to the foot of the bed, and there was a fireplace. A half-burned candle sat on the bedside table, and a long table had been pushed near the bed. Several pitchers and a large urn were abandoned there along with a stack of towels intended for the birth. Dust had settled over all of it.

"Come away, there are bad humors here. We should get a sin-eater to sleep here before anyone else enters the chamber and gets shackled with bad luck."

"Why hasn't the head of house already hired one?" Moira asked.

"We have no head of house," she explained. "The laird will expect ye to manage the duties. The cook runs the kitchens well enough. Ye'll be deciding who has a place."

Because she would be the laird's wife. It was slightly appealing until she recalled the way Gahan Sutherland had looked at her. Like a high-priced whore. She preferred to focus on the good her union might do for ensuring peace. But she'd have to try her hand at making Achaius think she liked his touch.

A shudder shook her, and she hurried after the maid.

The maid was leading her down a narrow passageway. The stones were older here, many of them pitted. There was only a single tin lantern to provide light. She pushed open a door and held it for Moira. The chamber was as dark as a cave. A little light spilled in from the hallway. Once Moira stepped over the threshold, the girl reached into her apron pocket and pulled out a flint stone. She struck it with a piece of iron until sparks flew onto the pile of tinder left on a small pewter plate. It flared up, and she held a candle over it until it lit. The golden glow spread out around the maid, and she carried it to another candle sitting on the far side of the chamber.

The maid returned the candle to the holder sitting by the plate. The tinder had burned away, leaving only a thin taper of smoke that lingered in the stale air. She walked to the window and opened the shutters. A cloud of dust billowed up as she pushed out the wide shutters. She wrinkled her nose, but then she turned and offered Moira a smile.

Moira smiled back. "What's your name?" she asked.

"I am Fann, milady," the maid said and lowered herself. There was a hopeful note in the girl's voice. She opened the doors of a wardrobe from which she pulled out a folded bundle of bedding and set to making the bed. Moira went to the other side of the bed to help her straighten the sheets. The work went much faster with two of them. A look of relief crossed Fann's face; no doubt the girl had worried her laird's new wife might be expecting pampering.

"The sheets are clean. A bit of time and the night breeze will freshen the air in here."

She moved to a chair that had a piece of Matheson plaid covering it. When she lifted it, the candlelight sparkled off the dust. The chair was a sturdy one, built in an X fashion. Fann picked up the seat cushion and beat it against her hip a few times.

"Do ye wish to take supper below?" She nibbled on her lower lip. "The laird is rather set in his thinking. He'll insist ye sit at the lower table, because of yer common blood, until ye wed."

The girl was flustered but obviously eager to help her new mistress adjust. The way she chattered so freely spoke of a household where the line between mistress and staff was very thin. In fact, the only difference might be that she had the church's blessing to share Achaius's bed. The Matheson laird clearly felt he was ruler and to be obeyed instantly.

She doubted any maid who caught his eye might tell him no.

"I'm weary. Would ye be kind enough to fetch me something?"

The girl lowered herself again and smiled. "Ye may rely on me and me two sisters. They are younger, but our mother has taught us well."

Fann hurried out of the chamber, likely intent on finding her siblings to help her bring up the supper tray. Moira understood the nervousness eating at the girl. Everyone needed to make sure they had a place. It might be spring, but there would be no new crops for several months yet. Even then, no one was provided for without giving something in return.

Moira would be striving to please Achaius for her keep.

With a sigh, she sat down in the chair but shot back up when she realized how sore her bottom was. She wasn't accustomed to riding a horse for so many hours in a row. Her cheeks colored as she remembered that she'd be expected to welcome her new husband into her embrace by the next nightfall.

Or sooner. Her cheeks reddened as she recalled the greeting her husband-to-be had given her. It was possible he'd happily claim his rights the moment the Church blessed them. She certainly wouldn't be the first bride deflowered in the light of day.

Or the first one accused of seeking a lover when she got a good look at her groom.

That fact didn't make her any less accepting of the accusation Gahan Sutherland had made. Achaius would likely be furious if he discovered she'd lashed out at his overlord's son, even if the man had deserved it.

Oh, he had. She smiled with satisfaction. Moira doubted she could find any remorse for her actions, even if she ended up locked in the stocks for daring to forget her place. Gahan might be bastard-born, but he was still a blue blood. The man was also a Highlander.

Bari liked to call himself one, but the truth of the matter had been there in the hardness of Gahan's body. Every retainer following the son of the Earl of Sutherland was lean and bulky with muscle. Sutherland was far north. Most likely, it was still covered in snow. Only the strong survived there. Like Gahan.

She shook her head. She was letting her mind wander into dangerous places. She'd learned long ago not to ponder how much better others' lives were. Such mental exercises were only going to take her to one place, and that was resentment. There was much to enjoy in her days, and it was best to remember that fact.

Achaius's face rose from her memory. His eyes had sparkled with glee as she blushed. His laughter echoed in her ears, destroying her attempts to find something positive about her plight. But she had to. Alba needed her to please the old laird.

Though it was clear he would not be making any effort to consider her desires.

❧

The bells from the church woke her.

Moira jumped awake because it sounded as if she was sleeping in the bell tower. She pushed the coverlet off her legs and ran to the window. The floor was chilled from the night air, and it stung the bottoms of her bare feet.

The church was inside the curtain wall, the bells eye level with her window. She certainly wouldn't be sleeping past morning Mass.

"Morning, miss." Fann hurried into the room and retrieved Moira's undergown. "This is me sister, Aife."

The second girl picked up Moira's overgown and stood behind her sibling as Fann helped her into her undergown. Once it was in place, Aife held up her overgown. Both were simple garments, no finer than what Aife or Fann wore.

"After Mass, we'll have to see what can be found for ye to wear for yer wedding. There will be nice things in the last mistress's chamber. Her family sent her with velvet."

The last bits of slumber evaporated as Moira recalled exactly what the day would hold. She'd spent long hours trying to fall asleep, and now she was paying for it. Her head hurt with fatigue already, and the sun was barely risen. Fann pulled a brush through her hair, and Aife offered her the linen cap.

"Come...come," Fann urged her.

The bells had stopped ringing, and the sound of song drifted up from the church. It wouldn't do well for her to be late to Mass. Plenty of lairds were forgiven of the same sin, but it was a wife's duty to be there even if her husband wasn't.

In fact, there were a great number of sins Achaius might be allowed that she was forbidden.

Moira followed Fann through what seemed

identical tunnels running inside the old keep. She stumbled as she tried to make sense of which direction they were going, but there appeared to be no markings of any sort.

Fann knew the way, though, and soon they were hurrying from the tower to the steps of the church. Others were also doing their best not to be late. There was no time for greetings or even to notice who was next to her. By the time she was in line with the rest of the female members of the congregation, the priest was beginning the Mass.

But there were plenty of people trying to get a look at her. It was by far the most attention she'd ever attracted, and it was more than unsettling. Her confidence tried to desert her, but the memory of the look on Alba's face kept her standing steady. There was no way she would achieve her goals if she crumpled. Being peeked at would certainly not be the worst of what the day would hold.

She wished she was marrying Gahan Sutherland and would be welcoming him into her bed later. Heat scorched her cheeks at the thought. She had no right to even think such a thing, much less during Mass. But the thought was there, inside her head, too bold to brush aside.

How would she even go about such a thing? A man like Gahan would no doubt have experience with women trying their hand at snaring his attention. He might even have a wife now, or be contracted for one. Without realizing it, she scanned the opposite side of the church. It wasn't hard to find the Sutherlands. Their plaid was darker in hue, because they used more dye, an expense they didn't seem to mind. But they were also larger.

Ye noticed that before, which is another thing ye should nae have done…

For just a moment, she allowed her gaze to rest on Gahan. He was several rows closer to the altar, so it wouldn't matter. Just a fleeting indulgence before she had to devote herself to duty.

The hall was bustling with people. The scent of hot porridge drew them once their souls had been cleansed for the day. The tables filled as maids delivered pitchers of fresh milk. On the high table there was also cream and dried fruit, but Moira sat at a lower table. She cupped her bowl to warm her hands and studied the contents of her morning meal.

Simple oats and barley, but it was hot, and that pleased her the most. After a long winter, it was easy to long for richer food, but the rules of Lent were strict. The high table certainly didn't suffer from a lack of tempting items to make the morning fare more palatable. It was a delicate balance between Church and laird. No laird wanted the Church outraged with him, but no priest wanted the laird irate with him. Still, Achaius poured a generous amount of cream into his bowl, then reached for the dried fruit.

"At least yer sister knows her place."

The hall quieted as Laird Matheson spoke. Moira looked up to find him staring at her. Bari was seated beside him at the high table. Gahan was there as well, but he'd sat at the end of the table, more than an arm's reach from the other two men. His mistrust of them was clear, and he didn't seem to care who knew it.

"She is honored by yer offer to wed her," Bari said.

Achaius laughed. He pounded the table and coughed several times. "Ye are a liar, Bari Fraser."

Moira slapped her hand over her mouth to keep her amusement from showing. Bari turned red.

"I am nae!"

Achaius was unimpressed with Bari's sputtering. The Matheson laird reached for his mug and took a long swig from it, then wiped his mouth across his sleeve.

"Then ye are a blind man. The lass is horrified, even if she has voiced no complaint. As I noted, she knows her place. A fine trait in a wife."

Moira fought the urge to look away from the high table. It felt like everyone was staring at her, and the hall had fallen as silent as the sanctuary during Mass. But she had to look him in the eye or fail completely. There would be no peace if he believed her discontent.

"She'll do her duty," Bari said.

"Aye, I believe ye on that account." Achaius put a spoonful of porridge into his mouth and swallowed. "Otherwise, I think she would have been much more welcoming to the good earl's son last night when he followed her down the hallway and tried to suggest she run away with him."

Her jaw dropped open, and the hall was stunned into silence for a moment that felt like an hour.

"Ye son of a whore!" Bari shouted. He was out of his chair in a flash, but he froze because Gahan had also risen, his expression deadly as he faced off with Bari.

"Keep the sharp side of yer tongue off me mother,"

Gahan warned softly. His tone was far more ominous than Bari's shouting. "Or I'll show ye what happens to men who insult me family."

"Ye seem to nae understand where yer hands do nae belong," Bari growled. "Ye need to leave."

"Sit down, ye whelp. This is my land and my tower. Ye do nae throw anyone out, especially me overlord's son. I know me place." Achaius's retainers instantly stepped to attention behind their laird. Bari returned to his chair.

"Yer sister did a fair job of dealing with the situation, and I found it interesting."

Achaius surprised both men. They watched him consume another spoonful of his breakfast, and then a second before Bari lost control.

"What do ye mean by that?"

Achaius turned his head and stared at him. A moment later he pounded his fist on the table, shaking everything on it.

"Are ye me king? Me priest? There are few men I'll stomach that tone from."

"I am yer fellow laird," Bari insisted.

"Blah!" Achaius pointed his spoon at Bari. "I should demand more dowry for that piss-poor reasoning. She's nae that pretty, and a virgin as well."

"Of course she's a virgin."

"Well now, lad, once ye've had as many maidens as I have, it tends to lose its appeal in favor of a woman who knows how to please. Half me retainers think she'll cry tonight. I'm looking for a warm welcome in me bed."

Achaius went back to eating, and Bari did too.

Speaking as he was, up at the high table, it was almost possible to believe they weren't discussing her. She had as much meaning to them as a mare. The unease that had kept her awake left her with a knot in her belly. It was as if she were disconnected from the moment; not really a part of it, and that made it possible to simply dismiss it as insignificant.

She would not cry. There were plenty of things she could not control, but she would master her emotions. Besides, she would not be wasting any tears on a situation in which she had so little worth. Her groom and her brother seemed content to discuss her wedding without her. Well, she'd offer them the same callous disregard. Their plans mattered little to her, and she would repeat that idea over and over until she believed it. Tears were for things she cared about.

She realized that Gahan Sutherland was watching her. His dark eyes were aimed directly at her as he ignored the conversation. Heat stung her cheeks, and she looked away because she realized she was blushing—again.

✦

Achaius sat in his private solar and belched. His captain waited for him to settle back into his chair before tugging on the corner of his bonnet.

"Do ye want me to assign an escort to yer bride?"

Achaius shook his head. "And I want ye to forget that ye asked me. Tell the lads outside the door that I'm sleeping."

His captain's eyes narrowed. "Gahan Sutherland is determined to corner her again, I'd bet good silver on it. She was watching him during Mass, those pretty blue eyes sparkling. He had his eye on her while ye ate, sure enough. There are nae many things that will pull a man's attention away from such a publicly issued insult as letting his mother be called a whore in the Great Hall. A woman he wants a taste of is one. Otherwise, I wager he'd be out of the gates by now."

"He's staying because of her and no mistake. Ye can see it in his eyes." Achaius nodded. "But do nae worry. That bastard is going to help me gain every last bit of Fraser land. It's a stroke of luck having him beguiled by me bride."

He laughed, and his captain grinned.

"Ye see it, do ye nae?" Achaius began to let his eyes shut. "Gahan Sutherland wants Bari's blood, and if I am wed to Moira, I'll have the best claim to the Fraser land once Bari is dead. There is nae a cousin or a bastard with a close claim. The earl will have to bestow the Fraser lairdship upon the legitimate issue of me union. I need Gahan to have a reason to kill Bari. A valid one would be even better."

"What if the lass does nae conceive?"

Achaius opened his eyes and waved a hand in the air to dismiss the worry on his captain's face. "I'll lock her in a tower and tell one and all that a midwife told me she's carrying and needs to conserve her strength. Then I'll buy some whore's brat to seal the deal. It can die in a few years, leaving the land in Matheson hands. Or live if I need it, but it will be raised to serve me."

The only way it would have been better was if the land were connected to his own, but he wasn't going to be picky. It was a stroke of luck, one he planned to enjoy. His breakfast helped him slip off into an early morning nap as his captain left. He needed the rest because he was going to enjoy doing his best to make sure everyone believed he still had the vigor to deflower his young bride.

For a moment, Achaius opened his eyes. His kilt lay smooth and even over his lower body. His member was still soft in spite of the juicy offering Bari Fraser had delivered to him. For a moment he was bitter, resenting what age had stolen from him. The thought of tossing Moira's skirts should have stiffened his cock and filled him with anticipation. Instead, he was left contemplating how to make sure the sheet was stained come sunrise.

Sutherland's bastard son had no problem getting stiff at the sight of young Moira.

Achaius forced his resentment aside. Gahan's interest in Moira might have more than one purpose as well. Not only was the man provoking Bari Fraser into a rage, he would certainly take the secret of any bastard he bred with Moira to the grave. That made him perfect for the chore of ensuring his bride conceived.

If nature wasn't going to let him enjoy his newest bride, at least age hadn't stolen his wits to keep him from being able to make sure he gained the most from his newest venture. Life was about profit. Everything else was drivel for women and servants of the Church.

Three

THE MEWS AT MATHESON TOWER WERE NICE. THEY opened up to let in the fresh morning air and looked to be swept every day. Athena had been given a perch with a water pouch hung from it. There was a long line of perches but only three other hawks. As soon as Moira removed the hood from Athena's head, she looked at the other birds and cried out in an attempt to accrete her dominance. Moira clicked her tongue.

"What the hell are ye doing talking to Gahan Sutherland?"

Bari was still spoiling for a fight. Moira put Athena back on her perch and turned to face him.

"I should give ye a beating," he threatened.

Unlike Gahan, Bari never curbed his impulse to strike her. Now that she had a comparison, in her mind, her sibling resembled a weak child.

"What manner of wife do ye expect me to be?"

Her question confused Bari.

"According to the maids, there is no head of house. I will be expected to shoulder the duties. I can hardly do that if I am too timid to hold a conversation with my husband's guests."

"Gahan Sutherland is different, and ye know it."

There was a rage burning in Bari's eyes that struck her as unnatural. It was too intense and had been there for too long now.

"Nay, I do nae understand."

"It is none of yer concern!" Bari seemed caught between the need to shout and crumble into despair. His nostrils actually flared with the intensity of his emotions. "Ye have been told what ye need to know. Stay away from Gahan Sutherland."

Moira dared to allow her amusement to show. "I can hardly control the man. He followed me, and he is the overlord's son."

"Ye'll mind me, Moira!"

Athena didn't care for the shouting and let out a shrill cry. Bari snapped his head around to look at the bird.

"Or the next time ye come out here, ye'll find yer precious bird with a broken neck."

Moira moved in front of Athena. Bari snickered.

"It seems a stroke of luck that ye insisted on bringing it along. Now get back to the keep and take a bath. There's nothing we can do for how ugly ye are with that common nose, but ye can be clean. Yer wedding is at sunset." He paused for a long moment. "And ye had best be a virgin. Because if ye aren't, ye are no use to me at all."

A feeling of helplessness was growing inside her, and she detested it. At least her temper burned it away, so she let it flare up. "I wish I weren't one."

Her brother's eyes widened with rage.

"And I do nae care if ye do nae like hearing me say it," she said.

Bari suddenly grinned. His shift in mood stunned her. "Maybe ye are nae such a pitiful peasant after all. There just might be some of our father in ye." His lips returned to a hard line. "But ye will never hold a candle to what Sandra was."

Her brother left, lost in his recollections. A chill went through her. Once more she noticed just how unbalanced Bari was. She spent so little time with him that the change was clear. Alba's desperation became easier to understand. Her brother ignored the maids who served him, but they knew what she had only just noticed. Bari Fraser was obsessed with vengeance. Moira had grown past fearing her brother years ago, but today she had a feeling of dread because it was very possible he was going insane.

Maybe she was lucky to be wedding, because no one on Fraser land would be resting easy if the laird went mad.

⤥

For all the grandeur Matheson Castle seemed to have on the outside, it was pitifully lacking in bathing facilities. There was no bathhouse and only a few small wooden tubs. Fann set one up in the back part of the kitchen where it was warm and closer to the wells. The cook sent the kitchen boys away so Moira might have some privacy. Somehow, she doubted such a courtesy was extended to anyone else. The cook used one of the keys hanging from her belt to unlock a chest. She pulled out a thick bar of soap, pausing to smell it before handing it to Moira.

The moment Moira stepped out of the tub, the cook climbed in and happily applied the soap to herself. Next went her assistant. Several more tubs were filled, and it seemed every maid was taking the opportunity to bathe. Or perhaps it was more that they considered they had permission, since the soon-to-be mistress had decided it was bathing day.

Mistress...She didn't feel like the lady of the house. The title "head of house" felt more fitting. It was clear Achaius was something of a miser. With his last wife dead, he should have elevated one of the staff to the position, but he'd held onto the coin.

Well, she was not used to being idle, so it was a blessing. She just wished it didn't come with the duty of sharing the old laird's bed.

It was odd, but she'd never thought much about what went on between men and women. Oh yes, she knew the names both kind and insulting. She understood the mechanics of coupling, but she had no idea of what it might feel like. Some women craved it. Many wives dreaded it.

She sighed and began to learn her way around. The hallways still looked the same to her, and soon she was trying to discover which one connected to which stairway. It was an old custom to keep the hallways identical, a last defense against the inner keep being breached. When the enemy entered, they wouldn't know which way to go to capture the laird. Those who lived inside the walls learned to find their way with tiny details. Moira tried to focus on finding some, but she was distracted and fretting about the approaching night.

"Ye enjoyed seeing yer brother called a liar."

Moira turned to find Gahan behind her. The man must have been leaning in one of the doorways. Behind him was the captain she'd come to recognize because he always seemed to be shadowing Gahan.

"And ye do nae deny it." Gahan lifted a hand and waved his captain away. The man frowned, but a quick glance sent him on his way after a tug on his bonnet. His footsteps stopped just around the corner. That was all the privacy he was willing to allow his laird. Even a man such as Gahan had restrictions placed on him. No doubt his captain wasn't willing to be the one to tell the Earl of Sutherland that his son had died on his watch.

"I am nae accustomed to being dishonest, in spite of what ye seem to think me nature is. And Bari says many things he should think on before letting past his lips." The lengthening afternoon shadows left her no attention to give to his attempts to needle her. She was more concerned with the wedding taking place at sunset. Still, Gahan was not a man who had time to waste. Nor was he an idle person given to wasting daylight. He'd sought her out, yet he might have had her summoned. Whatever he craved, he wanted to ask her in private.

"Ye want something from me. What is it?"

Gahan's expression changed. She ended up staring at him because he'd always been so intense around her that this transformation was startling. He'd dropped his guarded look and appeared almost uncertain.

"I want ye to give me yer hawk," he said at last. "Make a gift of her to me."

Surprise held her silent for a moment. Gahan drew in a deep breath and angled his head as he looked down at her.

"Me men will make sure she comes to no harm."

She gasped. "How do ye know about Bari's threat?"

He shrugged. "It's always wise to keep a few of the stableboys friendly with me. I'm sure they will put the silver to good use. Most of them do nae have shoes."

That was a shame in a castle as great as this one was. Those same boys would man the cannons should there be an attack. They should have been clothed. It was the duty of the laird to see it was done, and a shame that the overlord's son was noticing it was not done. Achaius was a miser, and that often destroyed loyalty. But she would soon be his wife, and she'd have the power to right the wrong.

"Thank ye for telling me. I'll see to the boys." Apparently they were as much in need of her doing her duty as Alba. If she failed to wed Achaius, the Matheson castle folk would continue to suffer, for no one would notice. Her throat tightened, like there was a noose knotted around it.

"And yer hawk?"

"Why do ye offer me help?" Maybe she was being foolish to question him, but she just couldn't control her curiosity. Maybe it was because he was the only person she could speak her mind to.

He shrugged, and for a moment she was distracted by the way his shoulders moved beneath his shirt. There was something about him that fascinated her and made her heart beat faster. She wanted to look at this man, actually stare at him. It was like being under a spell.

"Maybe I want to strike at yer brother any way possible. Or perhaps I'll admit that I've raised hawks since I was a boy, too, and cannae stomach knowing yer brother will harm one out of spite. I dare say, if he were in your shoes, he'd nae be standing as straight as ye are."

"He's never allowed me to call him brother, because my mother was common-born." It was a slip, an admission she had no reason for sharing with him. Bari hated her for her blood. She'd do well to remember that hatred...

"There are plenty of Highland lairds who have the same blood in their veins. There are many who claim it keeps the blood strong. Yer father wed her, so the matter should nae be questioned."

She was at a loss for a long moment, unsure what to say, for he was offering kindness when she had never expected it. Not from anyone—least of all from him.

"Athena is yers, and I thank ye." Her voice was full of relief.

"Ye should nae have to."

He half turned and let out a whistle. She heard someone around the bend in the hallway start walking away. Those footsteps threatened to send tears down her cheeks, for she knew Athena would be hers no longer.

She had to recall why and be content.

"Bari is a knave for bringing ye here. What else has he threatened to do if ye do nae wed Achaius?"

She was staring into his eyes again, this time because she just couldn't understand why he cared. His lips twitched into a grin that was beguiling. He was one handsome brute when he softened his expression.

She jumped and looked away, her cheeks hot with shame. "Well…hmm…does it really matter?" Her mind was cloudy, and her thoughts formed slowly. But she forced herself to focus and make sense. "What I mean to say is, doing me duty is something I will nae shirk. Wouldn't ye honor a contract made by yer laird? Even if the bride was nae to yer liking?"

She covered her mouth with her hand when she realized she'd admitted her true feelings. "Nae that I dislike Achaius." There really was no way to explain her way out of it. So she turned, intending to leave, but he blocked her way with one arm. His lightning-quick motion startled her. She'd allowed herself to trust him being so very close to her.

But the man was a Highlander, and one with vengeance on his mind. She was a fool to allow him so close.

"Sandra would have fluttered her eyelashes and done her best to beguile Achaius," he said. "She was a bitch with a calculating mind and a heart of stone. She used a woman's wiles like weapons."

Their gazes were locked, and she felt the burn of his stare all the way to her toes.

"Ye're nae trying yer hand at that game, but maybe ye are playing a different one," he pressed.

He was a man accustomed to getting what he wanted. She tried to lean back, but the wall was solid, and the pitted surface pressed into her palms. Her heart accelerated and, oddly, she was convinced she could smell his skin.

"What is so hard to understand?" she asked in frustration. "The Church preaches that a woman should follow the direction of her family and laird."

His lips parted. "Agreeing with the sermon is much easier when ye're in the house of God. Once ye are standing on the steps of the keep with an old man pinching yer bottom, that's when I'd expect ye to tell yer brother to go to hell."

"I wish—" She slapped a hand over her mouth to stop her words. But he gripped her wrist and pulled it away.

"Ye wish what?"

The contact of his grip caused a flood of sensation. It was like something was unleashing inside her, a hidden part of her that she had never realized existed, some instinct that told her to move closer to him.

"Release me," she breathed.

One dark eyebrow rose like a challenge. "Why? I am nae hurting ye. I know me strength and control it well."

"Yer touch unsettles me."

Something flickered in his dark eyes, and it frightened her because she felt an echo of it inside herself. It was worse than pain—that was something she knew how to endure. His touch was eroding her control and making her fight the urge to touch him back.

She wanted to but shook her head.

"And I will nae have ye accusing me of trying to seduce ye." She didn't sound as steady as she'd have liked, but at least she hadn't stumbled over the words.

She twisted her hand, trying to free herself, but he turned her arm up and placed a kiss against her inner wrist. It burned, but then the sweetest delight rippled through her from the contact.

"Ye are unnatural," she accused. She was almost breathless, but she was also frightened of him, afraid of what he was unleashing inside of her.

When he raised his head to look at her, his expression was purely sensual and strangely inviting.

"Because ye enjoyed that?" His gaze lowered to her lips. "So did I. And it was very natural, lass. We were made to respond to each other."

The delicate skin of her lips tingled. She was almost desperate to discover what his kiss felt like before she lost the chance forever by pledging herself to Achaius in holy matrimony.

"Well, ye should nae teach me such things. Ye should go before ye ruin everything."

His grip tightened, and she flinched. "Now ye are hurting me."

"What am I going to ruin?" he asked softly, easing his hold on her wrist. But he was still watching her suspiciously, and she knew he was lowering his voice to deceive her.

Her temper flared up, rescuing her from the flood of new sensations, and she jerked her arm away from him.

Moira gave him a withering look. "Any hope of happiness I might find here. Ye are a selfish man to show me what a kiss might feel like if me husband was nae so old. I do nae need to dwell on the facts that cannae be changed."

"This wedding is designed to cause trouble. I'm trying to make ye see it before it's too late," he argued.

"And just what do ye think will happen if I do nae take me vows?" She closed the gap between them with her chin out. "Do ye think the Matheson will be pleased to see me turning me nose up at their laird's offer? Will yer own father be happy to hear ye caused discontent in a match among his vassals? I do nae need the memory of yer kiss distracting me from me duty."

"If a kiss is all it takes, I am happy to do the honors."

His words didn't make sense to her, but a second later, she understood completely. Gahan leaned down and sealed her lips beneath his. The contact was jarring, like an explosion, and she jumped back. But he grasped her shoulders and pulled her close again. This time, he claimed her mouth, pressing his lips over hers without mercy.

Excitement twisted through her belly, and all of a sudden she wasn't thinking, she was responding. She reached for him, sliding her hands up his chest and delighting at the way he felt. Never once had she suspected a man might feel good, but Gahan did.

His kiss was even better.

After the first moments, he began to tease her lips, slipping and sliding across the delicate surface as he cupped her nape to keep her in place. He pressed her mouth until she opened for him, and then the tip of his tongue joined the assault.

She had no idea how long it lasted, for it felt like time had simply stopped. All she wanted to do was follow his lead and forget everything else.

But he suddenly pulled away, stiffening as though

he was just as spellbound as she. Suspicion glittered in his eyes, and it was colder than ice.

"Ye kissed me," she growled, surprised by how furious she sounded.

"And ye kissed me back."

She shoved at him, struggling when he held on to her. "When it comes to seductions, ye clearly have more experience than I. Perhaps ye are the one wielding a man's touch like a weapon."

She gained her freedom—or so she thought—until she tried to run and he pulled her up short by her wrist. The hold was unyielding, but it was clear he was in fact controlling his strength.

"Do nae wed Achaius, lass. It will lead to trouble."

She froze. Gahan Sutherland, son of the Earl of Sutherland, was asking her not to go through with the wedding. It was more tempting than she wanted to admit. She bit her lower lip to keep herself from saying how much she wanted to do as he asked.

He rubbed the inside of her wrist, the motion soothing and yet alarming at the same time.

"Ye know it is wrong. Bari wants the Matheson to help him feud against the Sutherlands. Yer wedding will seal the pact."

He released her, and for a moment, she stood with her eyes fixed on his. Uncertainty ate at her, and her lips tingled. She backed away before she gave in to the urge to say anything else. He was the son of the Earl of Sutherland. He would pursue what was best for his clan above all else, and she would be wise to remember that she was not a Sutherland. She was just a pawn. An obstacle he needed to move in order to achieve his goals.

"Ye have no reason to tell me the truth," she whispered.

His eyes narrowed at the insult. She hadn't labeled him a liar outright, but it was close enough for a man of his high station. Nobles did not suffer veiled threats. But she wasn't finished.

"I would certainly nae be the first bride played falsely by another clan, either. A few kisses in the shadows, and when I forsake me duty, me own kin will be attacked to pay for the slight. Ye can ride home with no one the wiser to the part ye played. Perhaps ye want to see the Frasers attacked because ye believe it justice, but it will be naught but blood spilling and good mothers crying over the graves of their sons."

She expected his anger to flare up, but instead he let out a soft grunt that sounded like he agreed with her.

"That is nae what I am doing, lass." He flashed her a grin. "But I suppose I cannae blame ye for nae knowing sense when ye hear it. Yer half brother never speaks any."

She was returning his smile when his expression became serious. It was almost like she could feel the shift in his emotions. Which was far too much of an intimacy.

"But ye are no girl. Ye are mature enough to understand me." His tone was solemn. "Listen to me, and I will make sure you have a way out of here."

It was so tempting—*he* was tempting. Moira shook her head. In a flash, the fragile trust she'd decided existed between them shattered, revealing the very real threat he posed. The man wanted his way and planned to get it by whatever means necessary. She raised her chin, refusing to cower.

"Ye praise me for being past me tender years, but somehow think I do nae know what becomes of girls who ride off with men they are nae wed to?" She settled her hands on her hips. "Best ye listen well, Gahan Sutherland. I was shocked by me first kiss, which is why I did nae slap ye for taking the liberty. But ye are a rogue to have done it, for ye have made no offer for me. Ye should be ashamed to do something like this on me wedding day. I am no less honorable than ye and will nae discard me duty the moment someone steals a kiss in the shadows."

It was exactly what she had been raised to believe, yet it felt wrong to chastise him.

Gahan chuckled. The sound was chilling, because it made her feel like a game animal being cornered by something very dangerous.

"First kiss? Well, there is another thing I can detest yer half brother for. As pretty as ye are, at least one of his men should have tried to win yer affection."

"I am nae pretty." She covered her lips when she realized she'd spoken. "At least, ye should nae be saying I am."

"Would ye have me lie to ye?"

He reached out and stroked her cheek. A shiver raced down her body in response.

"I'd have ye stop toying with me." She was pitifully close to begging, but he had such a devastating effect on her. "I must try and make the best of this match. Do nae fill me head with fanciful ideas of offers ye have nae made."

"I keep me word, Moira," he informed her in a hard tone. "I offer to make sure ye have a way out of this keep. I do nae need to promise nae to leave ye stranded on the road, for I am no villain. Never accuse me of dishonor again."

She backed away from him, holding up a hand when he began to follow. "I wonder, would ye like yer own sister riding off without the blessing of the Church? With someone ye know has reason to want vengeance against her clan? With no promise of anything, except the sure knowledge that she'd be dishonoring her own kin?"

She'd silenced him. It would likely only last a moment, but she took advantage of it and left. She listened for his footsteps behind her, but there were none. He might be many things, but it appeared Gahan was a man who understood sense when he heard it. Only children lived in a world where everything might be put aside in favor of their feelings.

So ye admit ye have feelings for him?

She cringed but continued out into the sunlight. Bari was her laird, and it would be her brother she had to depend on once Gahan Sutherland rode back to his father's land.

❧

"Ye kissed her?"

"I am nae in the mood to be lectured, Cam," Gahan growled.

His sibling wasn't put off by his tone. In fact, Cam reached out and placed a solid hand on his shoulder to keep him from following Moira out into the yard.

"I see what sort of mood ye are in. Have ye forgotten that she's kin to Sandra?"

Cam was incredulous, and his sobering words broke

through the spell Gahan seemed to be under. He'd never been a man who gave much thought to superstitions. But his forehead was moist with perspiration, and if Cam hadn't stopped him, he'd be standing behind Moira like a devoted slave. The woman was obviously more accomplished in wielding her feminine wiles than he'd given her credit for.

"I was trying to get her to refuse to wed."

Cam cocked his head to one side. "Well...that's more than I would have done, but I suppose it makes sense. No young lass wants to wed an old man."

"Unless she's scheming like Sandra did."

Gahan moved toward the doorway and frowned. Moira had vanished. His body tensed as though it mattered to him what became of her. The troubling sensation lingered as his eyes swept the yard, searching for her.

"There ye are."

Achaius made his way toward Gahan. "I feared ye'd ridden out before witnessing me vows."

He slapped Gahan on the shoulder and grinned.

"Why are ye so worried about me being here for yer wedding, Achaius? Bari Fraser has made it plain he'd like to see me horse's arse."

"That lad is young. He does nae yet grasp the full importance of being united with the Earl of Sutherland."

Gahan turned to face Achaius, suspicion tingling up his nape. "If me father is so important to ye, why have ye nae informed him of yer intention to wed Moira Fraser? It does nae speak well of ye when I hear of a union such as this through one of yer neighbors."

It was a bold thing to say, but Achaius only waved the veiled insult away. "Have ye seen me bride?"

Gahan nodded and pressed his lips into a hard line, because his memory was quick to remind him of the way she'd felt against him. He was interested in so much more than just how she looked. He should be ashamed of himself, but all he felt was a growing urge to make sure Moira took his offer of a ride out of Matheson Castle.

"She's a pot of honey." Achaius chuckled and pointed a time-withered finger at Gahan. "If Bari Fraser is going to offer her to me, well now, lad, me eyes still work well enough for me to want a taste of her. Young lads are nae the only ones cursed with impatience. The difference is, I know me days are few, and I want to enjoy every one of them."

"She does nae want to wed ye." His father was going to have something harsh to say about his comment, but Gahan didn't care. The entire situation stank of foul play. He wanted the truth, and polite comments weren't going to uncover it for him.

"Maybe nae, but she's hardly the first wife I've gotten a chilly reception from. Marriage is business, lad. Yer father knows it well. Why else are ye a bastard?" Achaius shook his head. "Because yer father wed himself a woman with a fine dowry, that's why."

"What is she bringing ye?"

"Land," Achaius informed him with glee. "Now I'm off to dress in me best before I get on me way to the church for a blessing. I hope ye'll be here at sunset to see it."

The old laird made his way up the steps with the help of his retainers.

"Land? Bari Fraser is willing to give up land?" Cam uttered disbelievingly.

"Which proves without a doubt there is something foul brewing here," Gahan said. "No laird gives away land for a half sister and a groom without a noble title."

But suspicions were not proof. He had no reason to stop the wedding.

&

Moira ran until she was on the front steps again. Her cheeks were burning, betraying to everyone what she had been about.

Well, what was so terrible about it?

She was slightly stunned by the fury of her thoughts, while at the same time she welcomed the rush of temper. Or maybe it was confidence. She liked the sound of that better.

"Moira!"

Bari was bellowing from the stables. She didn't need to answer him, because he spotted her and began to tromp across the yard toward her. His kilt swayed as he went, and she decided he looked like a lad getting ready to throw a tantrum.

Try as she might, all she could muster was annoyance.

He hooked her arm and pulled her into the keep again. But instead of taking her into the Great Hall, he headed for a small receiving room off to the side that had a solid oak paneled door. Bari sent it closed with a kick of his foot.

"What in the hell do ye mean by giving that damned hawk to Sutherland?"

Her cheeks were still warm, but now it was her temper fueling the flush. "I mean to make sure ye do nae harm her in a fit of childish temper."

Bari looked at her as though she'd struck him. Rage flickered in his eyes, and she recognized the signs of his slipping sanity immediately this time.

"Have ye turned slut so easily?"

"Do ye truly think no one heard ye this morning?" Moira countered. "Or that a man such as Gahan Sutherland is nae willing to part with a few bits of silver to learn what ye are saying? I wager the stable lads ran to tell him before ye finished threatening me. Ye forget, Bari, he has as much reason to wish ye ill as ye do him. He'll use me as surely as ye will."

"Ye will have naught to do with that bastard!"

"He came after me again only because of what ye threatened to do to Athena."

Bari's eyes bulged. He moved closer to her and lowered his voice.

"Is that all he wanted from ye?"

"Well, he also thinks ye are insisting on this wedding in order to have the Matheson join ye in a feud against the Sutherlands. He wants me to refuse. Are ye really plotting a feud?" She might be risking a great deal by provoking him in a closed chamber, but she refused to take her wedding vows without putting up a fight.

"All I care about is that Achaius is willing to help me gain vengeance for Sandra." It was an evasion, but it only proved what Moira suspected. Gahan was right.

Bari snickered. "Do ye think ye've escaped me hold over ye by giving that bird away? It does nae matter. Matheson will likely take a great deal of delight in raping ye if ye refuse to stand by his side. Do nae think ye will find a welcome back at Seabhac. If ye ever set foot on me land again without doing as I command,

I will make sure every person who shows ye even the slightest kindness is rewarded with ten lashes."

She clenched her teeth against the horror, and she wanted to gag because of the helplessness filling her. "Ye are nae worthy of the respect given ye by the Frasers," she spat.

"But I am still their laird—yer laird—and there is naught ye can do to stay me hand. The reasons for yer match do nae concern ye. Only the fact that I have given me word on the matter." He smirked at her, victory shimmering in his eyes. "Go get dressed for yer wedding."

Moira glared at Bari. Every muscle felt tense, and her mind was racing as she tried to think of a way around his dictate...but there was none. The noose was too tight to pull off. She knew that Bari would do exactly what he promised. The only choice she had was to wed Achaius and hope she could make him happy enough to refuse to go feuding.

But she admitted to having very little faith in how content she'd be. Sometimes, doing the right thing brought little satisfaction. She wondered how long it would be before she committed the ultimate sin of counting the days until she was a widow.

She'd resist the urge, because it would make her more like Bari, and that truly was a fate worse than death.

❧

Gahan walked through the hallways on his way down from his chamber. He wore a doublet with silver buttons that were closed for a change.

He'd rather be riding across the hills on his way

north, but he had his duty to attend to as well. Witnessing a vassal laird's wedding was a time-honored tradition. To ride off would be an insult. Highlanders tended to hold grudges longer than most.

The scent of roasting meat drifted past his nose, reminding him that the Mathesons were making ready to celebrate their laird's fourth wedding. There was excitement in the air. As he passed the huge arched doorway that opened into the Great Hall, he could see the brewmaster happily overseeing the placement of a hogshead of ale for the feast. He directed the men moving the large barrel into position, and only when he was satisfied it was steady did he open the spout and draw off a sample. The men grinned as he held it up, and they all took a whiff.

It didn't interest Gahan, but it should have. After a long winter of nothing but what the storeroom offered, a feast should have pleased him. Instead, he moved out onto the steps and looked at the gate longingly.

"I like the direction of yer thinking," Cam said from behind him. He stuck a finger into his collar and tried to loosen it. "I've never cared for a doublet once spring begins. I'm roasting like that pig."

There was a rustle behind him, and they both turned to see the last of the sun's rays illuminating Moira. Gahan's breath froze in his chest. Somehow he'd missed just how truly beautiful she was. She wore a pair of gowns made of fine wool and dyed a spring green. He realized he'd never seen her hair. It was brushed out now into a wave of golden silk that fell to below her waist. A wreath of early spring greens sat on her head and looked grander than any golden crown.

But the look of impending doom in her eyes cut

him deeply. Still, she held her chin steady as she lowered herself in front of him. Then, drawing a shaky breath, she descended the stairs.

"I hope ye enjoy the wedding," Bari Fraser sneered under his breath at Gahan. The cad didn't offer his sister his arm and left her to make her way to the fate he'd engineered.

She did it admirably. She was as regal as a queen and as determined as any Highlander going into battle, doing what had to be done for the good of her kin. No matter how much he detested the circumstances, Gahan was struck hard by how much grace she conducted herself with. By the time she arrived at the church doors, her feelings were hidden behind a smooth expression. She reached for the basin holding the holy water and dipped a delicate finger into it. There was only a brief pause at the door as she lowered herself in deference to the house of God, and then she made her way to Achaius's side. The strength it took for her to face her future without tears in her eyes was not lost on him.

May God forgive him, but Gahan entered the church, craving Bari Fraser's blood for forcing his sister to such a fate.

Despite it all, Gahan reminded himself that Moira wasn't the only one who understood duty. He took up a position behind the couple and maintained his composure. He was the son of the Earl of Sutherland and had his father's expectations to uphold. In that moment, as the bells began to ring above them, he realized how much he and Moira had in common. They were both their father's children, bound by duty to remain in their places. Both the Church and the rest of the world maintained order by such methods. He'd been raised to respect it and to fear what happened when there was no order.

But at that moment, he felt more like becoming a savage than he ever had in his life.

The Matheson clan knew how to celebrate.

Her brother's retainers joined in, and the Great Hall was a swirling mass of jubilance.

"More cider!" Achaius bellowed. His mug was still full enough for some of the amber liquid to slosh over the rim, but a maid hurried up to the high table to fill it.

"Bari Fraser, yer father did nae teach ye how to drink like a Highlander," Achaius declared, to the amusement of his kin.

Moira's new husband stood up and lifted his tankard high. His people hooted with approval, pounding the tables as their laird emptied his mug in one long draw. He wiped his mouth on his sleeve and threw his arms up in victory to the delight of his clan.

"That's how it's done, lad!"

The assembled company pounded on the tables until Bari stood. He drained his mug, slammed it down, and the musicians began to play. Pipers and drummers played merry tunes.

Moira tried to let it take her dark mood away. She tapped her toe and clapped her hands but couldn't seem to keep in time. She looked for the children and watched them attempting to mimic the dance steps of their elders. One mother noticed her interest and promptly brought her baby up the steps of the high table to place it in Moira's arms.

The Matheson clan members applauded. The baby was a little bundle of life, a tiny miracle that smelled sweet. It watched her with big, glassy eyes while sucking on its fist. She tried to wish for a child, hoping the promise of a babe might brighten her mood, but she just couldn't banish the distaste of how that child would be conceived.

"Miss, we'd best leave before they get much more cider into them. They'll lose all sense soon," Fann whispered from beside her and lifted the baby away. She handed it to her clanswoman, then turned around and waved Moira toward the arched opening at the back of the hall.

Fann seemed to know her kin well. A cheer went up as Moira left the high table. But she hesitated in the hallway, looking toward the large doorway that led into the yard. The doors were still open to allow people who were finishing up their duties to join the festivities. The retainers manning the walls would be listening to the music and lamenting their poor luck at drawing duty tonight.

Moira cursed her own poor luck, because she was dreading the duty waiting above stairs for her. Still, some duties were best done quickly, so she turned and left the hall behind her.

"Second thoughts? Is that why ye hesitate?"

Moira jumped. "How do ye blend with the shadows so well?"

Gahan moved only slightly, so she could make out the mocking grin on his lips. "It's me dark hair."

The color of midnight.

Fann had continued on up the stairs, but it wouldn't take her long to realize Moira wasn't following. A lump formed in her throat as she faced the fact that there was no escape.

But Gahan extended a hand, offering it to her palm up. It looked like an invitation, and she longed for it to be one. Except there was no way she might accept it. She gripped the front of her skirts and lifted them to climb the stairs.

"Ye do nae want to go up those stairs."

"Nay, I do not," she admitted.

"Then come with me."

It was so tempting. She'd never felt so trapped, so desperate in her life. Her mouth went dry, and she stared at his hand as she faltered.

He moved, reaching out and clasping her hand. The contact was explosive, and she recalled how easily the burst of awareness might transform into excitement. She didn't want to jerk away; instead, her fingers closed around his, and it sent a rush of sensation through her.

Back in the hall, Bari roared with laughter, but the sound of his voice broke the spell.

"I cannae."

She opened her fingers, but Gahan tugged her forward. She stumbled into the shadows with him, like falling into the mythical world of the Fae.

His embrace was warm and secure, and she might so easily allow her senses to become beguiled. He leaned down, angling his head so their lips met. There was no reason to resist this time, and every reason to meet him halfway. The desperation threatening to smother her sent her rising up onto her toes so she might have a last taste of him.

He groaned when she moved toward him, a deep sound of male approval and surprise. His lips settled onto hers, softly coaxing at first, gently instructing her. He teased the seal of her mouth with the tip of his tongue until she parted her lips, opening her mouth wider. He took instant advantage, deepening the kiss as passion began to flare. She jerked back, stunned by how quickly their kiss transformed into something ravenous.

"We cannae."

His hands firmly held her hips. It was bluntly intimate, making her more aware of her passage and its purpose than she'd ever been before.

"I will take ye away."

"But to where?" She was letting her thoughts spill over her lips once more, but it sobered her. She pushed against his chest, and he released her with a soft grunt.

"I'll take ye away and make no demands upon ye, Moira. Just do nae go up there and unite the Matheson with yer brother's plans for a feud. I know the Church would have something to say about me asking ye to leave, but I still am."

He'd crossed his arms over his chest and looked like he was resisting the urge to reach for her again. Not many men were willing to swallow their pride so completely. Too many preferred the glory of battle to logic.

"Ye make too much sense, Gahan Sutherland, and I'm tempted, for I am no blind to the fact that Bari is intent on making trouble with yer kin. But ye have every reason to want vengeance on Bari. I'd be a fool to no see how taking me away would satisfy that need."

She backed away, moving back into the hallway where the lanterns offered her some light.

"I would nae take me vengeance through a woman." His voice was hard as he followed her into the half light. "Ye are questioning me honor again, lass."

She'd be mad to trust him, but the way he looked at her made it seem so possible.

"If ye are acting with honor, ye must understand that I have me own to uphold."

"There is naught honorable about yer brother wedding ye to an old man."

"I agree." She took a deep breath. "But I do nae see the Mathesons taking kindly to ye stealing their laird's bride. No one will debate the wisdom of the match. They will see only that ye stole me away while Achaius made ye welcome. He'll feud with ye or with me brother."

"Yer brother would deserve it."

"But me clanswomen would nae, and it would be the women of the Fraser who will weep for their sons."

She expected him to argue with her. Instead he cursed, low and viciously, but not at her. She'd never thought to find something in common with him, but at that moment, they were both caught in the web of circumstance.

"Ye are nae like Sandra."

It was the finest compliment she had ever received. Her cheeks warmed with a blush as she lowered herself in front of him.

"Good-bye, Gahan Sutherland. It might be a sin, but I thank ye for giving me my first kiss."

The men who had wagered against her composure lost their bet, because she didn't weep on her
way up the stairs. She smiled as the words Gahan
had praised her with sank into her memory and left
her feeling proud.

⁓

"She's a surprise," Cam muttered as soon as Moira was
out of earshot.

Gahan turned on his brother, but Cam only raised
an eyebrow. He reached up and smoothed the three
feathers secured to the side of his bonnet with a silver
brooch and made sure one of them was pointing up.
It was the symbol of his position as captain, a rank he
held for the sole purpose of protecting the earl's son.

"I'd be little good to ye if I failed to notice when ye
slip away. There's more than one man here who would
enjoy hearing ye were found with yer throat slit."

His brother was speaking the truth, but it felt like
the point of a dagger was indeed at his throat. Too
many truths were cutting into him. He had to force
himself to walk away. He had never cared enough
about a woman to think about her when he was gone.
To have it happen with a woman he couldn't have was
a foul twist of fate. There were more than a few who
believed a child born on the wrong side of wedlock
inherited their parents' sin.

At the moment, he felt like the curse of his birth
would never leave him.

Four

"THERE'S NO NEED TO BE NERVOUS."

Fann sounded more uncertain than Moira felt. Aife was poking the fire and adding wood. Soon the chamber was overly warm.

Or maybe she was more nervous than she wished to admit.

"I found this dressing robe for ye. It's made of thick wool and lined in the softest linen. It will feel grand against yer skin."

"Against me skin?" Moira questioned.

Fann's smile was, without doubt, wicked. The lump returned to her throat and stayed there as the girls began to take away the fine overdress and under-robe. She understood the reason for the large fire now.

"Sit, so I can take yer stockings."

Aife brought over a stool, and Moira lowered herself onto it.

She had to face her responsibilities. Maybe she should think of Gahan. Why had the man said such things as *lover*? Such boldness was certain to send her thoughts places they shouldn't go. If she had never tasted sugar from the Indies, she could not long for it.

Fann knelt and rolled one stocking down her leg. The warm air teased her skin, making her feel vulnerable. When the second stocking was removed, she felt completely exposed.

Gahan's dark features filled her thoughts as Aife began to loosen the wreath in her hair. But Achaius's face came to mind, and she felt the sting of tears when she realized just whom she was going to be lying with tonight.

She could not think of Gahan. It had been unkind of the man to tease her. To be so close that she wondered what his kiss would feel like. Such curiosity was sure to shred her determination. Well, not if she refused to allow any thought of the Highlander to enter her mind. She was wed. The wife of another man now. Gahan was forbidden.

"Ye are sweet as a spring morning," Fann murmured and reached for the neck of her last garment.

Moira hugged herself to keep her chemise. Fann worried her lower lip for a moment before she lifted the dressing robe and held it up. It almost felt like a trap as Moira uncrossed her arms and pushed into the sleeves. Fann moved in front of her to tie it closed.

Aife set two slippers on the floor for her.

A shiver went down her back as she pushed her foot into a slipper. She ground her teeth as she forced herself to put on the second one. But once it was done, she was able to draw a deep breath again.

Her throat constricted when she was led into the hallway. Fann guided her up two more flights of stairs to the laird's chamber. Two retainers stood guard. They grinned at her as they opened the double doors.

Just beyond the doors was a different world. The outer room had Persian carpets and ornately carved furniture. Hung on the walls were tapestries, and beeswax candles burned, filling the air with sweetness. Through the open doors, which led to the bedchamber, she could see a huge bed with a canopy and thick bed curtains.

As she passed two thronelike chairs, she realized they had the crest of another clan on their cushions.

"The laird's second wife was a Sinclair," Fann explained on her way to the bed. "The first was a Campbell…"

The bed curtains were embroidered with the Campbell insignia. As she looked around, most of the lavish adornments held the crests of other clans. Achaius knew how to play the marriage game well.

"Quickly now, miss. The men will be delivering yer groom soon."

The bedding was pulled back, and Aife untied the dressing robe. She stepped behind her to remove it gently and drape it over a chair. Fann stepped up and took hold of the chemise collar, and Moira jumped back. Fann looked surprised, and Aife looked to her sister for direction.

"Ye are wed now, so there is no reason to wear the chemise to bed," Fann offered gently. "The laird will nae like it."

"Of course." Moira tugged the garment off herself and handed it to Fann. "It is simply a habit."

Fann nodded and looked toward the floor to hide

her feelings. "The laird will nae summon ye often. In yer own chamber, ye may do as ye please."

With her last garment stripped from her, she slipped into bed. The mattress was soft and felt like goose down. The sheets were fine and smelled of heather as Fann pulled them up to cover her. There was a small mountain of pillows behind her, so many that she wasn't really lying down.

Fann and Aife both lowered themselves before quitting the chamber. Both girls had bright cheeks and hurried from the room. Once the outer doors shut, there was only the crackle from the fire to listen to. And her own thoughts.

She'd never been nude in bed before. Her skin was ultrasensitive, and she wiggled about, trying to become comfortable. But it was impossible for her to relax. Time felt suspended, every minute a tiny eternity while she strained to hear the doors opening again. A log fell in the hearth, sending sparks flying in a scarlet shower. The flames drew her attention as they danced, consuming the wood until it all collapsed into a bed of glowing red embers. The thick coverlet warmed her feet, and her eyes slid shut, the last few restless nights taking their toll on her.

〜〜

The church bell woke her again.

Moira rubbed her eyes and sat up, her body protesting after two nights of restlessness.

"A right fetching sight ye are, Wife."

The blood drained from her face, and she turned to look at Achaius. He was lying back on the mound of pillows, splotches from his supper marring the sleeve of his shirt. He still had his boots on, but his kilt was tangled around his feet.

"And yer tits are mouthwatering."

She crossed her arms over her chest a scant moment before the door burst open.

"We've come for the sheet!" one of his captains announced.

Horror stifled any protest she might have made, and she was tugged out of the bed while still fighting to speak.

"Have at me, lads! Yer laird still knows how to enjoy a juicy treat!"

Achaius's retainers helped him out of the bed. Moira's heart was pounding as she waited for the accusations to begin flying. Bari might well beat her to death, and there would be no one to believe she was still a virgin.

But the sheet wasn't clean. Marring its creamy surface was a dark stain that delighted the men. They tore it off the bed and took it to the window. Moments later, it hung outside the window of the keep, and a cheer rose from the yard.

How? It made no sense.

Was it a miracle? She scoffed at herself. The Lord above certainly had more important things to use His divine power on.

The retainers filed out with smiles on their faces as Fann gently placed the dressing robe around her shoulders.

"Come with me, mistress."

Moira looked back at Achaius, expecting to see rage on his face. Instead, he licked his lips and winked at her.

"I do enjoy being wed, lass, indeed I do."

The men dressing him chuckled. "The sheet proves that sure enough, Laird," one offered.

Fann urged her toward the door as Moira tried to recall the night hours. Try as she might, there was no memory of her husband's arrival.

Yet the sheet was bloodied.

When they were back in her chamber, Moira stole a moment to check the insides of her thighs. But they were clean, proving that her monthly courses hadn't arrived at the most inopportune time.

To be sure, more than one bride had flown a bloodied sheet and not been pure on the night of her wedding. But she hadn't employed any decep-tion—not that anyone would believe her if it were discovered she was still a maiden. She sat down on a stool and rubbed her forehead. Her wedding night was behind her, and still the worst was yet to come.

When had she angered fate so badly?

Achaius laughed for a long time. He flexed his hand, looking at the cut between his fingers. It would heal soon enough, and his little bride had never noticed it. He began to cough, this time the fit lasting for quite some time.

Mornings were becoming harder, his coughing fits more prolonged. His lungs seemed to fill at night. But it was nothing good whiskey wouldn't cut through, so he poured himself a measure and swallowed it. His throat was burning as he poured a second cup, then sipped at it. He was celebrating.

Achaius knew Moira Fraser had a fire in her belly, one that would see her refusing to settle for watching life pass her by. All he needed was to dangle her in front of Gahan Sutherland. Once the man made a grab for her, she'd take what she thought was her only chance to know the touch of a young man. Every woman was a wanton at her core. Just as every man was a savage.

When thrown together, they would not be able to resist answering passion's call.

"Can we leave now?"

Gahan shot a dark glare at his brother. The wedding sheet was flapping in the morning breeze to the delight of the Mathesons and Frasers. Their glee disgusted him.

He had to stop to determine why he was so furious. It should have been because the two clans were united against his own. But the truth burned in his gut. It was jealousy, pure and simple. The stained sheet drove home the fact that Moira had given herself to Achaius. The man was her husband, for Christ's sake. Gahan knew he should have been able to use that fact to temper his rising envy, but it wasn't having any effect.

"Aye, we're leaving," he snapped. At least distance would help get Moira out of his thoughts.

"Nae so fast, young Gahan. I insist ye stay a bit longer."

Gahan turned to find Achaius making his way toward them. Cam tugged on his bonnet, but Gahan's hands were clenched into fists at his sides. There was a smirk on the old laird's face that made him want to hit Achaius.

"I have matters to attend to, Laird Matheson. We have already lingered here too long. I will inform me father of yer wedding," Gahan told him.

"No, no." Achaius reached them and had to pause a moment to catch his breath. "Ye were right, lad."

"About what?" An insane twist of excitement flared through him, but behind Achaius, the soiled sheet flapped in the morning breeze, confirming there would be no announcement that Moira was free.

"Right to scold me for nae sending word to yer father of me union with sweet Moira. When ye are as old as I, every day becomes more precious." He chuckled and coughed. "At least that's the best reason I've got."

"The deed is done." The words stuck in Gahan's throat.

Achaius licked his lips. "Aye, I know it well, but I've a mind to ride back to Dunrobin with ye to tell yer father of me actions."

"I can do the telling."

The old laird straightened and looked him in the eye. There was a gleam of something in the old man's eyes that sent suspicion snaking through Gahan's gut. It looked almost like the man was only playing at being feeble.

"I know me duty as surely as ye do. Yer father is me overlord, and I need to tell the man meself. The weather is fine, and a ride would do me well. There is nothing like a new bride to restore a man's vigor. Me men will be ready to ride out after they fill their bellies."

Achaius turned and made his way into the keep again. Cam stepped up beside Gahan.

"Are ye really going to allow him along?"

"Do ye have a reason to tell him no?" Gahan shot his sibling a hard look. "One me father will nae have a problem with?"

"Since he's united with the Frasers, aye, I can think of one," Cam hinted.

Gahan's expression became grim. "I wonder if I should nae have mentioned that little fact last night. I think Laird Matheson might just be interested in knowing he isn't wed to Bari's only sister."

"I'd bet on that. Tell them both that Sandra is still alive. At least we'll have an end to this."

"An end that would happen when Bari Fraser tries to kill me." Gahan indulged himself in a pleased grin. "But me father would nae be pleased with me spilling blood under a vassal's roof."

Cam shook his head slowly, but Gahan didn't regret his words. "This game is nae to my liking. I prefer me fights out in the open. Nae with secrets clinging to me boots."

"Most men do," Cam said, "but ye are nae a common man, and the nobles are always waging their battles in the shadows."

"Aye. Which is why I cannae tell Achaius no. If we do, he'll cry to one and all that we slighted him."

"Bari will no doubt make good use of that," Cam agreed. "At least it will remove ye from here and the fascination ye seem to have with Moira Fraser."

"She's another man's wife now."

Cam shrugged. "Ye say the words, but the look in

yer eyes tells me ye want to smash Achaius in the jaw.
She's under yer skin."

"Nay, she is nae."

Gahan turned his back on his brother, but it wasn't
so easy to brush aside the truth of his words. He was
spoiling for a fight. Maybe he'd let Bari Fraser know his
sister Sandra was still alive and locked up in the oldest
tower at Dunrobin Castle. The bitch should be dead,
but neither he nor Norris had the stomach for hanging
her. It was not the Highlander way. Maybe Bari and his
father had no reservation about sending a woman to do
their dirty work, but in the end, Gahan hadn't been able
to bring himself to order her execution.

So she stayed at Dunrobin.

Taking Achaius to Dunrobin could well see that
fact uncovered, because servants talked. No castle was
without spies or those looking to improve their lot by
selling secrets.

❧

"What do ye mean ye are heading to Dunrobin?"
Bari asked.

"It is simple enough," Achaius said. "I failed in me
duty, and I intend to apologize to me overlord."

"We have an alliance."

"Indeed we do, lad." Achaius finished his breakfast
and belched. "I always keep me word when the dowry
has been paid."

Bari leaned closer to him to keep their words from
drifting. "Then why are ye going to Dunrobin?"

"Ye truly are newly weaned from yer mother's tit,"
Achaius replied. "If I have the opportunity to inspect

the defenses of me foe before the fighting begins, I would be a fool nae to take it."

Achaius slapped the table. "Someone go wake me bride! I've no doubt she is nae here because I gave her little chance to rest last night, but we have duties to attend to."

"Ye intend to take Moira?" Bari asked. "I do nae think that is wise."

Achaius was on his feet and making ready to leave the high table. He froze and shot a hard look at Bari.

"She is me wife now. She's going to help me soothe the ruffled feathers of me overlord—something ye should be doing too, since yer sister Sandra tried to kill him. Remember yer place, Bari Fraser. The Earl of Sutherland is also yer overlord. Get yer men together and saddle the horses. We're riding north."

"Like hell Bari Fraser is riding with us."

Cam was furious, and so were half the Sutherland retainers. They clustered around him as they waited to see what their orders would be. They might be bound to obey him, but more than one Highlander laird had learned that loyalty was best earned. Highlanders did not follow fools for long.

"Let him. It will save us the trouble of watching him." Gahan surveyed the faces of his men. "It's going to be entertaining to see him try to convince me father that he had naught to do with Sandra's actions."

A few grins appeared, and most of the men nodded. Their eyes were bright with their hunger for vengeance. He moved toward his horse, but Cam followed.

"And Moira? Ye are set to allow her to ride with us?"

Gahan tugged on a strap. "Aye," he answered. "There is no reason to deny her." He knew he shouldn't feel glad about her traveling north with them, but he was filled with satisfaction all the same.

"Oh, there is reason—and a good one." Cam smoothed a hand along the neck of Gahan's stallion. "Ye watch her like a hungry wolf. Are ye thinking to follow yer brother's example in bringing home a woman to keep?"

"She's another man's wife now. I won't be doing any more watching."

Gahan shot his brother a hard look. Cam held his stare for a long moment before nodding. He reached up and tugged on the corner of his bonnet before going to see to his own horse. It granted Gahan a moment to relax his grip on his emotions. Hiding his pleasure was hard because Cam was right; he did watch Moira too closely. The reason eluded him, but the need to continue to be near her remained.

It was almost suspicious the way fate was keeping her near him, but he wasn't in the mood to question forces beyond his control.

⬦

She was leaving.

Moira had to squelch the urge to skip down the stairs like a little girl. Two Matheson retainers trailed her, making it imperative that she maintain dignified behavior. Yet it was almost impossible.

She was going with Gahan after all…That idea gave her pause. She stopped on the steps, and Fann bumped into her. The stairs were narrow, and she went stumbling down them until someone hooked her around the waist to stop her fall. He lifted her off her feet then set her gently down on the bottom step.

"I hope that is nae a sampling of how adept ye are at traveling, Lady Matheson."

Gahan's tone darkened when he spoke her title. It sounded wrong and felt wrong, too. Unconsummated meant the union might be dissolved. Which filled her with happiness.

"Nay…I am normally sure-footed."

But ye are a deceiver…

The sunlight didn't quite reach inside the keep yet. She was grateful for the poor light, because she felt her cheeks flushing. The burn increased when she realized Gahan was scowling because he thought she had bedded her husband.

No man had ever been jealous of her.

But he wasn't jealous, she reminded herself. He was scheming against Bari…

"Good. We need to depart. It will take us most of the day to make MacLeod land."

"I understood we were bound for Dunrobin," she said, puzzled.

Gahan hooked his hands into his belt and watched her. He seemed even more formidable today—and disapproving. His harsh expression stung.

"I know who me friends are and will be spending the night on their land. Nae out in the open."

"Oh, of course."

He was on guard this morning; his captain stood only a foot from his back. There was a formality that made her long for the man she'd encountered in the darkness. But she would not see him again.

Because ye refused him…

"Yer mistress will need a surcoat," he said, addressing Fann. "There is still snow at Dunrobin."

"What do ye have on yer feet?" he asked gruffly.

Moira hesitated to show him her shoes. He and his retainers wore thick, well-made boots that laced over antler-horn buttons up to their knees. They had to be wonderful to wear when the snow was blowing.

"Show me." His tone rang with authority, and there was no mercy in his expression, only the unrelenting look of a man who was accustomed to being obeyed. She caught the fabric of her overdress and tugged it up.

"My sister's shoes are nae yer concern," Bari said from the doorway that opened to the yard.

"They are when I'm taking her north. I've no need to hear ye saying she took ill because of me actions. Ye've already said far too much about me, and none of it was good. The Sutherlands do nae crave trouble with the Frasers."

Gahan turned in a flash, the longer back pleats of his kilt whipping up. Bari jerked back, clearly surprised by how fast Gahan moved. Her brother's lips curled into a snarl.

"Ye'll stay away from her, bastard."

"She's a wed woman now and beyond yer control," Gahan replied. There was a touch of satisfaction in his voice that clearly enraged Bari.

"Indeed she is wed," Achaius agreed from behind Bari. "And I'm a good provider for those who are mine." He pointed at Fann. "Get yer mistress ready. The sunlight is wasting."

Fann reached for her elbow, but Moira found it hard to turn around. The air was thick with tension. Achaius turned and left, leaving the two men facing off. Bari looked like he might lunge at Gahan.

"Try it," Gahan taunted. "I'm the one who handed the poison to yer sister Sandra, and I'll be happy to have ye know it."

"Ye did what?" Bari screeched.

Gahan shrugged. He reached behind him and pushed Moira up the stairs and out of the way. She gasped, because he seemed so intent on her brother, yet he knew exactly where she was. A pair of Matheson retainers snapped out of their daze and reached down to grab her and lift her several steps above the impending fight.

"I thought it rather fitting. Sandra poisoned me father, so I gave her enough poison to end her own life."

"That is suicide," Bari roared. "Ye damned her to hell, ye bastard!"

"That's where she belongs."

Bari threw a punch at Gahan's jaw, but it never connected. Gahan lifted his foot and planted it in the center of Bari's chest and sent him flying through the doorway. Gahan's men surged after him as Moira twisted free and followed.

Bari was facedown in the dirt. He bellowed with outrage as he scrambled to his feet. But Achaius shouted over his sputtering.

"How dare ye attack me overlord's son in me castle!"

Matheson retainers rushed Bari and had him

restrained before the Frasers realized their intent. There were more Matheson retainers than Fraser, and they pushed Bari's men back.

"He gave me sister poison!"

"I tossed it onto the bunk next to her. Which is less than she deserved for coating me father's goblet with it. Hanging was too simple for her crime."

"Ye had no right to deny her soul salvation!"

Achaius smacked Bari across the mouth. There was more strength in the old man than it appeared, because Bari went stumbling. Matheson retainers hauled him up from the ground and held him for their laird.

"He had every right," Achaius declared. "I would have broken every one of her fingers and left her alive for a month before I hanged her. Ye'll ride north with us and make yer peace with the earl, or I will send this sister back to ye."

"Ye cannae undo what has been done," Bari argued. He shook off the men holding him, but they only eased off, remaining a half pace behind him as a warning. Her brother pointed at the sheet. "Ye are wed."

"I am laird here. I can do as I will. Nae many men would fault me for turning out the kin of a poisoner. If ye do nae make yer peace with the earl, I say ye knew of yer sister's treachery. I'll keep no kin of yers as wife."

She should have been horrified. But she found herself hoping Bari would refuse to bend. It was more than a hope; part of her was desperate to escape. What had seemed impossible was suddenly a flicker of possibility.

Bari glared at Gahan. "I did nae know what she was about."

"Good," Achaius said. "I would have been sad to let yer sister go. She's a juicy treat."

Achaius turned to face Gahan and licked his lips. Disappointment raked its claws across her gut, it was so intense. She thought she saw Gahan stiffen in anger, but she realized she was seeing only what she wanted to.

"Come, mistress." Fann was tugging her up the stairs once more. Achaius was smirking at Gahan. The suggestive nature of his expression turned her stomach, so she relented and let Fann lead her away.

But she wrung her skirt all the way up the stairs.

Was Achaius so feeble-minded he didn't realize he hadn't consummated their union? Or was he playing a game with her brother?

Both options promised her grief. Bari would not have her back if Achaius turned her out, while Gahan's offer had been an empty one. She needed to forget about him. No good could come of giving in to her desire for the man. Except that taking a lover would solve the problem of her still being a maiden. Achaius would have no trouble turning her out if a midwife testified she was still a virgin. She'd be accused of soiling the sheet too.

Gahan would make a fine lover...

The idea was intoxicating. It was balm for the fear burning through her. He'd hardly admit to their liaison.

She stiffened. Her thoughts disgraced her. Gahan had honor, and she was thinking of ways to tarnish that noble trait. Bari might have dictated the circumstances of her life, but he did not control her morality. No matter what happened, she'd face it.

Even if the idea of having a reason to let Gahan kiss her again was nearly impossible to resist.

❧

"Mistress?"

Gahan's captain stepped up beside her mare once she was mounted. He offered her something, and when she took it, she realized it was a leather gauntlet. Athena was perched on his forearm. Her hand shook as she pushed it into the thick leather glove.

Cam offered her the hawk, and she cooed softly to her. Athena fluttered her wings in greeting as she climbed onto her arm. Cam tugged on his bonnet, then strode away to mount his own horse.

The Sutherland retainers were an impressive sight, mounted and bristling in the morning sun. Each man wore a leather jerkin that was studded with brass for protection. She was used to seeing Gahan with his collar undone, but today he wore a stiff leather collar closed around his throat. Archers wouldn't find it simple to pick him off his horse. Behind his left shoulder, the hilt of his sword gleamed, the heavy weapon strapped in place across his back.

All his men were dressed the same, a blunt reminder that Sutherland had the coin to ensure their retainers were well outfitted. The Matheson retainers did not have as much; neither did the Fraser ones. Many of them had doublets that were worn or patched. Not every man had a sword on his back either. Many of the younger ones had only knives. Bari might sneer at Gahan for his illegitimate birth, but there was no denying he had greater standing. Gahan guided his horse forward and raised his hand.

"MacLeod land!"

His men roared with approval, then followed their leader out of the raised gate. Most of the inhabitants of the castle had come out to watch them leave. The Matheson retainers kept Moira in their midst as they followed, leaving the Frasers to fall in behind them.

Horse hooves pounded the road, and Moira discovered herself smiling. If it was wrong, so be it. But she was happy to be leaving Matheson land.

Five

GAHAN KEPT THEM AT A HARD PACE. HE WAS RACING the sun and knew it. But he didn't push the horses past their endurance. He was everything a noble son should be, everything a leader should be. Moira could see that his men followed not just because his blood was blue, but also because he knew how to lead them. As a result of his careful management, the miles fell behind them quickly. They crossed onto MacLeod land, and the tops of the keep came into sight.

The fields around MacLeod Keep were already being turned. Men were working the plows as the troop of men rode past. They looked up, most of them taking the opportunity to wipe their brows. The scent of newly broken earth tickled Moira's nose, but it was a good smell, one that announced spring and new beginnings. Weddings normally gave her such a feeling, but hers hadn't.

The sun was already hugging the horizon when they gained their first view of MacLeod Tower. Bells began to ring along the curtain wall of the stronghold. Gahan pulled them to a stop just beyond the range of the archers and waited for his standard to be recognized. Moments later, the gate was lifted. Gahan led them through, and soon the inner yard was full of horses and men dismounting.

Moira was grateful to be stopping. She made sure Athena was settled on the saddle perch before getting ready to slide off her mare. Cam caught her on her way down, ensuring that she touched down softly.

He offered her a nod, then resumed his post behind Gahan.

It should have been a Matheson retainer who saw to her, but none of them were anywhere near her. Somehow, she'd ended up surrounded by Sutherland men. She lifted her arm for Athena, and the moment the hawk was settled on her arm, a Sutherland man led her horse away.

Bari stopped to glare at her, but the men around her shifted, cutting him off. He snorted then made his way to the steps of the keep, where Saer MacLeod was welcoming Gahan.

Saer MacLeod was an imposing man. His dark hair hung to his shoulders. The cool evening breeze clearly didn't bother him, given that his shirtsleeves were rolled up and tied at his shoulders. His arms were brown from the sun. His kilt was held in place by a worn belt that lacked any showy decoration, like the one Bari wore. Saer was hardened, the muscles of his arms clearly defined. He had a great deal in common with Gahan; both looked like men who earned everything they had, including respect.

Achaius made his way to where Saer stood. The MacLeod laird didn't look at him. Instead Saer MacLeod turned to look at Moira, his unsettling gaze sweeping her from head to toe. Achaius gestured her forward.

She should have thought of him as her husband but just couldn't. The label stuck in her thoughts, refusing to let her thoughts flow.

With Athena perched on her arm, she made her way up the steps and lowered herself in greeting. The new MacLeod laird wasn't interested in her manners; his eyes were on Athena.

"The hawk trusts ye," Saer MacLeod remarked.

"I raised her."

"Yes, yes…me bride has many skills," Achaius said.

Saer extended his bare forearm, but Athena let out a shrill warning. Her feathers ruffled, and she lowered her head to make sure he knew she had no liking for him.

"Calm the bird," Achaius ordered, "and hand it to Laird MacLeod."

Saer's eyes narrowed. Moira bit her lip and said, "A hawk cannae be ordered into submission. They must be trained to do so."

"Aye, the lass is right. Ye must earn its respect," Saer said, nodding. He withdrew his arm. "Ye are welcome in me home."

He turned and walked through the double-door entrance into the main tower. It was nowhere near as grand as Matheson Tower, but it felt more welcoming. Achaius and Bari followed him without a backward glance, while Gahan remained behind with Moira.

"Ye are less than dirt to the Matheson," Gahan remarked. He kept his voice low, but there was rage in his eyes. "Did he hurt ye?"

It was a question he had no right to ask, an intimate one that sent heat to her cheeks. She seemed to be forever blushing in his presence, but instead of being irritated, she discovered she was pleased.

She would certainly never blush for Achaius.

Gahan pressed her. "Tell me the truth, Moira."

"Ye should nae ask—"

His dark gaze cut into hers. "Answer me."

"He didn't…" She couldn't finish the sentence because she knew she was lying—or at best, she was willfully deceiving him.

She lifted her foot to climb another step, but he moved in front of her. The man was imposing enough without towering on a step above her. She felt goose-flesh prickle her skin in response. Behind her bodice, her nipples contracted into hard points, and her heart increased its pace. Time felt frozen. She was trapped between breaths, noticing all the details of his face. It felt as though he could read her thoughts as easily as a book.

"Ye are hiding something," he stated.

Gahan's accusation brought Moira back to the present, giving her such a start that she jostled Athena still perched on her arm. The hawk let out a shrill cry, and Cam came up the stairs at a run, managing to lift the hawk off her arm as Moira regained her balance.

"I'll take Athena to the mews," he said, and was gone with a swish of his kilt, leaving her to face the formidable glare of his master. There was some unnatural connection between them. She lowered herself and ducked around him.

Inside, her husband waited. She looked at Achaius,

insisting that she focus on him. With a determined step, she closed the distance between them.

It was time to act like a woman.

And a wife.

⤳

Moira sat at the end of the high table. It was a place of honor, one she'd often wondered about as the half sister of the laird. The reality didn't fit the image she'd created in her girlhood fantasies. She didn't feel honored. Instead, all she noticed were the looks of pity being cast toward her from the women of the MacLeod. They were no fools. Her union was a cruel joke, and they narrowed their eyes when they gazed at Bari for arranging the match.

The fare set out on the high table of MacLeod Tower was simple. The surprising fact was that every table was served the same meal. Saer MacLeod seemed completely at ease and content with the common fare, as did Gahan. Only Bari and Achaius occasionally looked longingly toward the kitchens to see if something more might be coming.

"I hear yer land was raided after Sauchieburn," Bari remarked at last. "Little wonder yer table is light."

Saer turned to look at his guest. "The fare is filling, which is more than some must make do with. The land I inherited is fertile. I am used to earning what I have."

"I suppose it is better than what ye had living on the isles."

"Among the savages?" Saer inquired. "I found them more trustworthy than some of me fellow Highland lairds. The men of the isles will fight ye face-to-face, nae slip poison in yer drink."

Bari's face reddened. "That was me sister's doing." He reached for his mug and took a large swallow before nodding. "I'm off to set it straight with the earl."

Saer didn't respond. Bari finished his meal and departed for his chamber. Achaius remained, entertaining those willing to listen with tales of his youth. Moira sat by his side, determined to begin acting like a wife. To leave before her new husband would set tongues to wagging about the validity of her marriage. The candles burned low before he finally stood up.

"Forgive me for retiring so early, but I've a new bride to enjoy."

No one corrected him on the time, and Moira found herself worrying her lower lip as she stood to follow her husband. Her reprieve might be over. But there was nowhere else to go. She followed Achaius up two flights of stairs to a chamber. Someone had made sure it was ready. A fire crackled in the hearth, and candles cast their yellow light over the bed.

The linens were turned down, and Moira felt her throat tighten. A young gillie helped Achaius strip off his clothing until he wore only his shirt. The young lad laid everything neatly aside then tugged on his bonnet and left. A lump began to form in her throat, but she forced it down. She reached for the button that held her sleeve closed at her wrist.

"Still in yer dress, lass?" Achaius crawled into bed, propped himself up on the plump pillows, and smirked at her. "Well then, take yerself back to the kitchens and have the cook mull me some cider."

"Cider?" Her fingers froze on the button.

"Aye, aye." He waved her toward the door. "Me belly is troubled."

"Of course."

She might have spoken too quickly, but he didn't seem to notice. Moira forgot to lower herself before spinning around and heading toward the door. Her determination was no match for the flood of relief that swept through her.

"Ye are a dutiful lass to hurry so."

She was already out the door when his words reached her ears. She was in fact running, but she seemed unable to control the urge to flee. It was only a reprieve…and a short one at that.

She walked down the stairs to the kitchens like a woman on the way to her execution. All too quickly, steam rose from the small copper pot the cook used to warm the cider. The cook unlocked the spice cabinet, taking only a small piece of cinnamon and a single clove before locking it again. When it was added to the cider, she leaned over and inhaled deeply.

"It's been a long time since I used any of the spices. We have little left. I adore cinnamon, but there are more essential things to be buying this season. Our new laird does nae waste coin on comforts. That is a blessing, for there are many needs here since we were raided."

She smiled, blissfully ignorant of the turmoil filling Moira. For a moment, Moira was jealous of the other woman, envious of the fact that she was not dreading the coming night. Then she chided herself for being childish. Everyone had their duties, both pleasant and not. She'd not go hungry on Matheson land.

Moira carried the cider up the stairs, her steps echoing in the now-quiet tower. Only a single lantern was left glowing in the hallway, the light making its way through slots in its tin sides. A torch would have provided more light, but the fire risk was much greater. The MacLeod land had been raided, but the tower had not been breached, or the lanterns would have been carried away. A castle and its grounds were expensive to maintain. Her dowry would no doubt go toward improvements of Matheson Castle. Gahan would be expected to increase Sutherland holdings when he wed.

She sighed and climbed the last step. The dread was beginning to annoy her. So she lifted her chin and entered the chamber with a determined stride. Once it was done, she would not worry about it any longer.

But the chamber was filled with snoring.

Achaius had the coverlet pulled up to his chin and his eyes closed. He was so deeply asleep, his snoring bounced off the stone walls. The scent of cinnamon filled her nose, and she turned around.

The cook was in luck, it seemed, for she would be getting a taste of the cider after all. There was no reason to let it go to waste.

Gahan lingered at the high table.

"Yer brother suffered from the same affliction," Saer remarked.

"And what might that be?"

His host wasn't offended by his sharp tone. Saer chuckled and leaned against the side of his chair so he might look straight at Gahan. There was a devilish look in his dark eyes and a grin on his lips. Gahan laughed.

"Being in the company of Bari Fraser has soured me sense of humor."

"Laird Fraser does have a stench about him." Saer's expression became pensive. "One I do nae trust."

"Nor do I."

"It makes the fascination ye have with his sister a bit complicated. Nae that I would allow that to stop me from taking what I wanted," Saer said suggestively.

"I do nae have a fascination with her."

Saer picked up the knife he'd used to carve his dinner and slid it back into the top of his boot. When he looked back at Gahan, his dark brows were raised.

"Ye are correct," Gahan relented. "But she's wed now, and that is nae a line I intend to cross." Disappointment left a bitter taste in his mouth, but he didn't reach for his mug of ale. The drink held no appeal for him. All he craved was Moira, and he could not have her.

"She is nae *that* wed," Saer replied. "Standing at the church door for the blessing is nae wed. Nae to my way of thinking. Insincere words do nae make a bond. A Highlander is a man of his words and actions."

Gahan frowned, earning another chuckle from his host.

"Look at her, man. She's still a maiden. I'd bet me last coin on that. She still looks at ye like sweet kisses are the only thing lovers share. There was also the look of impending doom on her face when her husband called her above stairs. Her fear was of the unknown."

Her words rose in his memory.

"He didn't…"

"Christ," Gahan swore. "She still flew a soiled sheet."

Saer cocked his head. "Did she, or did that old man have a hand in it? Laird Matheson doesn't seem the type to admit time has stolen anything from him. Her brother should be lashed for wedding her to such a creature. Have ye noticed how little interest the Matheson retainers have in her? They do nae care if she ends up dead. Her usefulness was in bringing them her dowry."

"I have noticed." Gahan curled his fingers into a fist. "It does nae surprise me. Bari Fraser had a hand in his sister's attempt to poison me father. I'm sure of that and will nae rest until it's proven. Wedding his sister to an old man is exactly what I expect of him."

"But ye are taking the man to yer home?" Saer asked.

It was Gahan's turn to grin at Saer, but it wasn't a pleasant expression. "If Bari is fool enough to enter Dunrobin, I'll be happy to let him through the gates. I make no promise he'll ever leave as anything but a ghost."

Sear shook his head slowly, distaste showing in his eyes. "I admit I'd rather fight a man and be done with it."

"Yer new position will force ye to temper that impulse and face the fact that many do nae share yer preference," Gahan said. "I've listened to me father say such over and over, yet I still want to balk. Bari Fraser has forced me to see the truth of me father's teachings."

Something moved to their right. Both men turned to look, because the hall was quiet. There was a flip of skirt and a glimpse of Moira as she passed by the opening to the hall on her way to the kitchen. Gahan lost interest in the conversation. It was annoying how fast his thoughts returned to how much he wanted another taste of her.

"Ye're besotted, just like yer brother. But me point is made. She is nae being enjoyed by that old man." Saer stood and stretched, then slapped Gahan on the shoulder. "Life is too short to lie with the wrong woman."

"Ye sound like ye know that from experience."

Saer shrugged. "Both our mothers were lemans. It makes sense that we inherited their will to have love in their lives. Some call that a curse. In yer case, it might prove to be so."

"Even if it is a lie, her wedding vows separate us."

"A curse it will be then," Saer offered solemnly. "No man chooses who draws his interest. The only thing ye have power over is whether or nae ye let those opportunities slip through yer fingers. They are rare, though, so think upon the matter before making yer choice."

"Do ye nae think I have?" Gahan snorted. "I asked her to run away with me. Me sire would have a great deal to say about that."

Saer raised an eyebrow. "Yer sire cannae change the fact that ye have the same fire in yer blood that he did, and that it is his fault. As for the lass saying no to ye…" His lips slowly raised and parted to flash his teeth. "Are ye sure ye do nae want to try to change her mind? Lasses can take a bit of persuading."

"That is a dangerous idea, my friend."

Saer shrugged. "If I wanted her, I wouldn't care."

He moved off, his kilt swaying as he went. There

was no doubt in Gahan's mind that Saer would do exactly as he claimed, but what bothered him the most was the spark of irritation that came from even the mention of another man being interested in Moira.

He couldn't be jealous.

Shouldn't be.

But he stood, and in spite of his better judgment telling him to join his men, Gahan moved toward the kitchen.

Toward Moira.

The kitchen was quiet. The maids had climbed into their bunks on the far side of it where they might enjoy the heat from the large hearths. A couple of young lads were sleeping on pallets on the floor. The cook had already removed her overdress and was brushing out her hair when Moira appeared.

"Me husband has fallen asleep." She offered the cider to the cook.

"Ye do nae want it, Lady Matheson?"

The cook was forcing herself to ask. Hope brightened her eyes, and she wrung her hands to keep from reaching for the cider. Moira shook her head and handed it to her.

"Enjoy it."

The cook smiled and lowered herself, then lifted the small lid off the mug and inhaled the scent. She hummed and carried it back to the large worktable she spent so many hours at. She perched herself on a stool, the embers from the fire turning her cheeks ruby, and sipped at the cider.

Moira smiled as she turned and left the kitchen. There was a bed above stairs for her, but it seemed less than welcoming. She moved into the shadows slowly, in no hurry to get to the stairs.

She'd rather meet Gahan in the shadows. It was a wicked thought, one that warmed her cheeks, but she didn't believe the blush was one of shame. No, she needed to be truthful. It was excitement warming her. But she would be disappointed tonight.

She sighed and lifted her skirt to mount the stairs.

"What were ye hiding from me, Moira?"

For a moment, she thought she must have conjured Gahan from the darkness with her longings. She stared at the shadows as they parted, still unbelieving. He moved forward, and her fingers connected with him. She jumped, not realizing she'd reached out to touch him.

"Thinking about me?" he questioned suggestively.

"I—" She clamped her mouth shut and tried to force her wits to return.

He stepped closer, and she retreated. "Ye what?"

She bumped into the wall. Gahan took advantage of her position, flattening a hand on the stone surface next to her head. He was impossibly close.

Yet still forbidden.

"Ye must stop asking me personal questions." She was breathless and certain he heard the tattletale sound.

"Ah, ye are referring to when I asked ye if Achaius hurt ye?" His tone was husky, and it awakened all the yearnings she'd tried to smother since he had kissed her. "What I really wanted to ask was did he please ye?"

He gently stroked her cheeks, sending a jolt of

delight through her. It was so intense, her knees felt like they were wobbling. The wall behind her was suddenly welcome support.

"Or make ye blush, as I do?"

He didn't give her the chance to answer. His warm breath teased her lips a moment before he satisfied her longings with a kiss. She trembled, unable to control her body. He cupped her cheek as his lips began to tease her. The tip of his tongue traced her lower lip, then pressed her to open her mouth for a deeper kiss.

There was no considering her actions. She reached for him, slipping her hands into the open collar of his doublet and shirt. His skin was incredibly warm, hot really, and impossible to resist.

She wanted to touch him and kiss him. His kiss became demanding, his tongue thrusting into her mouth in an intimate invasion. Excitement knotted her belly, drawing her thoughts to her mons. Hidden between the folds of her sex, her clitoris began to pulse. Gahan pressed her against him, smoothing a hand down her back until he could cup one side of her bottom.

It was bold and exactly what she wanted. But the hard outline of his cock broke through the spell.

"No...no...I cannae do this to ye." She shoved away from him, bumping against the wall again. Gahan didn't give her any more space than that.

"Do what to me, lass?"

Only a sliver of moonlight made it through an archer's slit to break the darkness. But it was enough to cast his features in silver. His expression was dark and unyielding, demanding an answer.

A confession...

She had no will to deny him, only the need to be done with Bari's pretenses.

"Use ye." She shivered. "I cannae deceive everyone."

"Deceive in what way?"

He wasn't going to allow her to escape easily. But the truth was often harsh. Yet she found it more bearable than the torment of guilt.

"Achaius didn't…didn't…I fell asleep before he arrived."

Gahan cupped her jaw, his eyes steady on hers. "Who bloodied the sheet?"

"I do nae know. Yet it was nae me. I would have done me duty."

She could feel him weighing her words. He was a man who lived by his instincts, and they served him well. But she stared into his eyes, for she had nothing to hide.

"I believe ye."

Three words had never pleased her so much. She smiled, caught in a rush of relief. But she also had to recall the facts of the matter. She pushed at his chest and ducked under his arm.

"I should go now."

He chuckled, the sound full of promise. "Nay lass, that is nae what ye need." He reached out and gripped her wrist. "But since ye're a maiden still, I suppose it's something ye would nae understand just yet."

He didn't give her a chance to answer him. With a firm tug, he pulled her toward him, but he leaned over, and she went right over his shoulder. A second later he was striding down the dark hallway with her hanging over his shoulder like a new kill.

"Gahan—"

He pushed open a door then kicked it shut behind them. Wherever they were, it was dark. He reached for something, and a moment later he opened a window shutter that allowed the moonlight in. She had only a brief moment to notice it was a window before he pulled her off his shoulder and caught her in his arms.

"Stop talking, Moira. Ye and I agree far more often when we are nae talking."

He turned, and she saw the bed for the first time. It was far less grand than the one Achaius was snoring away in, but Gahan tossed her onto it and followed her. His weight was so pleasing. She gasped as he settled on top of her, taking some of his bulk on his elbows. Clearly he was more experienced in bed sport than she.

"This is wrong." It was what she should say. What the Church would demand was right. Yet that was so opposite of what she felt.

Gahan stroked her cheek and angled his head to place a kiss against her neck. Sweet sensation went rippling through her body, and she reached for his shoulders to keep him near.

"It feels very right to me, lass." He kissed her neck again and again until he found her collarbone. She arched toward him, anticipation threatening to drive all sense from her head.

His hands settled over the swells of her breasts, stroking the sensitive flesh. Suddenly he pushed back and stood up, cold air rushing across her body. But Gahan quickly pulled her up and tugged at the laces holding her overgown closed. Her undergown followed, and he shrugged out of his doublet, then pressed her back down on the bed.

"No protest?" he teased.

"It would be a lie," she admitted. The last few days had been too full of deception. So she reached for him, for the one thing she craved, and Gahan didn't hesitate.

His kiss was stronger this time, more demanding and more purposeful. Somehow, she understood what he wanted; in some deep part of her mind she longed for it, too. But she didn't know what to do, her hands moving clumsily as she tried to touch him in return.

He groaned, and she jerked her hands back.

"Now do nae do that," he admonished gently. "That was a sound of enjoyment."

He rose up onto his knees again and unbuckled his kilt. It fell down to cover her, then he sent it over the edge of the bed. The buckle made a sharp sound when it hit the floor, but she was too absorbed with watching him strip his shirt off to care.

She'd seen a cock before—at least she thought she had.

Working with the hawks had afforded her a few accidental viewings of the Fraser retainers chasing the maids. Gahan didn't look anything like them—and she'd never been fascinated before.

She reached out, gently touching his erection. The skin was smooth as glass, but warm.

"Sweet Christ."

He groaned again, but she gained confidence from the sound and an amazing sense of belief in her own ability. She closed her fingers around his shaft and pressed her hand all the way to the base of it.

He sucked in his breath, then settled down on top of her again. "Two can play that game, Moira."

He captured her lips in a kiss that drove the last of her wits away. She didn't try to recall them, either. Instead, she twisted, trying to press herself against him completely. Need and yearning were pulsing through her, flooding her to the point of drowning, and all she wanted to do was sink into them. She parted her thighs and clamped them around his hips. The next groan that filled the room came from her as he settled against her spread sex. Her clitoris erupted with pleasure, urging her to raise her hips.

"If all I wanted was a quick tumble, I would nae have brought ye here. The wall behind the tapestries would have done well enough." He moved down her length, pulling the neck of her chemise low to bare her breasts. His warm breath teased one puckered nipple as he hovered over it. "I want more."

His eyes glittered as he locked stares with her. "Much more."

He cupped her breast, sending delight across her skin. How had she failed to notice how sensitive her breasts were? His touch lit a new flame of need inside her. It was deeper, hotter, and more intense. Her heart raced, but she didn't care if it burst. Her lungs struggled to keep pace, and she smiled, because her rapid breaths drew his scent into her senses.

He smelled good. Like solid strength.

The moonlight showed her the tip of his tongue as he extended it toward her nipple. Anticipation held her in a tight grip before the first contact made it snap. She cried out, unable to remain silent. Her body had never felt so much, so deeply before. It was swirling through her, pooling in her passage. Gahan captured her nipple between his lips, and it felt like the hard point was connected to her clitoris.

The little bud throbbed for attention—a demand, not a request. He kissed a trail to her other nipple, sucking it as intently as he had its twin. Her eyes closed as she arched up to offer her breasts to him. But it wasn't enough. She reached for his head, threading her hands through his hair. She tightened her legs around him, pulling him toward her. He released her nipple and smoothed a hand down her body. Her skin was ultrasensitive, and his hand felt perfect against it, as though she hadn't realized what her body was for until that moment.

He paused at the top of her mons, teasing the curls. It was such a forbidden place that she lifted her head and looked toward him once more. Anticipation brightened his eyes, and the silver moonlight bathed every hard muscle covering his body.

"I do nae care to cause ye pain."

He pushed through the curls and between the folds of her sex. She gasped, frozen by the sheer shock of the intimacy.

"Since it cannae be avoided, I will give ye pleasure before I take me own."

His tone was thick with promise. She shivered, anticipation returning to needle her, but the reason was unclear. "You have already given me pleasure."

His teeth flashed at her. "But a taste of true rapture, lass."

His meaning still eluded her. She opened her lips to ask him to explain, but his finger moved. Positioned directly on top of her clitoris, the single movement sent a bolt of delight down her passage. It thrilled her, yet at the same time increased the need twisting inside her.

"Let me show ye, Moira."

He wasn't asking permission. It almost sounded like a boast, but he began to move his finger again, making thought impossible. He rubbed her clitoris and then circled it. She jerked, her hips rising up to press against his finger, but he trailed it through the center of her slit. Sweat popped out on her forehead as he circled the opening to her passage. Inside her body, the walls of it felt like they were tightening in an attempt to grasp him.

But she wanted more than his finger. She curled up off the bed, desperate to gain satisfaction.

"I want…more."

Gahan captured her mouth, kissing her hard as he returned to rubbing her clitoris. She fell back, unable to do anything but experience the waves of delight rippling through her.

"I know what ye crave."

She lifted her hips, and this time he pressed down harder in response. The pleasure was white-hot now, so intense she wasn't sure if it was pleasure or pain. She needed something so badly, she whimpered. Her passage was so empty. She fought against his hold so she might be filled.

"Then give it to me," she demanded and pulled him toward her.

He growled softly and returned her fervor. "It will be me pleasure."

He lifted his hand away and leaned down over her. His weight was intoxicating, and she reached for him. The head of his cock slipped easily between the slick folds of her flesh. She felt him shake as he fought the urge to thrust deep.

"Slowly, lass…it must be slow at first."

His voice was tense. He held her hips, keeping her still as he pressed forward. Her passage was hungry, but he entered her only a tiny amount at a time. She growled with frustration, but a moment later, the walls of her passage protested. It felt like he was too thick to enter, pain beginning to burn inside her as he pressed forward. Her fingers curled into talons, her fingernails digging into his shoulders as she tried to escape.

He held her steady, pulling free before thrusting back into her again. This time his cock tunneled deeper, inflicting more pain. It was red-hot and pulsing, but she still wanted him inside her.

"Breathe, lass."

She sucked in a gulp of air, not realizing she'd been holding her breath. It eased the pain, sweeping most of it away. Relief washed over her, and she drew several more rapid breaths until she realized she was clawing him.

"I did nae mean to scratch ye."

He chuckled and withdrew from her body. "I do nae care, lass."

A moment later he thrust deeply into her, a low rumble from his chest telling her how much he enjoyed it. Her thoughts scattered again, the need burning inside her finally getting what it craved. The hard presence of his cock soothed her yearning. But she wanted more, she needed friction, and Gahan did not deny her.

He began to move in a steady motion, giving her time to learn the rhythm before he increased the pace. Beneath them, the bed ropes creaked as he drove his length harder and faster into her body. It didn't matter. Nothing mattered except raising her hips for his next thrust. The hard shaft pressed against her clitoris, moving her closer and closer to some sort of zenith.

When it came, it felt like something snapped inside her. Pleasure exploded beneath the pressure of his thrusts. It flung her into a vortex that twisted and wrung her without mercy. Gahan growled and pressed against her, releasing his seed. It was all-consuming, and she had no idea how long it lasted, only that when it released her, she was helpless against the surface of the bed, her entire body spent.

Gahan collapsed on top of her but shielded her from his weight with his arms, then rolled off her. The bed rocked again, making an ominous sound, but the ropes held. She doubted she could have moved if they had snapped. Her heart was still beating too fast, making her light-headed. Gahan was in no better condition. His chest rose and fell rapidly as well. What had felt like a cool night was now too hot, the thin layer of her chemise irritating against her skin.

She closed her eyes, drifting away on waves of satisfaction. As her heart slowed, her skin cooled, and she sighed. The sound was one of deep contentment. She had never felt so good. If she had, she didn't recall it. Even the dull ache coming from her passage failed to interrupt her enjoyment. So she let herself drift into sleep, only muttering when Gahan slipped an arm beneath her and rolled her over so her head rested on his shoulder.

She finally understood what perfection was.

❧

But perfection never lasted. At least not on earth.

Her mind became restless as Moira tried to wake and do something important. It needled her until she jerked awake, confused because she had been so deeply asleep.

Gahan jumped when she moved so suddenly, his huge body jerking off the bed as he pushed her to the side of the bed away from the door. He reached for something leaning against the wall, and she realized it was his sword.

"What is it, Moira?" he asked as he swept the room twice with his gaze before looking back at her.

"I fell asleep." The moon was still only part of the way across the window, telling her most of the night was yet to come.

He released his sword. "Aye, as did I." His attention dropped to where her chemise was still gaping open to expose her breasts. "But I am nae complaining about being roused."

She pulled up the fabric, earning a frown from him. "We'll be discovered," she said.

"Good." He began to pull on the lace that closed his boots. In their haste, he had never removed them.

"It is nae good." She stood up.

Gahan reached over and struck a flint against iron. Sparks dripped down to a pile of tinder, giving birth to a flame. The orange-red light illuminated his face, the hard features striking her as solid. He held a candle over it until its wick caught. Warm golden light washed over him, gifting her with a full view of just how perfect his body was, as well as how strong it was. There wasn't a single bulge of fat on him, and every muscle was hard. There was something savage about him, but it served only to enhance his appeal. She shivered and hugged herself.

He stood up and held the candle over the bed. A dark stain marked the sheet.

"Deception is nae good, Moira. Let us be discovered, and let yer brother and Achaius receive what they are due for insisting on the farce that is yer marriage."

His tone was just as solid as his body.

"To what end?" She stooped down and picked up her undergown and shrugged into it.

"The end of yer marriage, to begin with." He placed the candle on a table and stood up. But he didn't seem concerned with his lack of clothing. Instead, he began to close the distance between them.

"Everyone will say ye stole the wife of one of yer vassals." She lifted her overgown and put it on, but there was no way to close it because the ties were down the back.

"Achaius is nae yer husband," Gahan growled and pointed at the stained sheet.

"Neither are ye. So if we are discovered, I will be shamed, yet rightfully so."

He was the son of the Earl of Sutherland. Allowances

would be made for his lustful wanderings. Horror filled her as she realized what she had forgotten in the grip of passion. It had been so simple, so very much like being enchanted. But reality was hard and full of consequences. He was the earl's son, and as such, he would not be alone.

She turned in a circle, looking into the darkened corners of the chamber. Off to one side was a doorway leading to another room enclosed in blackness. "Where is he? Yer captain? Ye are never alone."

"Sometimes I am."

She looked back at Gahan in relief, but his hard expression didn't put her at ease.

"Cam stayed outside the door until we fell asleep."

"But he is here now."

And the man knew full well that they had been enjoying bed sport.

Gahan reached for his shirt and shrugged into it. "With yer brother in this tower? I doubt me captain would leave me even if I ordered him to."

The shirt had been draped over the arm of a chair, and Gahan's kilt was no longer lying on the floor but pleated and waiting for him on a side table. A shiver went down her spine. Cam had been in here. Moira looked back at the side door, blinking several times as her eyes showed her what she had already known to be true. Gahan's captain stood there, partially hidden in the shadows. He didn't look at her, but her cheeks burned scarlet anyway.

She turned to leave, but Gahan captured her wrist and pulled her back to him.

"Ye do nae have to return to Achaius." His

embrace was solid and tempting. But Moira knew the sun would rise, and with it, the harsher side of life.

"I won't be another link in the chain. Bari wants to fight with ye so badly, and he will if I don't go through with this. Sandra was very important to him, and I share blood with him. 'Tis something I cannae change."

His expression turned stony. "Did ye know about the poison?"

"Nay." He was weighing her answer, his dark eyes glittering with the need for justice.

She sighed then pushed away. She wanted to think she was leaving to protect his good name, but the truth was she couldn't bear to see the suspicion in his eyes. It tore a hole in the trust that had grown between them, sweeping away the confidence that had seen her sharing his bed. Which left her no reason to stay.

None at all.

Cam spoke. "I do nae think the lass cared for how long ye considered her answer."

"Keep talking, and I'll smash ye in the jaw, Cam."

His brother grinned, but Gahan wasn't in the mood to jest. He turned around, feeling like the walls were closing in on him. It took every last bit of discipline not to go after Moira. But the stained sheet was a glaring reminder of her.

She shouldn't be so important.

The words and the idea that she mattered to him didn't sink in; they just crossed his mind before disappearing. He tugged the sheet free and folded it.

"What are ye planning to do with that?"

"Keep it." Gahan lay back down. "And do nae ask me why, because ye already know that I do nae understand why. Only that it is going to Dunrobin, and I will never tell Moira I am sorry you are witness to how it was stained."

"She's right. If ye show that to anyone, there will be talk of yer stealing from a vassal," Cam warned. "As well as making it public."

"Exposing deception is nae a thing to be avoided. That's why we are here, to prove Bari Fraser is the villain we know him to be."

Cam grabbed the sheet and handed it to another retainer. "Somehow, I think that reasoning will gain ye naught but grief as well." He pinched the candle out then returned to the second chamber to get some sleep.

At least someone would sleep, but Gahan doubted he would. He hadn't needed to hear Cam softening toward Moira. It was too close to his own feelings for her. He grunted and punched the pillow.

He didn't have feelings for her.

She was a Fraser.

But her scent still lingered, and the echo of her soft cries as he'd pleasured her followed him into slumber.

◈

Everything was quiet when she climbed the stairs back to the chamber where Achaius slept. She entered the rooms provided by Saer McLeod. The small receiving portion of the chambers had a single candle burning for her. The retainers had lain down near the curtains that separated the receiving room from the bedchamber. They were thick, wool ones that stretched from ceiling to floor to provide privacy. The retainers were lying across the floor to prevent anyone from crossing into their laird's bedchamber without stepping over them. They had the portion of their kilt that was draped over their right shoulder raised to cover their heads and keep them warm throughout the night.

But they'd wake if she walked past them and opened the door.

A reckless urge to do so rose up inside her. She didn't even want to fight it. Frustration with her current predicament threatened to help her make sure the retainers knew how late she was returning.

At least it would be an end to her sham of a marriage.

But there would also be an end to Bari's civil behavior.

A curtain was pulled aside on the side of the room. Another candle burned inside a tiny alcove. A cot took up most of the space. It was intended for a groom or a captain, but the candle had been left there for her.

Her husband's retainers didn't expect her to join Achaius.

It wasn't an uncommon thing. Especially among noble unions. Her cheeks stung with a blush as she realized just how relieved she was. It was wrong, but it felt so wonderful.

She let the curtain fall over the doorway and lay down. The ropes strung through the wooden frame of the cot groaned and needed a good tightening, but the bedding smelled fresh enough. She pinched out the candle and tried to sleep.

Her thoughts were churning, but at least she was

alone. It was a small mercy, but she was grateful for it. Dawn would be soon enough to deal with reality.

⁕

Achaius opened his eyes when his captain stirred. The man rolled over and settled back into sleep. The fire was only a bed of coals now, a faint red glow coming from them. His toes were still warm, and he grinned as he realized his wife had returned. Beyond the curtain, he watched the faint light go out.

Yes, his young wife had returned. In the darkest hours of the night too. There was only one reason for that.

He savored the victory, his mind full of the opportunity it afforded him. As soon as he was sure her belly was full, he'd let his captain tell Bari of the lovers' secret. The Fraser laird was no match for Sutherland's bastard. Gahan was a bear of a man and much harder than Bari. The moment Bari gave him a cause, Gahan would snap his neck.

Achaius grinned and chuckled. It would be perfect, and he would have the Fraser land. A laird was only as good as the profit he gained for his clan. It was the Highland way.

⁕

Moira was sore the next morning.

She noticed it the moment she sat up. Deep inside her passage, she ached. But the gray light of dawn was welcome because her sleep had been fretful. She fingered her underrobe, contemplating the thoughts that had troubled her sleep. She was torn between the need to be truthful about Gahan and her sham of a marriage, and the very real threat of giving her half brother what he wanted: a reason to feud with Sutherlands, not to mention with the Mathesons alongside him. Perhaps truth was supposed to be the only path a true heart should walk, but she just couldn't stomach the price.

She could do little more than drag herself out of bed and pat her hair down before pushing the curtain open.

"There ye are," Achaius remarked.

"Good morning, Husband," she said dutifully. The bright light of day reminded her of all the reasons why she needed to please Achaius.

"That cook must have taken impossibly long with the cider," Achaius said, laughing. "No doubt because her laird is nae a man who enjoys his comforts. She's out of practice in brewing up such things."

Achaius's gillie was tending to his master with the help of two other youths. The first one directed his dressing, and one brought forward a large, polished brass mirror for Achaius to see himself in.

"Get yerself ready to ride," Achaius said as he inspected his appearance. "We've two days of riding before making Sutherland. It will be the ground for beds tonight."

Moira let out a breath when Achaius did not pursue the subject of her late return, and for the first time in her life she was grateful to hear there would be no warm bed to climb into at sunset. No walls meant Gahan could not surprise her in dark hallways.

She knew her thoughts were cowardly, but it was

better to admit it than allow herself to be in a position to fall under his spell again.

❧

Dunrobin was far, far in the North.

On the journey, the rivers they crossed still had ice in them, and the going had been further slowed by mud. Snow still lingered under trees and on the shady sides of slopes, but much of it was melting and making the ground difficult to traverse.

Soon the roads would be filled with merchants moving about to sell what they had crafted during the winter. Only a few of the fields were turned, the nights still too cold for planting.

But construction had commenced on the castle.

When they neared the village that surrounded the castle, the sound of hammers and picks filled the air. Wagons with their beds weighed down with stone made a slow but steady trek up to the new building. Three large cranes were in position, and it looked like well over two hundred men were working on a new section of the castle. The road was packed hard from the constant traffic.

Dunrobin Castle was already massive. There were three tall towers and two older ones, short and square. The newer ones were round, to make them harder to hit with war machines. A thick curtain wall connected them all, and the back of it dropped off to the ocean.

The prosperity of the Sutherlands was clear. Gahan pulled up and turned his horse so he might make eye contact with Bari as her brother got a good look at Dunrobin. Some might have accused

Gahan of appearing arrogant, but Moira decided he was justified.

Bari was a fool to trifle with a clan like the Sutherlands, especially when he did not have to. Sandra had been a beauty and had many suitors, but she'd set her sight on one who didn't care for her. Greed was deadly.

Bari stiffened and rode straight for the entrance of the curtain wall. The wall would double the size of the inner yard. The castle would be huge, and she doubted even the English king had such a fine fortress.

She expected the Sutherland retainers to take their horses toward the stable, but they continued on into the inner yard. The earl stood on the steps of the largest keep, his face set into a frown. Next to him was a younger man, one every bit as toned as Gahan, but with light hair. Gahan climbed the stairs to talk to him. They had a heated debate, which the lighter-haired man clearly lost. He nodded at last, then turned and spoke to the retainers guarding his back. There was a shift and then a snarl as a petite woman with a swollen belly was guided away.

She didn't go before shooting a scathing glance at the blond-haired man.

"Ye did nae have to send yer wife away, Norris Sutherland," Bari declared.

The blond-haired man clenched his hands into fists. "Ye were made welcome here last season, and ye betrayed that trust. I promise ye one thing, Bari Fraser, ye will nae get another chance to harm any member of me family."

Bari hesitated, fighting the urge to argue. The

muscles in his neck corded, and many stopped what they were doing to stare at the standoff. But he finally ducked his chin and lowered himself in front of the earl and his son, Norris. "I'm here to make amends for me sister's actions."

Neither Norris nor Gahan looked impressed. The retainers behind them moved in closer.

"Aye, it's true," Achaius said as he made his way up the stairs. "I won't be having traitors in me family. Since I wed Laird Fraser's younger sister, I insisted he come here to smooth over this difficulty."

"Ye wed his sister? And come here after the fact?" Norris Sutherland asked incredulously. "That is nae how ye prove yer intent to be a good vassal."

Achaius made it to the top of the stairs and took a moment to catch his breath. Norris wasn't going to give the man time, but his father held up a hand. Achaius reached up and tugged on the corner of his bonnet before performing a shaky reverence. One of his men caught his elbow to help him straighten back up.

"At my age, ye do nae go to sleep at night and assume ye will be granted another day to enjoy life. For my impatience, I offer ye an apology. Yer father will likely understand me better than ye, young Norris," Achaius admonished the heir to the earldom with a note of glee. "I've always been a bit of a fool for a sweet lass."

Norris looked past Achaius to Moira. His gaze was much like Gahan's, sharp and knowing. "She could be yer granddaughter," Norris declared bluntly.

Achaius didn't look ashamed. "Marriage is for

begetting children. I need a young, healthy lass for that. I'm looking forward to seeing her belly as round as yer own wife's."

"Let us take this to me private chamber," the earl decided.

His sons didn't agree. Both Gahan and Norris glared at Bari suspiciously. Their father turned and walked into the keep. Both Matheson and Sutherland captains followed, as did many of the retainers.

Once most of the men moved inside, Moira sighed, realizing it was the first moment of peace she'd had in days. There was a great deal of activity in the yard. Younger boys were leading the horses away, while the retainers who had ridden with Gahan greeted their families. There were squeals from children being lifted high in their fathers' arms.

"The men have their minds occupied with dark thoughts they need to settle with the earl, and since the mistress was sent away, that leaves welcoming ye to me, my lady."

Moira turned to see an older woman standing behind her. She wore an overgown of fine wool, and a ring of keys was secured to her belt. Moira lowered herself.

"I am Asgree, the head of house at Dunrobin, and ye owe me no deference, Lady Matheson."

"I am simply Moira. My mother was common-born."

"Still, ye are wed to a laird." The older woman studied her for a moment. She snapped her fingers, and a young gillie came quickly to her side. "Perhaps ye would like to bathe?"

Just the mention of the word made her tremble. The gillie tugged on his knitted bonnet, then extended his arm out for Athena. She let him take the hawk, the idea of a bath too much to resist.

"I did nae see any clothing packed for ye."

"Nae." Moira followed the head of house into the keep. Maids in livery lined up as their mistress passed, and then followed behind. Each one wore a linen cap and apron.

"It is just as well. Yer gown is too light for Sutherland. Alice? Go find something warm enough for Lady Matheson."

The maid fixed her with a keen, knowing look that sized Moira up before the maid turned and mounted a set of stairs without a single question.

She didn't feel like Lady Matheson. *What ye are is Gahan's lover*, she thought. Well, that wasn't entirely true either. One liaison did not make them lovers. Sinners, to be sure, but nothing else.

Asgree led her into a bathhouse built alongside the kitchens. The window shutters were open to allow the fresh air in.

"The light will be gone soon, but we'll stoke up the fire if ye wish to wash yer hair," Asgree told her.

Two maids were already working at the hearth. One added a thick log while another picked up a bellows and used it to fan up the flames. The log crackled and popped as it caught. The room was soon warm as a summer day.

There were several tubs leaning up against the wall, large and high-backed. The maids set one near the hearth and soon had it full. They added hot water from a kettle. Moira disrobed and sighed as she stepped into the hot water. She gleefully cleaned the dust from the road off her skin, dunking her head several times to rinse her hair. The water was pure bliss, and she sank down into it with a happy smile upon her lips.

"There is no one in here for ye to worry about."

The door opened, and the blond-haired woman with the swollen belly came through in a huff. The maids all turned and lowered themselves. But she stopped two paces into the bathhouse when she noticed Moira. The retainers with her had stopped at the door, but they moved up beside her the moment they realized who else was in the bathhouse.

"This is the *women's* bathhouse," Daphne MacLeod groused at the men beside her.

"Yer husband wants ye watched so there can be no more trouble from the Frasers," one of the men offered. He was fighting to keep his tone respectful, but the look he aimed at Moira was full of hatred. "It was her sister who poisoned the earl. They cannae be trusted."

Daphne glared at the retainer, and suddenly her eyes filled with tears. The retainer looked appalled and backed away, unsure of what to do with a pregnant, weeping female.

"It's nae her fault. It is just the babe making her temperamental," Moira chimed in. She remained low in the tub to hide her nakedness. She bit her lip when everyone stared at her. "I'm sorry. I suppose ye are nae interested in what I think."

"It is the truth, nae yer opinion," Asgree offered before turning to address the retainers. "There are many here to see to the mistress. Stand outside the doors."

The retainers hesitated, but the head of house

pointed them toward the door, and they finally left, but reluctantly so.

Daphne rolled her eyes and rubbed her lower back. "Me husband ordered them to cling to me skirts like pups. I thought this would be the one place I might have some peace."

"I will leave." Moira sat up. "I hear a warm bath is soothing for the backache."

Daphne looked at her for a long moment. "What do ye know of the pains a woman is burdened with when she is heavy with child?"

"My clanswomen spoke freely of it."

"At the high table?" Daphne questioned suspiciously.

Moira wrapped a length of toweling around herself and moved closer to the fire. "I am only a half sister to Bari. I never sat at the high table. He forbade it because me mother was common-born. I admit to appreciating nae having to suffer him and Sandra."

None of the maids offered to assist her. Moira rubbed her hair dry and put on her chemise. Daphne moved toward her and fingered her overgown where it was lying.

"This is threadbare." Daphne handed it back to Moira, and she slipped into it.

"It is all she has," Asgree said. "There was naught brought along with her, and she had shoes on her feet with holes in them. Alice, where is that gown I sent for?"

The maid from before had returned with an overgown in her arms. It was plain, but made of thick, warm wool, and looked like it would fit Moira well enough.

"Sandra had the finest of everything," Daphne said, a lingering glint of suspicion in her eyes.

Moira could hardly blame her. It had been Daphne who stood accused of poisoning the earl, and she would have been hanged for it if Sandra had not been found out.

"I'll leave so yer husband's men do nae have a reason to look in on ye." Moira put on the overgown and picked up her arisaid. She stopped and lowered herself politely before Daphne. "I thank ye for making me welcome."

The retainers watched with narrowed eyes as Moira left, and every Sutherland she passed sent her scathing looks. The ill will and suspicion was to be expected, but that did not ease her way through the hallways. So she walked out of the keep, heading toward the only creature she might expect a warm welcome from. Dunrobin boasted fine accommodations for its hawks.

There were over thirty raptors in the clean and spacious mews, and perches for at least twenty more. The window coverings were open wide, and there were long poles fitted into the stone wall outside the window where hawks could enjoy the sun on their feathers. In the yard beyond, there were at least a dozen falconers working with birds while younger boys watched the art of training raptors. Some of the birds had leather ties on their talons because they were being trained to carry messages.

Athena lifted her wings in welcome, and Moira hid her unhappiness against the hawk's feathers. There was a familiar comfort in the moment. But it wasn't enough to banish the unease twisting her insides.

The earl's private study was brimming full of tension. The men glared at one another, distrust clear on their faces. The earl held up his hand to keep them all quiet as he walked around the large desk at the far side of the room and sat in the padded chair. There was a hearth behind him, demonstrating that firewood was not considered too great an expense for the master of Dunrobin.

"Now, Bari Fraser, I'd like to know what part ye played in yer sister's schemes," the earl asked smoothly.

Bari huffed but bit back the first words that sprang to his lips. "I knew naught of me sister's plans, only that she was found in yer son's bed. I was angry, sure enough, but I sent her here for ye to deal with the matter."

Lytge Sutherland didn't look impressed. He kept Bari standing in front of the long table which served as his desk. Norris stood behind his right shoulder, and Gahan had joined him on the left. Bari didn't miss the unity being displayed, and Gahan didn't miss the lightening color of Bari's pallor.

"That was part of her plan," Norris snarled. "She made sure we were all under the spell of a sleeping draught so she might slip into me bed and cry foul against me. I did nae seduce her, and I know me cock never touched her."

"It sure enough looked that way to us all." Bari drew in a deep breath and lowered his voice. "I was brought low by her deeds meself. When I saw her in yer bed, what else is a brother to do? But I still sent her here to Dunrobin to have the matter settled. There are plenty who would have challenged ye to a fight on the spot."

"Do nae quell the impulse on me account," Norris suggested savagely.

"Enough," Lytge cut in. "There will be no fighting. It is a fact ye sent her here. On that point, I'd be wrong to question yer loyalty."

"Good…good…" Achaius was quick to join the conversation, but Lytge raised a single finger to quiet the man. The earl studied Bari for a long moment, resting his chin on steepled fingers.

"Bari Fraser, ye may swear yer fealty in the Hall," Lytge said, "if that is indeed what ye came here to do."

Bari pressed his lips into a tight line, but Achaius slapped him on the shoulder. "Ye see there, lad? I knew this was the way. I'm sure ye're right glad ye took me advice and came along."

"Ye gave me little choice," Bari complained.

"Yet a choice all the same," Achaius insisted. "Life is a matter of decisions." He turned his attention to the earl. "These lads do nae understand that fact as well as we do."

The earl held up his hand. "Now I will speak with Laird Matheson alone."

Bari stiffened, his complexion darkening, but the retainers near the doors opened them wide for him to depart. He turned around and left, the retainers closing the doors behind him.

The earl fixed Achaius with a hard look.

"An interesting comment ye made there in front of young Fraser. And yet ye offer me a very paltry excuse as to why ye wed so quickly," Lytge said. "Where is yer great understanding of how life should be, Achaius?"

"Yer son was there for the wedding. A grown son has always been enough in the Highlands," Achaius offered. "Or is the problem in the fact that it was yer bastard son?"

The earl bristled. "Gahan is a son of Sutherland."

"Then there should be no difficulty," Achaius declared. "Me last wife died a full half year ago. I am nae going to waste me remaining days on waiting for the snow to melt so I can come to yer door. Lord Home has me sons at Court, and me hall is empty."

The earl let out a sigh. "Where I am discontented is in the choice of yer bride. For all that ye have brought Bari Fraser here, I doubt he would have come on his own. He's angry, and that's clear as day. Ye also rode against me at Sauchieburn."

"Aye, it's true about Sauchieburn," Achaius admitted. "I followed me king, and for that, I will nae make any excuse. Lord Home is making me pay for that, and I'll take me penance. But an empty castle is a hard thing to live in. Too hard for me. I want a wife and family, and I do nae have the time for letters to be making their way all the way up here. The lass is nae from so great a line as to be one ye would have wanted to go to another."

Lytge drew in a deep breath and tapped a finger on the top of his desk for a few moments. "Her blood concerns me more than if she'd been of a finer lineage."

"Bah!" Achaius spat. "She's a half-blooded sister Bari kept on his land in case he ever needed her to settle an argument. Ye know it as well as I. Look at the way she is dressed. He considers her naught but a vessel for gain."

"Exactly," Lytge agreed, heat edging his tone. "Bari Fraser has an argument with me, and I do nae need yer retainers riding with his in some vain attempt to avenge his sister. The bitch poisoned me at me own table."

"A fact which I'll admit I'm using to me own advantage."

The earl's eyes narrowed, but Norris spoke up before his father did. "How is that?"

"Simple, lad," Achaius replied. "Bari Fraser has a stink clinging to his kilt from his sister Sandra's doings, and I'll admit I've let him think I'm sympathetic to his cause. I wanted a young bride, but I have never wed without keeping me eye on the gain it will bring me clan. There are nae many who would take an offer from Bari Fraser, because they know ye are nae pleased with him."

"Yet ye did," Gahan spoke up, "and with a lot of haste."

"And ye were riding along Bari's borders at the first hint of spring weather, lad," Achaius accused. "Ye were looking for trouble."

"Because we have every reason to be suspicious of Bari Fraser," Gahan answered.

The room was silent for a long moment. Achaius chuckled, surprising the rest of the occupants.

"Well now, I've got him through yer gates, so it seems like ye should be grateful. I doubt there is another of yer vassals who could have done the same." He leaned forward, locking eyes with the earl. "Now ye do nae need to go looking for him."

"And ye get to keep the dowry," Norris finished.

"And the lass," Achaius interrupted with a smack of his lips. "She's a sweet treat."

"She's far too young and does nae want to be wed to ye. In fact, I question—"

"Enough!" Lytge interrupted Gahan. The room went silent again as the earl considered the man before him.

"If what you say is true, ye are welcome at Dunrobin, Laird Matheson. For the time being." The earl held up his hand to dismiss Achaius and keep his sons from commenting. Norris cut Gahan a look behind their father's back. Achaius stood up, reached for his bonnet, and made his way out the door on shuffling steps.

"He's lying," Gahan said the moment the double doors were sealed tight once more.

"About what?" Lytge demanded. "Nae that I did nae get that impression meself."

"As did I," Norris added as he came around his father's desk. Gahan followed him.

"I did nae raise ye to use such a hard tone unless ye had evidence," Lytge said, pointing at Gahan. "A son of a laird must always remember that others may act upon the words he allows past his lips, so ye'd best think before opening yer mouth. Being right is nae always the most important thing. Maintaining balance and peace is."

"He did nae consummate his union but flew a soiled sheet anyway," Gahan said.

Norris exploded. "The bitch is just like her sister Sandra."

"No, she is nae," Gahan countered. "She swore she had naught to do with the soiled sheet."

"And ye believe her?" Norris asked, incredulous.

Gahan nodded. "I understand ye clearly, Father. This matters because Bari is trying to shift power in his favor. An unconsummated union is no union. At least not here in the Highlands."

"Sandra was a master of deception," Norris remarked.

"I remember it well," Gahan growled. "But Moira is nae like Sandra."

Lytge held up a hand when Norris would have spoken. Gahan found himself bearing the full weight of his father's scrutiny. "How do ye know Achaius failed to consummate his marriage?"

Gahan took a deep breath. "Because Moira was a maiden when I took her to my bed at MacLeod Tower. I have the sheet to prove it."

"Ye did what?" Norris demanded. "Are ye mad? She might have poisoned ye while ye slept."

"Cam best nae have left ye alone with her," his father warned.

"He did nae," Gahan confirmed, "and it is the only thing I lament, for the lass did nae deserve to have her modesty trampled."

"She's a Fraser," Norris reminded him.

"I know it well. She confessed that she was virgin and tried to tell me to let her be. I cannae explain me actions, only that I did take her to me bed, and I am sure there is deception in this marriage."

"Agreed," Lytge said firmly. "And I think ye have done the right thing to bring them here. It allows us to plot the next move."

"While giving them a clear shot at our backs," Norris argued.

"It's that or let them choose the timing," Gahan replied.

The earl nodded in agreement. Norris grunted, clearly not pleased.

"Norris, ye make sure Daphne takes to using the hidden passageways. I do nae want Bari Fraser knowing where she is." His father pointed at Gahan. "Ye stay away from Moira Fraser. I believe ye are correct. Achaius is scheming, and ye are playing merrily along by trifling with his new bride. Do nae hand him a valid reason to join Bari in a feud against us."

Gahan opened his mouth, but his father shook his head. "Mind me, Gahan. I'd tell ye to find a willing maid to ease yer lust, but I'd rather ye were keeping a watchful eye on our guests. There is going to be trouble, mark me words on that."

"Yet if we control when it happens, there will be an end to this which does nae include a feud."

His father nodded, but there was a grim look in his eyes. "It will be no easy task."

Gahan knew it. He tugged on the corner of his bonnet and left his father's study. He was fighting the impulse to look for Moira. Cam fell into step behind him, but that wasn't enough of a deterrent to keep from thinking about her. Maybe she was just playing a part, drawing him in with whispered words and innocent looks.

Innocent or not, he was still a damned fool, because as the sun began to set, all he wanted was another taste of her lips.

❧

"She's been scratching at the door all day," the retainer said by way of greeting to his replacement coming up the stairs, "whispering all sorts of enticements she claims to have learned at Court. It's enough to make ye think ye're losing yer senses. It might be in the laird's favor that he has no stomach for hanging a woman, but this one is a demon."

Having made it to the top floor of the oldest tower in Dunrobin with a pitcher of water and sack of bread, the Sutherland retainer relieved his comrade outside the barred and locked door. The hallway was narrow and the stairs steep, and the two retainers switched places with some difficulty.

"Be on yer way then. I'll ignore the bitch," the new guard said as the old retainer disappeared down the stairs. The guard looked at the small door cut into the main one that would allow him to pass food to the prisoner. Duty demanded he open the hatch and pass the sack and the pitcher he held inside the chamber. He slid the wood panel to the side, opening a one by two foot opening in the door. The bar was removed only twice a month when a tub was brought up for Sandra Fraser to bathe.

"Take yer supper—"

He froze in midsentence, blinking as he tried to believe what his eyes were telling him. Sandra Fraser was laid out on the small cot in the cell wearing nothing at all. Her hair was flowing down onto the pillow as she beckoned to him.

Sweat popped out on the retainer's forehead. "Take yer meal or starve."

She stood up, her auburn hair swinging like a silk

curtain behind her. Her face was drawn, but her tits were still plump and tight, making the guard's cock stir. In spite of her crimes, she was still well fed.

"I'm coming…but I'd rather be making ye come." She stroked her lower lip as she walked slowly toward the doorway.

"Take yer food."

She reached for the pitcher and bag but stroked his fingers as she took them. "Join me. Ye will nae regret it."

He slid the door shut and wiped his forehead across his sleeve.

"Yer duty is to keep me in this chamber. I swear I will stay here. All I ask is for ye to tell me brother I am alive. Relieve the torment of thinking me dead. That is all. Nae so much to ask, and I will reward ye well."

"Enough!"

Frasers were nothing but trouble.

Curse them all.

❧

Dunrobin had a huge Great Hall, which was presently full of hundreds of retainers. As the supper service was held back, Moira noticed the women were pushing their way inside too. Candles flickered in the chandeliers, but there was an uneasy silence tonight. Bari Fraser stood before the high table, waiting while the earl and his sons took their places.

Gahan wore a fine doublet with silver buttons. On the side of his bonnet was a gold brooch with a large emerald set in it. The earl wore a chain of office that left no doubt that he was the head of the massive Sutherland clan. Lytge settled himself as Bari waited.

Only after Norris and Gahan took positions behind the earl did he nod at Bari. Achaius waited at the foot of the stairs that led to the high table until the earl's business was finished.

Bari stiffened, the muscles in his neck cording, but he bent his knee and lowered himself before the earl.

"I pledge ye me loyalty, even if it may cost me life. I condemn me sister Sandra for her actions and beg yer forgiveness for the slight me blood has done against yer noble person."

The earl didn't comment for a long moment. Tension filled the hall as everyone waited. Moira stood beside Achaius, feeling as out of place as Bari was.

"I accept yer pledge, and ye are welcome at me table," Lytge finally said.

Bari shot up and climbed to the high ground. Soft conversation began to flow, but it didn't sound welcoming.

"Bring on supper," Lytge bellowed, proving time hadn't stolen his vigor just yet.

Achaius sat down next to Bari, taking the last two seats at the high table. It suited Moira, because she didn't think she could sit still up on the dais with everyone's eyes upon her. Daphne MacLeod was of the same mind. She pushed her chair back, but her husband caught her arm. She leaned toward Norris and whispered something. He released her, but his lips were pressed into a hard line. Daphne shook her head and stopped and stared at the retainers ready to follow her. She rubbed her back again and finally turned and disappeared through one of the arched doorways at the side of the Great Hall, the Sutherland retainers at her heels.

Women began bringing in platters of food, and Moira joined their ranks, but they were not welcoming.

She refused to let them intimidate her. She took a place at one of the lower tables, keeping watch on the ones that seemed most interested in making her evening difficult. It kept her mind off Gahan.

When it came time to clear the tables, the Sutherland women were no less hostile. They made no effort to hide their distrustful comments and glances even as Moira helped gather dirty platters and mugs. A few of them smirked at her as they boldly sat down and began chatting while she worked. It was a bold action, one the Church might even give them time in the stocks for.

Asgree appeared and snapped her fingers at them. "Unkindness has no place here," Asgree said. "Leave the feuding to the men. We'll have to endure enough grief from their quarrels without adding our own."

It was so similar to what Moira's own kinswomen had said. She felt guilt tighten around her. So far, she hadn't been able to hold Achaius's attention for any length of time, let alone please him. He was still sitting at the high table, talking away to those willing to listen.

He was her husband, and yet he wasn't.

Her thoughts strayed to Gahan and how much she preferred him. It was the truth, and it shamed her. Achaius may be guilty too, but it was her duty to take up the position of his wife. Moira noticed that Gahan, however, was watching her from the high table. He drew her attention, and it took true effort to look away. Then Achaius laughed, slapping her back into reality.

She could still try to attract Achaius away from his scheming. She had to. It was time to be in her place.

She moved in front of him and lowered herself. "I find I am tired and wish to return to our chambers. Would ye join me?" Moira said, smiling at him.

Achaius stopped talking and grinned at her. "Ye head off to bed, lass. Best sleep while ye can, for when I join ye, there will be no rest for ye." The Matheson retainers chuckled, but none of the Sutherland men did.

She drew in a deep breath and straightened. Dreading her duties was irritating her now. She was not a coward. She didn't want to have to keep steeling herself for something that never happened, but it seemed she couldn't seduce Achaius even if she wanted to. She left the hall with a heavy feeling of defeat.

The steps were much wider than in Fraser Tower. There was even a railing to hold on to. The walls were freshly plastered, and between the archer slits, large hooks held lanterns. Everything about the tower declared prosperity.

The floors were also farther apart. She grinned when she reached the third floor. It was split into two chambers. Instead of two doors at the top of the stairs, there were four. Two angled west, and two faced east. The ones facing east opened, and she stepped inside. The first room was a receiving chamber. It wasn't very large, but tapestries hung over the wall. Achaius's gillie was sitting near the hearth, enjoying a thick slice of bread and cheese.

"Mistress." He tugged on the corner of his bonnet but looked at her in confusion. "Did the laird send for ye?"

For all of his bluster, her husband didn't seem to enjoy a warm bed as often as he claimed. Otherwise, the gillie would be expecting her to be in his master's bed when Achaius arrived.

"He told me to sleep while I could," Moira replied truthfully.

The gillie shifted. "Then ye should go into the outer chamber until he sends for ye. He is master, and it is best to wait for his instructions."

It wasn't so much what the boy said that made her abandon her resolve to take up her position as wife as it was his tone. He was worried. Deeply worried that she'd not do as his laird wished.

"Ye will tell me husband that I await his command," she instructed firmly.

The gillie grinned and tugged on his cap. "Yes, mistress." He pointed to the outer chamber. "And there is a fine bed there for ye, on the other side of the receiving chamber."

The receiving chamber was dark; only a single candle burned near the door. She made her way across the thick carpet to the double doors and opened them onto a bedchamber. A fire had died down, but the coals still glowed warmly. Moira chided herself for how relieved she was, knowing she'd most likely spend another night without having to share Achaius's bed.

The bedding was turned down, indicating that the staff of Dunrobin was accustomed to noble unions that lacked passion. It was no doubt the reason the earl had a bastard he favored so much. Gahan's mother had been the woman he truly loved.

For a moment, she was caught in the grip of jealousy. Men had so much more freedom. For the first time in her life, Moira understood why women took lovers in defiance of the Church. Cold beds were very unwelcoming, a fact she'd been innocent of just two days ago, before she'd taken Gahan as a lover. Well, that was a memory now.

Moira draped her overgown on the back of a chair and sat down to take off her shoes. Her stockings had new holes in them, but she'd leave the repair until morning. She reached for a brush sitting on the bedside table and drew it through her hair several times before she climbed into the bed. It was chilly, but not for too long. The sheets were clean, and she pulled them up to her nose as she tried to use the hint of lavender to drive the memory of Gahan's scent from her mind.

It didn't work very well, but at least the comfortable bed lulled her into sleep—even if Gahan was waiting there in her dreams for her.

Gahan emerged from one of the secret passages, joining Norris in his private chambers. Their father sat in an armchair in front of the fire.

"Bari Fraser is in the north tower, well away from us," Gahan reported. "But he is nae happy. It seems none of our women are interested in sharing his bed."

"Sandra seems to suffer the same difficulty," Norris remarked. "The men set to watching her door report she's taken to trying to seduce them so they will tell her brother she is alive. I suppose I should have put her in a tower overlooking something other than the main gate."

"I'd prefer it if she left Dunrobin," Daphne interrupted. She was fussing around in the bedchamber beyond the open curtains of the receiving area, but she noticed the stares being sent her way and moved into the doorway. Her swollen belly looked huge, and she began to rub it slowly. "Well, I would, and ye are having yer meeting in our private chambers, so do nae expect me to keep silent. But I know why ye're here. To make sure no spies overhear ye."

Every castle had its spies. Daphne turned around and returned to fussing with a length of cloth. The earl waited until she'd moved away a good ten feet.

"I'd like to be rid of Sandra as well, but I will certainly nae be handing her back to her brother," the earl remarked. "She's a blot of bad luck."

"Bari is nae much better," Gahan said. "I wager he does nae know his sister's marriage went unconsummated. He does nae have the union he wants with the Mathesons."

"Achaius might never admit such a thing. He wants the dowry." Norris grunted. "On second thought, though, I think it might be better to have him know ye took Moira to yer bed. At least the man would try his hand at killing ye, and we might be rid of him."

"Ye must never assume the outcome of a fight," Lytge warned. "I've seen a few surprises in me years and would nae like to lose one of me sons. I warned ye to keep away from Moira Fraser, and ye'll do it, Gahan. Achaius may yet consummate his union. The man talks of it often enough."

"He's past the age," Gahan replied. "I'd wager me last bit of silver that Moira is sleeping alone right now."

"Ye cannae have affection for a Fraser," Norris declared. "None of us could."

Lytge chuckled and stood. "As if ye listened to anyone when young Daphne took yer interest. I know the look, because I still see Gahan's mother in me dreams. Ye are both me sons, cursed with the need to love." He pointed at Gahan. "Stay away from her, at least until she is no longer a wife—and I'd appreciate it if her husband died on his own land, nae on mine."

"She is nae his wife," Gahan insisted.

His father nodded slowly. "I agree that an unconsummated union is no marriage, nae in Scotland, that is. The English might disagree, since they let the Pope tell them what to do, but the only witnesses to such a thing cannae be the man who wants the bride for himself. The Matheson will have reason to feud with us."

"Her brother will hardly agree to ending the sham of a marriage either," Norris added.

"Why is this so bloody complicated?" Gahan groused.

"Because ye are me son and too much like me," Lytge informed him. "No man has everything. There are plenty of men serving as me retainers who may chase the lass of their choice, but they long for the position ye enjoy, and make no mistake about that. But that same position has a cost, for naught is free in this life. Yer actions gain responses…Ye must think before ye act, else watch the men serving ye suffer for a rash act. Fate tests us all."

It was the truth, but Gahan had no liking for it.

The only thing that made him nod in agreement was the sound of regret in his father's voice. His sire wanted what was best for him, but being the Earl of Sutherland meant thinking of duty before all else.

Fate did indeed want to test him.

❧

Moira was jerked out of sleep, certain she'd heard someone calling. The chamber was dark, only the faintest glow coming from the hearth. The nights were still long. She didn't think it was past midnight. Drapes covered the windows, so there was no light from the moon to help her see into the corners of the room.

"Help…I need…help…"

The sound was muffled, like it was coming through the walls. She crumpled the bedding in her hands in fear. Dunrobin wouldn't be the first Highland fortress with restless spirits.

"Moira…I need help…"

She sat up and swung her legs over the edge of the bed.

A Dunrobin ghost wouldn't know her name.

She grabbed a candle and held it against the coals until it lit. A warm glow surrounded her, but it also showed her that she was alone. "I hear ye…"

"Here…I'm here…"

It was Daphne MacLeod's voice, but muffled. Moira moved slowly toward the far side of the chamber and heard the woman groan.

"Where are ye?" Moira called out.

A thump sounded against what looked like a doorway to the garderobe. Moira pressed on the wood, and it popped open, releasing a draft of cool air that made the candle flicker. Once the flame grew bright again, it illuminated a hidden passage with narrow stairs spiraling down into darkness. Daphne MacLeod was sitting on the stairs, her hands fisted in her skirts. Her face was drenched in sweat.

"Thank Christ…"

"My lady, why are ye here?" Moira sputtered.

Daphne groaned long and low before opening her eyes and sucking in a deep breath. "I was spying on ye. Christ forgive me! But I was, for I just had to know if ye were only pretending to be sweet-natured." She gasped, and her hands clenched her skirts tighter.

"I'll go get help," Moira said quickly.

Moira started to stand, but Daphne cried, "Do nae ye dare leave me! There is no time! This is what I get for spying. Me babe is coming now! I can nae even make it to me own chamber. Ye have to help me!"

She let out a cry and leaned back on the narrow steps. Moira set down the candle and peered at Daphne for a moment. "Ye are right, my lady, the child is being born. I see its head." Her heart began to race, but she bit her lower lip to steady herself.

"I know I'm right!" Daphne shouted.

Moira knelt between Daphne's knees and gathered up her undergown to catch the baby. "Do nae worry, I'll catch the babe. Push with the next pain."

Daphne groaned as she bore down, and the baby's head came all the way into view.

"Breathe, lady! And push!"

The baby was slick, and Moira used her skirts to get a good hold on it as Daphne pushed again.

"Good…well done, lady. The shoulders are out."

Daphne yelled with the last push needed to birth her baby. Moira gently clasped the infant's head and ankles before turning it over to clear the fluid from its nose and mouth. The baby gasped, and its arms began to flail as it let out a squeal.

"It's a lad, lady! A fine, strong little boy," Moira declared.

Moira wiped the baby's face clean and looked up, but Daphne had collapsed back onto the stairs. Her chest rose and fell, but terror knotted Moira's insides. *They'll hang me if Daphne is found dead…*

But her hands were full with the baby, and it was still attached to its mother. The doorway to the hidden passage was still open.

"Help!" Moira drew in a deeper breath and yelled. "We need help!"

The wind whipped up the stairwell, and she cuddled the baby close to keep it warm. Another gust of wind came up the stairs, and she looked down into the darkness. There had to be a door open below to let the night breeze in.

"Help us!" she yelled down the stairs, the sound bouncing between the stone walls. "Someone! Please!"

Every second felt like an hour. The baby settled down, making small noises as the candle flame flickered. Her heart was racing, and sweat trickled down her back beneath her clothing. Daphne lay like a broken doll across the steps. But there had to be retainers charged with watching her chambers.

"Who's up there?" a man's voice asked.

"Lady Sutherland needs ye!" Moira shouted.

She heard him coming, the hard pounding of boots against stone. She reached up and pulled Daphne's skirt down just before a Sutherland retainer emerged from the darkness.

He took in the scene and growled at her. "Ye will nae touch the laird's wife, Fraser."

"We have no time for that!" Moira snapped. "I need a knife to cut the baby's cord so we can move the lady to my bed."

The man's eyes grew round as he looked at the baby. He bumped into the wall as he cowered away from the scene of childbirth.

"A knife, sir!"

He reached down and took one from the top of his boot. Moira cradled the baby in one arm and cut the cord with her other hand.

"Ye must move her gently, as though she is made of straw." Moira stood up carefully, nodding toward her room. "Into this chamber, for we dare nae move her more than necessary."

"I should take her to her own chamber," the retainer argued.

"Ye cannae. She must nae be jostled, else she might bleed. Each step is a risk."

The man made the sign of the cross over himself before gently scooping Daphne up off the stairs. He angled her through the doorway that led to Moira's chamber and settled her in the bed.

"Fetch a midwife—and quickly," Moira instructed him. She held the baby in one arm and plucked a candle from the table. She knelt down and held the wick against the embers to light it. A golden pool of light illuminated the newborn.

"I cannae leave the mistress with ye," the retainer said.

"What do ye know of childbirth?" Moira growled at him. "Ye know nae how to help at all, so *I* dare nae leave her with *ye*. Shall we both stand here, then? Get on with ye!"

Daphne made a soft sound of pain, her head moving from side to side as her face drew tight. Yet it was a sweet sound, for it meant the lady still drew breath.

"Get me hot water and linens and some experienced women!"

Moira grabbed her overrobe and swaddled the baby with efficient motions. The retainer hesitated only a moment before he was running through the dark chamber.

"Where...where am I?" Daphne blinked, trying to see in the dark.

"Ye are fine, lady, and have a new son." Moira carefully gave the child to Daphne. "He's strong and well, Lady Sutherland."

Daphne clasped her arms around her baby and studied his face for a long moment, then looked up at Moira. "I fainted."

"Aye, but many do." Sure the baby was secure, Moira released him to his mother's embrace.

Daphne tried to sit up, but Moira pressed her back. "Ye must nae, lady. Ye must stay still."

"Get yer hands off me wife, Fraser!"

Norris Sutherland didn't wait for Moira to obey him. He grasped her shoulder roughly and pulled her away from Daphne. Moira went stumbling across the floor; the retainers following Norris Sutherland let her fall in a heap.

"Do nae raise yer voice, Norris!" Daphne snarled and sat up.

"Ye must stay still, Lady Sutherland!" Moira gasped. "Ye might tear yer insides and bleed."

"Do nae tell me wife what to do!" Norris shouted at her.

"Yet, she is correct." Asgree appeared in nothing but her shift and nightcap. The head of house was out of breath but still took command. "This is no place for raised voices." The baby started crying, all the shouting disturbing him. Asgree flicked her long braid over her shoulder as she leaned in to look at the new baby.

Moira jerked her skirts out from beneath her feet, but someone lifted her off the floor before she was untangled.

"Thank ye…" Her words trailed off as she looked up into Gahan's dark eyes. He was straight from his bed, his shirt untied at the neck, granting her a view of his chest.

She recalled all too well the perfection of his flesh and what it felt like against her own.

"Ye men need to leave," Asgree informed them.

"The Fraser goes too," Norris declared.

"Stop lashing at her, Norris!" Daphne said, then gasped. "It's me own doing I'm here, and right glad I was to have her help! I was spying on her because of yer suspicions."

"Well-founded suspicions," Norris argued. "Which is why ye should have been nowhere near a Fraser."

"I'll nae be shackled like a hound." Daphne slapped the surface of the bed. "Now stop yer growling and tell me ye're pleased with yer son."

Norris turned to Daphne and instantly transformed. His face beamed with joy as he sat on the edge of the bed and peered down at his newborn child.

Asgree tut-tutted, making a shooing motion. "I need ye gone, so I can attend to the mistress."

Norris glared at her. Maids were flooding into the chamber, their hands full of things to help with their mistress's birth. Daphne began to groan and kick at the bedding. Norris stood but refused to back away from his wife. Asgree had to lean past him to wipe the sweat off her mistress's face.

"I'll go, if that is what it takes to get ye to leave," Moira said. She brushed off Gahan's grip and made her way to the door.

The receiving chamber was brightly lit now, and Achaius stood in the doorway to Moira's chamber in nothing but his shirt, surveying the scene.

"Well now, me bride has made herself useful, it seems," Achaius remarked, noting Moira's appearance. Her gown was covered in blood and fluid from the birth, and her hair was a tangled mess. Her bare toes were turning to ice now that her heart wasn't racing anymore.

"Yet ye brought naught else along for yer bride to wear," Gahan muttered darkly. "For a man who claims to be so happily wed, ye spare her little of yer attention."

Achaius merely blinked in the face of the reprimand. "A wife sees to her husband's needs, lad. Nae the other way around. If I wanted a fancy woman, I'd have gone to Court. I like her in her skin, and do nae care what dress she wears during the day." He turned and made his way back to bed.

"Bloody selfish bastard ye have for a husband." It was a bold thing to say, even for the son of an earl, but people were rushing in and out of the chamber so quickly, no one seemed to take notice. Gahan shook his head then scanned her from head to toe. "Ye look like ye rolled across the stables."

"Thank ye so very much," Moira said, brushing past him. Her heart had stopped racing, but the sting of Norris Sutherland's words rose in her memory, and tears stung her eyes as she remembered just how unwelcome she was at Dunrobin.

Norris Sutherland stomped out of the bedchamber, Asgree standing in the doorway with a thin, age-worn finger pointed at him. "It's time for women's work." Noting Achaius's closed door, Asgree spoke to one of the maids standing by. "Seeing as Lady Sutherland is occupying Lady Matheson's chamber, escort her to the star chamber."

Asgree closed the doors firmly, and the maid stepped forward to escort Moira away. Norris turned with a swish of his kilt and stopped when he caught sight of her. His eyes narrowed, but Gahan stepped between them. Whatever idea she'd had of standing firmly in the face of his displeasure dissipated as shock tore through her. She wasn't the only one stunned. Norris looked at his brother, astonishment showing on his face.

"I'll take her," Gahan said to the bewildered maid, who lowered herself and scurried away from the two men staring daggers at each other. For a long moment, they held each other's stares, then Gahan captured Moira's wrist and pulled her behind him out of the chamber. They were halfway down the stairs before she recovered her wits.

"Where are we going?" Moira asked.

"The star chamber," Gahan grunted. "So called because Norris's mother painted the walls with constellations. It's often used for guests, so no gossip will come from ye being there."

Moira followed him down two more flights of stairs to the door of a chamber. When she hesitated on the bottom step, Gahan turned in a flash, giving her a look at his furious expression before he pulled her over his shoulder. Gravity aided him, since he was below her.

"Nay...ye'll ruin yer shirt!"

He ignored her warning, taking her weight easily. Even though they were alone, she felt ridiculous hanging over his shoulder and tried to straighten up. He smacked her bottom in response. She collapsed back over his shoulder with a gasp as he carried her across the landing and opened the door.

He set her down and kicked the doors shut, plunging them into darkness. She was still stumbling away from him when he cupped the sides of her face and sealed her mouth beneath his. There was too much heat in the kiss, and she recoiled from the sheer volume of sensation. Gahan followed her, renewing the contact between their lips. Shock was replaced with passion as he slid his arm down to clasp her against him.

Dreaming about him hadn't been nearly as good

as being pressed against him. It was pure delight, and she reached for him, returning his kiss. He pushed her until her back hit the wall. His shirt frustrated her, preventing her from feeling his skin. The ties at the collar were loose, and she slid her hand inside to stroke his skin.

"Ye enchant me, Moira," he muttered against her neck. "I think I should be afraid of yer effect on me."

"So should I," she whispered. She was caught in the grip of need again. It was a torment she enjoyed, but one that completely consumed her. The darkness of the room cloaked them, offering sanctuary from reality.

He stroked her thighs, from her hips down, and then gripped her gown to pull it up. The night air offered relief from the heat threatening to consume her. Her heart raced, but this time, the scent of his skin was there to intoxicate her.

"But all I can think about is how much I want to get back inside ye." With her gown raised, he caught the back of her thighs and lifted her.

His kilt moved to accommodate him, and his cock nudged between the folds of her sex. A jolt of need tore through her, making her gasp at its intensity. She ached with emptiness, her clitoris throbbing for attention. His cock was hard against her folds, seeking the opening to her body as he pressed up against her. She arched toward him, clasping him between her thighs.

"Christ in heaven!" he swore as his length penetrated her.

She gasped, gripping his shirt so tightly the fabric began to tear. The sound only fed the wildness churning inside her. She dug her nails into his skin and arched her neck, straining toward the next thrust.

It was hard and sent the breath from her lungs. But pleasure twisted through her, and she tightened her grip on his hips, trying to pull him closer. The pace was frantic, each thrust deep and hard. He held her thighs tightly as he used his body to pin her against the wall.

There was no delaying the moment of climax. It broke like a storm wave, the frothy bubbles racing up and over her in a rush that made her thrash. She cried out, the intensity too much to contain. Gahan grunted and thrust hard against her a few more times until he growled and his seed spurted into her womb. The hot fluid set off another ripple of delight. This one was deeper, feeling like it moved through the very core of her body. It left her senseless, her arms refusing to hold onto him.

But he trembled too, pressing her against the wall as though he lacked the strength to stand.

"I wanted to drag ye away from the hall tonight." He stroked her cheek, threading his hand into her hair and gripping it. "I wanted to drag ye away because ye were going up to his bed."

Her breath caught. It was pitch black, but she didn't need to see his face to feel his intensity.

"I had to…" She hated the hesitation in her voice. "It was me duty."

And she was failing at it again. She pushed against his shoulders, but he held her still.

"He is nae yer husband, Moira." His tone was hard and edged with authority. "He's a miser who wants what yer brother will give him, but he's past the age of being a husband to any woman."

"Yet he has broken no law." She shoved at him again.

He hissed at her but let her down to her feet and stepped back a pace.

"He's broken the code of honor," Gahan said, "and the Church would agree ye are nae wed."

"That does nae make it right for us to be…"

"Lovers?" he finished. His tone was hard, and he moved off into the chamber and struck a flint stone. Light illuminated his face, and soon there were several candles flickering.

"There is no affection between us." She shouldn't have shared such a personal thought with him, but it just refused to remain unspoken. "Ye want yer way. That is the reason ye kissed me."

He moved back toward her, not stopping until he had a hand pressed against the wall next to her head. She was pinned just as surely as if he were touching her.

"Aye, that was true the first time I kissed ye." He leaned in and pressed a hard kiss against her mouth. She twisted away, but he followed her, demanding surrender. Resistance might have been on her mind, but it dissipated beneath the motion of his lips. "When ye kissed me back, it became something more, Moira."

"Kissing ye back only confirms I lack morality."

Gahan cut through her argument. "Flying a soiled sheet and claiming he is enjoying ye is far worse. Achaius is either a greedy man or one plotting to feud. There is no other reason for wedding ye."

She ducked beneath his arm. "Neither reason absolves me of my sins."

Gahan cupped her shoulder and turned her around. "Ye went to his bed tonight. I saw the determination in yer eyes. What happened? Why were ye sleeping in the other room?"

"That is hardly proof of anything, Gahan. Many couples do nae share a bed past coupling."

"Answer me question." He might be bastard-born, but he was clearly the earl's son. Authority edged his words. "Did ye go to his bed?"

"I tried." She sighed. "I had to try, had to attempt to perform me duty. Achaius's gillie told me to wait until I was summoned. Ye should go before everyone knows what we're about."

Gahan ran a hand through his hair. "Don't worry, I'll be leaving, lass." He held up one finger. "But I am leaving only because ye are correct to worry our liaison would cause trouble. I want peace as much as ye do."

For a moment, she offered him a genuine smile. Gahan didn't return it.

"I give ye fair warning, Moira, if I discover an opportunity to expose yer husband for the liar he is, I shall." He paused at the door. "And I promise ye this, I will nae rest until I find the means to end yer marriage."

She covered her mouth as her jaw dropped open. Gahan took one last look at her before opening the door and leaving. Determination flickered in his dark eyes, leaving no doubt that he meant every word.

No doubt at all.

Six

HER EYES BURNED IN THE MORNING. MOIRA RUBBED THEM and forced herself to sit up. A scent teased her nose, and she drew in a deep breath then scanned the room.

"Good morning, Lady Matheson." A young girl offered Moira a soft smile as she opened one of the window shutters, spilling bright morning light into the chamber. "Asgree had the cook mull ye some cider. It will help wake ye."

The cider was on the bedside table, but Moira didn't reach for it. She hugged the bedding close to hide her nude body.

"I am Alanna, and Asgree sent me to look after ye, since ye have none of yer own maids with ye." Alanna picked up Moira's undergown and wrinkled her nose. "It was wise of ye to discard this before crawling into bed. The sheets would have been ruined, and that would have been a shame." Alanna's cheeks reddened, and she cast a nervous look toward Moira. "Forgive me, Lady Matheson, me mother always said I talked too much."

"Do nae worry," Moira assured her. "It is a happy morning."

Alanna smiled wide. "Oh, it is indeed! Ye need to dress so ye can see the young lad be baptized."

She opened one of the wardrobes that sat in the room. There were a great number of them set between the windows, and all standing as high as Alanna's head. With the doors open, Moira could see that the wardrobe was full of garments. She couldn't help but be jealous of such plenty. She'd never owned more than one chemise at a time.

With the morning light, Moira was able to enjoy the beauty of the chamber as well. It was indeed a star chamber. She sipped at the cider as she looked at the constellations painted so perfectly on the walls.

"The last countess enjoyed painting," Alanna remarked. She held out an undergown in a soft blue color that complemented Moira's blond hair and matched her eyes. "She also enjoyed fine clothing. This will suit yer coloring well."

"It's silk," Moira said and shook her head.

"Asgree told me to dress ye finely. Lady Sutherland has decided ye shall stand as godmother."

"I could nae." Moira's mouth went dry just thinking of the fit Bari would have.

Alanna's eyes rounded. "Oh, but ye must. I've got a silver penny bet on ye." She slapped a hand over her mouth—but too late.

"What do ye mean?" Moira set the cider aside and left the bed. At least she was getting a little more accustomed to being nude in front of other women; her cheeks warmed only slightly.

Alanna shrugged and shook the underrobe so it rippled welcomingly. "Lady Daphne is a spirited lass.

She told her husband that ye would be the godmother because ye caught the babe. The young laird was quite set against it, but she did nae back down. She promised him she'd be off to visit with her brother, Saer MacLeod, if he did nae soften his heart toward ye."

She gathered up the underrobe and helped Moira into it.

"Mind ye, I think it is a shame ye are wed to so old a man. Yer brother is the fiend I've heard he is, and more for making such a match. Men think themselves so important. I laid down me silver against the laird, and I am nae sorry. The retainers all want to sully yer name, but what do they know of yer nature? We females are so often caught in the web of their doings. I am nae the only one betting ye will accept Lady Daphne's offer of becoming the babe's godmother and stand up to the laird's ill thinking of ye."

Alanna went behind her to begin lacing the gown closed. "This silk is fine against the skin. It fits ye well, Lady Matheson."

Then Alanna went back to the wardrobe and withdrew a velvet overrobe.

"I've never worn something so fine," Moira protested.

Alanna brought it to her anyway. "All the more reason to try it. The laird's first son is a grand occasion. It's worthy of velvet."

Alanna carefully let the gown fall over Moira's head. It was pleasantly heavy against her chilled skin. A full-length mirror granted her a look at herself as Alanna secured the ties.

"Ye're quite fetching," Alanna said. The girl

brought a brush over and began to straighten Moira's hair. The glimmer of enjoyment in her eyes made it impossible for Moira to argue with her anymore. That silver penny was likely all the girl earned in a month.

That wasn't the only reason she wanted to do it, though. Norris Sutherland had wounded her pride. Oh, the man had cause, she would grant him that, but Alanna had a point, too. Women so often had to suffer for the messes men made. Even if the current tension was due to Sandra, who'd been acting on instructions from Bari. They had both been raised to be calculating and dishonest in order to better their station, making Moira forever grateful for her common-blood mother who had taught her to be content.

Alanna put up her hair in a velvet French hood. "The countess kept these things for receiving lairds and nobles. She always had the current fashions sent to her." A pair of stockings and a fine set of leather shoes completed her wardrobe. Alanna rubbed her hands together. "The priest will be waiting for ye to come for a blessing before ye go to take the babe from his parents. Saer MacLeod is going to be the godfather."

"Saer MacLeod cannae be here!" Moira exclaimed.

Alanna nodded. "He is. That man is unnatural. Laird Norris sent a hawk within an hour of the babe's birth, and Saer MacLeod was here with the dawn. Nae many would brave the night spirits."

"I doubt Laird MacLeod fears anything," Moira said.

Alanna nodded and went to open the chamber doors. The undergown rustled as Moira moved toward the doors, and she set her shoulders firmly.

Perhaps she had not been raised in silk and velvet, but she would not disgrace her father.

Nor would she forfeit Alanna's penny.

⊱⊰

"Ye are causing quite an uproar, Moira Fraser," Saer MacLeod observed in a low tone. He was wearing a fine wool doublet, and cocked his head from side to side, chafing at the irritating collar.

But what Moira noticed most was that he did not call her Lady Matheson. A chill touched her nape, because she realized he was no fool. He knew the truth of her union.

"Standing as godmother was nae my idea, Laird MacLeod," Moira said. "Nor was delivering Lady Daphne's child in a stairwell."

He flashed her a grin that wasn't kind at all. "Me sister is a formidable woman, for all that she looks like a Fae princess. I was nae surprised to hear she'd gone to make her own judgment of ye. "

They were kneeling at the steps of the altar as the priest began the service.

The priest frowned at them as he finished his prayers and made the sign of the cross over them both. Saer didn't look repentant, in spite of the holy man's attempt to shame him for talking during their blessing as godparents.

"Now bring me the babe," the priest instructed solemnly.

Moira rose from her knees and took the arm Saer offered her. They made their way down the main aisle of the church while the Sutherland clan watched, and went back into the castle. Tradition demanded the babe be brought to the church without its mother, so it was Moira's duty to bring the baby for its cleansing and return it to Daphne.

Daphne would not be allowed back into the church until she'd been churched, which wouldn't happen until a fortnight passed and she had her "sitting up" day. Until then, she'd rest and do her best not to move so her body could recover. At her churching, she'd be blessed and cleansed as well, for no one wanted to risk letting someone back into the house of God who might have made a deal with Satan to ease the pain of childbirth.

Saer and Moira climbed up to the chamber Daphne had slept in, and found her already sitting up in defiance. Despite the fact that she was still abed, lavish robes were laid over Daphne to make it appear that she was dressed in them. A ruby necklace was secured around her neck too. Norris stood beside his wife, formally attired as well, and surrounded by Sutherland retainers.

Moira lowered herself before entering the room.

"Ye are set on this?" Norris asked his wife.

Daphne gave her husband a hard look. "I have learned to have respect for fate when it intercedes in me life. I do nae understand why Moira was the one who caught our son, but I will nae argue. She is part of our son's life."

Norris didn't appear convinced, but he looked at Moira with something other than seething anger for once. He gave her a curt nod and lifted his son with gentle hands. "Then it will be as ye say."

The baby was sweet and settled into her arms with a soft sound. It sucked on its finger as it watched her with cloudy blue eyes.

"He's scrawny," Saer informed his sister.

Daphne pouted. "That shows how little ye know, Brother. He's a fine big boy, according to the midwife."

Brother and sister shared a look before the church bells began to chime. Saer groaned and pulled on the corner of his bonnet.

"The priest is getting impatient," Saer said, cupping Moira's elbow and guiding her from the bedchamber. Achaius had appeared in the receiving room.

"Ye've pleased me well, lass. I'm proud to call ye me wife," he said to Moira.

Moira didn't know what to say to this rare praise from her husband, who was almost as much of a stranger to her as Saer was, so she just smiled and lowered himself, letting Saer guide her down the stairs.

They made their way down the stairs with Sutherland retainers trailing behind them. Saer leaned close to her ear. "I am curious, Moira Fraser, just how long are ye going to proceed with the deception that is yer marriage?"

She hesitated, and he locked gazes with her for a long moment.

"Nothing happens beneath me roof without me knowing. At least, naught so important as the fact that ye were still a maid when Achaius made it known he had ye."

Shock felt like it was strangling her. He gently eased her forward, and the retainers caught up to them as they passed through the castle doors. At the bottom of the stairs, Gahan and Lytge waited. Moira lowered herself but did not stop.

The yard was full of people who had come up from

the village surrounding Dunrobin. The bells along the walls of the castle were ringing as she took the baby toward the open doors of the church. Saer escorted her and, for this single occasion, took his sword into the sanctuary. A baptism was the one exception to being armed inside the house of God. As godfather, it would be his duty to strike down anyone interfering with the holy ritual.

Moira's duty was to take the baby to the church without any interference from his family, so she passed Gahan and Lytge at the doors without stopping. It was an old tradition one obeyed to ensure the new baby was cleansed completely of any influences of evil.

Once she'd walked down the long aisle, Moira handed the baby to the priest. The Sutherland people let out a cheer the moment he dunked the baby, who howled to release the devil. The baby turned red as he bawled, and his arms beat back and forth with his outrage. But Moira smiled, relieved she wouldn't have to pinch him. If he didn't cry, it was a bad omen. Even though she knew it would have been necessary, she was still relieved not to be handing Norris back his son with a mark on him from her hands.

After the ceremony, Moira returned baby Duncan to Daphne.

The new mother beamed. "Thank ye, Moira, and I'm sorry I was spying on ye. I pray ye shall forgive me. The midwife assures me that women do the strangest things when their time is near, but I am still shocked by me actions. "

"This is yer home. A good mistress always knows what is happening inside her keep," Moira replied. She had to bite back a denial that she had anything to hide, because she did: her nighttime trysting with Gahan.

"That does nae make it right, and fate showed me what she thought of it, sure enough." Daphne smiled down at her baby. "Yet it is all well. I think I would like to use the birthing chair next time, though. Those stone steps were hard on me back."

"Next time ye will nae mistake the signs of labor," Asgree said. "Ye are blessed to nae feel the pain until it is almost time for the babe to enter the world."

The baby began to fuss now that he could smell his mother's breast. Moira lowered herself and left the chamber, looking back in surprise, because the countess was opening her own robe to feed her son.

Saer was waiting for her in the receiving room, and Gahan appeared as well. Gahan reached up and tugged on the corner of his bonnet in greeting, and she actually looked behind her to see whom he was addressing, but it was for her.

He chuckled softly. "How could I fail to show respect for me nephew's godmother?" He held out his hand, the invitation clear. For all their intimate moments, none of them had been in the presence of others. She had to make herself place her hand in his, and her heart began to increase its pace as he closed his grip around her fingers. A shiver rippled across her skin, and her knees weakened.

He pressed the lightest kiss against her hand, then released it.

I will nae rest until I find the means to end yer marriage. His words rose in her memory as his eyes echoed the same look of determination he'd had when he said them.

Then Gahan and Saer clasped wrists and exchanged grins.

"My thanks for sending the hawk, Gahan," Saer said. "I would nae have missed this moment. I have been separated from me sister for too long."

Saer sent her another promising look before Achaius interrupted them. He made his way into the room with a slight scuff of his feet.

"There's me bride!" he said. "Do I know how to select the best the Highlands have to offer, lads, or no? Come, lass! I'm ready to sample the celebration fare the cook will be setting out."

As Achaius headed toward the door, Moira looked around and found Saer and Gahan watching her, although it would have been more truthful to say they watched the way Achaius made his way down the stairs without noticing whether or not she followed.

Her blush irritated her. It was frustrating to feel like a toy being fought over by children. With a rustle of the silk undergown, she followed Achaius.

At least Bari was nowhere to be found. Small comfort, but comfort nonetheless.

❦

"A Fraser for godmother." The earl didn't sound pleased. He scowled over his desk at his sons.

"Do nae forget midwife," Gahan added before turning on Norris. "And what do ye mean by handling Moira roughly?" he demanded of his brother.

Norris grunted and crossed his arms over his chest. "I was nae thinking clearly."

"No man does when his children are being born,"

Lytge said. "At least nae the men in this family. We care for our women. It makes us fools when they are suffering to give us babes."

"That does nae make me actions acceptable," Norris admitted. "I owe Lady Matheson an apology."

"Do nae call her that," Gahan grumbled.

"Enough, Gahan!" Lytge scolded. "We are nae the ones who put this charade into motion. We must let Bari play out his plan or risk being judged by our other vassals."

"Nay, Father, I do nae have to stand back and watch."

"What are ye thinking?" Norris demanded.

"I brought Saer MacLeod here because he's a witness."

"To what end, Son?" the earl asked softly. "Take another man's wife, and there will be trouble."

"There will be trouble if she remains his wife," Gahan said.

The earl nodded. "Aye. It is nae a situation that can be solved without consequence." He drew in a deep breath. "Let us leave it be for the moment. Time can be a very effective elixir, and Bari Fraser is nae a man with much patience."

Gahan nodded. It was a reprieve, but one that would allow him time to act. He agreed with his sire, but he wasn't going to wait for Bari to grow tired. No, Gahan was going to press the man until he broke and exposed his true purpose.

❧

"Where is me undergown?"

Alanna wrinkled her nose in response. "That was ruined beyond cleaning."

"It was all I had," Moira protested and glanced around the star chamber, frowning. "Where are me shoes and stockings?"

"Gone by the mistress's command," Asgree said as she entered the chamber with two maids trailing her. Their arms were full of folded garments. "The godmother to the Earl of Sutherland's heir does nae wear rags."

The maids shook out the clothes they had brought. There were undergowns and overgowns, and even a newly fashioned dress with skirts and bodice.

"Please sit down so the cobbler may measure yer feet." Asgree's request was perfectly polite, but there was a core of strength in her tone that sent Moira onto a stool without protest.

An older man entered and tugged on his cap. A younger man followed him with a wooden box. He set it down and opened it up to reveal measuring sticks and all sorts of tools.

"Ye seem to know a bit of the art of midwifery," Asgree said.

Moira looked back at the head of house and found her watching the cobbler with a critical eye.

"Aye. On Fraser land, I led a simple life. I learned the arts the rest of the clan girls did."

"Simple can be useful, it would seem." Asgree moved to inspect the garments lying out on the bed. The cobbler finished and tugged on his bonnet as he left. The head of house clapped her hands the moment the doors were closed.

Alanna and the other maids began to unlace the fine velvet and lifted it away. She knew it was not hers to keep, and yet she was sad when they took the undergown away, for it had been a delight to feel the silk against her skin.

"The silver one, I think," Asgree decided, and her staff lifted an undergown the color of moonlight off the bed.

It was the softest linen she'd ever felt, yet it was not thin. The garment settled around her ankles, and she sighed as it warmed her. The laces were on the side, which was quite useful. Most undergowns didn't have side laces, because the two long sets of eyelets took more work and time to lace. But it would be nice to be able to remove it herself—very nice.

An overgown of wool was next. The fabric was fresh, with no hint of mustiness to suggest it had been stored away. Once it was on Moira, Alanna brought a pair of sleeves and used long ties to secure them at the shoulder.

"This is truly too fine a gift." Yet she adored it. The tone of her voice betrayed her. In the Highlands, cloth was expensive.

"It seems a fair trade," Asgree noted. "Since yer clothing was ruined during the birth."

"Yet mine was nae so fine."

"Sutherland is blessed to have sheep that produce strong wool," Asgree offered. "And ye are much the same size as the young laird's wife. Let's finish. They will be waiting in the hall for us."

The first meal of the day was always the simplest, but the kitchens were in a flurry as the cook prepared for the evening. The scent of cooking meat teased Moira's nose as she entered the hall and made her way down the aisle. Achaius spied her and pounded the table.

"There ye be! What mean ye by making the earl wait?"

Moira lowered herself and felt the weight of those filling the lower tables staring at her. No one had waited on her; the meal was half-finished. Achaius was scolding her to impress the earl. Many a husband did the same with their wives, but she still bristled. She bit her lip to contain her displeasure.

"She was being seen to by me daughter-in-law," Lytge said. "Young Daphne does nae think it fitting that the godmother of her son goes about wearing rags. Raise the lass, man."

Achaius gestured her forward, and she climbed the stairs on the sides of the platform on which the high table stood to take a seat next to him. She noticed there was room for her at the high table because Gahan was not there. It was just as well; she didn't need him distracting her at every turn.

Bari sat near the end of the high table. "She was nae wearing rags. We provide well enough for our women," he insisted.

Several of the Sutherland men sitting at the high table sent him dark looks, but it was Daphne's brother who turned and smirked at him.

"I'm sorry to hear yer land is worse off than mine," Saer MacLeod responded. "Perhaps the coming season will be kind to ye."

Bari growled. Achaius pounded the table again. "Enough about me wife. We're thankful for the gift from the countess. She'll wear it tonight for the celebration. Right fine of yer daughter-in-law to have that baby while we're here. It will provide me the opportunity to linger another day. At my age, ye must take the chances to be merry when they come."

Moira felt herself caught between the calculating looks of Saer, Bari, Norris, and the earl, and she looked down at her food. She'd been hungry, but her appetite had vanished, replaced with the tension lingering at the head table.

Your real problem is that Gahan is missing…

That much was true.

Moira tried to look pleasant and pick at her food, but not knowing where Gahan was made her glance over her shoulder every few minutes, so she excused herself and made her way to the stables.

Athena was restless, crying at Moira and refusing to stand still. Moira ruefully noted that the only person who would notice her absence was Gahan, so she saddled her mare and left Dunrobin, looking for a place to let the hawk fly.

She had to ride away from Dunrobin to find ground that wasn't being broken for crops. She rode to the rocky high ground and gave Athena her freedom. The hawk let out a cry as she took flight. Someone had already fed her, but it was in the bird's nature to hunt. She soared on the morning breeze, looking for prey.

Moira took the opportunity to walk. The open ground ended at a forest. The trees were thick, but Moira wandered among them to cut the climbing afternoon sun. Water rushed by somewhere, and snow still sat in clumps where the thick branches shielded it from the sun. For the first time since Bari had informed her that she was getting married, she was at ease.

There was also no one to criticize her or suspect her of wrongdoing, and no one to tell her not to admit she preferred Gahan over Achaius.

She laughed softly at herself. It was an unfair comparison at best. Gahan was in his prime, and Achaius had bid farewell to that time decades past. Yet it was more than his physical attributes which made him superior. Achaius was a self-serving man, while Gahan had honor.

Athena cried, and Moira shielded her eyes to look for the bird. A second cry came as another hawk appeared in the sky. The birds began to circle each other, spiraling closer and closer together.

"Hawks are more honest than humans."

She jumped, whirling to face her company. Gahan was watching the hawks, a leather gauntlet protecting his hand. He leaned against a tree and looked at Moira, his gaze slowly slipping down her length.

"The hawks are nae concerned about what anyone thinks. They will mate if the courtship goes well," he continued.

"We have hardly had a courtship." Moira had no idea what she was saying. It made no sense, and yet it felt like she was finally speaking the truth.

Gahan flashed her a grin. "We've circled each other, tested each other, judged the strength of the other…" He pushed away from the tree and closed the distance between them. "Just like our feathered friends up there are doing."

As he approached, every inch of her skin became sensitive. He didn't stop until he was an arm's length away, making her look up to make eye contact. She felt breathless, her heart accelerating just from his nearness. No, it was because he was looking at her like she was something he wanted to taste.

She wanted a taste, too.

"So my question is, sweet Moira, since I have made sure to sneak away and will likely catch hell for it from Cam, do ye want to give me a chance to court yer submission?"

She realized with a start that he was saying he'd sneaked away specifically to court her. He'd previously overwhelmed her, but now he was asking. There was a sweetness to him she never would have guessed existed. It was so tempting to believe that, even though she was suspicious that was he still just manipulating her.

"Ye will catch hell. That captain of yers is nae a fool."

Gahan shrugged. "He's me half brother. So, aye, I agree with ye. He will have naught good to say of me taking the opportunity to be alone with ye." His features darkened as he looked past her to the tops of Dunrobin's towers in the distance. "When I saw ye ride out, I wanted to give Achaius hell for letting ye stray so far, but the honest truth is, I recognized it as the chance to be alone with ye. So I am guilty and unrepentant."

He reached out and stroked her cheek. She shivered, moving away, but she didn't jerk. Instead, she took a few steps away and looked back over her shoulder at him. Excitement was threatening to make her giggle, so she moved a few more steps away to try and control her emotions. Of course, when it came to Gahan, there was no such thing as control.

"I do nae think we have ever truly been alone," she said.

He followed her with a lazy pace. "Last night we were. Yet it was a stolen moment. Too quickly finished."

Her cheeks heated, and she looked away from him, searching for her self-discipline. He caught up to her and cupped her chin, turning her gently around to face him. It felt so right to be wrapped in his embrace, as though she'd been longing for it since he left her.

"This is no different," she said.

He reached up to gently rub the nape of her neck. "Because ye are going to be leaving soon?"

She bit her lip. "Of course."

He pressed a kiss to her lips, lingering before breaking their embrace just long enough to let her nipples pucker. "I would show ye the difference, Moira." He stepped back and offered her his hand. "Come with me. Come, because ye know ye are nae Achaius's wife."

"Because I want to be yer lover?" she questioned softly.

He nodded, his eyes narrowing.

She knew she shouldn't, but it felt wrong to refuse. Like she was lying to herself. The hawks were still circling above and would be for hours. It seemed Athena had the right idea.

She placed her hand in his, and satisfaction filled his eyes. He turned and began to lead her deeper into the forest. The sunlight filtered through the trees, and the birds called to one another.

A stone house came into view, the walls made of smooth rocks from the river. There was a huge water wheel on the side of it, waiting for the harvest and the grinding of flour.

"No one will bother us here," he said.

Gahan opened the door and pulled her inside. He

slid the bar across the door and winked at her as he took the long sword off his back and laid it near the door.

"I doubt we are the only couple who finds this a good place to spend an afternoon," he offered in a wicked tone.

Suddenly shy, she took a hesitant step away from him and looked around the mill. There was a large grinding stone with gear shafts that ran through the wall to the wheel. Large levers were set into the wall for lowering the wheel. It would take at least four strong men to operate it. Long tables lined the walls. There was a stack of empty sacks on one, waiting for the next season's grinding.

"Come here, Moira." His tone was soft and inviting.

But when she looked at him, she shook her head and bit her lower lip.

He pulled on the fingers of his gauntlet and set it aside on one of the tables. She expected him to disrobe, but he crossed his arms and considered her first. His silence prompted her more than a probing question might have.

"I just realized that I do nae know ye at all."

Understanding dawned on his face. "So ye wonder if ye are a fool for trusting me?"

"I know I am a fool." It was an admission, a confession that came from her heart. "I should be trying to catch me husband's eye, but…"

"But he leaves ye cold?"

She sighed. "Ye are being overly naughty, Gahan Sutherland. Have ye no shame?"

He had only been toying with her, letting her think she had left him behind. With a burst of speed, he captured her once more and began pulling the pins from her hair.

"Shame? Nay, Moira, I have naught when it comes to ye." He combed his hands through her hair, freeing it of the braid. He gathered it up and lifted it in a bundle and buried his face in it, drawing a deep breath.

"Ye draw me to ye with an intensity that overrules everything I know I should do. The right and wrong I've been taught dissolves into the pure rightness I feel when I touch ye."

He backed up and undid the few buttons on his doublet that were closed. He tossed the garment aside, and it hit the table with a thud.

"I want to strip ye and see the sunlight on yer skin." He pulled on the end of the wide leather belt that kept his kilt around his lean waist. With a tug, it loosened, and he caught the pleats of tartan before they slithered down his legs. He tossed the plaid on one of the side tables.

"I want to stretch ye out on me plaid and see me colors behind ye as I sink into yer body again."

He yanked his shirt off and tossed it aside. She couldn't resist letting her stare slide down his body. Every muscle was defined, and his cock stood erect, making her crave him.

He cupped her chin and raised her head so their gazes locked. "Shame? Nay, Moira, I have naught. All there is when I am near ye is desire, and it is thick enough to choke me."

"Ye make me tremble," she admitted.

Gahan chuckled as he spun her around. He attacked the laces on her gown and pulled the wool garment over her head. Her undergown didn't pose any challenge to him either. It fluttered onto one of the tables, and she discovered herself hesitating before turning around.

Gahan embraced her from behind, tucking her head beneath his chin. His cock nestled against her back and his skin was warm. For a moment he held her still, and a shiver shook her, raising gooseflesh along her limbs. He smoothed them with slow strokes of his hands before gently cupping her breasts, making her moan with pleasure. She turned, needing to be able to touch him.

Approval flashed in his eyes, making her bold. She reached out and stroked his cock. His lips thinned, filling her with confidence. She closed her fingers around his shaft, gripping it gently as she stroked it from base to head.

"Where did ye learn to do that?" His voice was husky, and he groaned as she repeated the motion. It seemed impossible to be affecting him so intensely, and it made her feel powerful.

"Bari sent me to the mews, and there are many who thought it a fine place to tryst. Some did nae care to check very carefully that they were in fact alone." She stretched up to kiss him, wanting to be the one setting their pace for a change. Need was twisting through her, but she felt in control of it this time, and she stretched up to press her lips against his more firmly.

He held her face in his hands and teased her mouth with the tip of his tongue. Opening her lips was a natural progression instead of the surrender it had been before. She stroked his cock again as he thrust his tongue into her mouth. The combination of control and invasion was enough to make her knees weak, but she refused to surrender.

She craved companionship, and for that, she would need to give as much pleasure as she received. Her memory offered up something else, something so forbidden she'd shied away from thinking about it until now. She broke their kiss and resumed toying with his erection. "I saw a few other things, too." His eyes widened, but she didn't give him the chance to question her. Her confidence was high, making her bold beyond measure. "Ye are nae the only one who wants to see the other by the light of day."

She sank to her knees, maintaining her grip on his erect staff. It was ruby-red and stiff, but the skin was soft beneath her fingertips.

"Moira…ye cannae mean to…"

She looked up at him, stroking his length as she locked eyes with him. "I know men like it, whatever it's called."

She didn't wait for him to tell her the term. She returned her attention to his cock and opened her mouth. She licked it first, a tiny lap at the slit on its head.

"Sweet fucking Christ!" he swore as he jumped back.

"Christ never did such a thing." She got to her feet and followed him. "And do nae bring Him up. There is naught here that is permissible."

He took her back in his embrace and toyed with her nipples and the globes of her breasts. "I think the Almighty has a great deal to do with the pleasure we find in each other's touch," he said. "Who else might have created such a need to seek it out when the reality of life does nae favor it?"

She didn't know, but she feared talking about it. She didn't want to discuss anything, because that would take her back to reality. She turned in his arms, reaching up to slip her hands over his short-cut beard.

"I'm a coward, Gahan, for I do nae want to talk. There are too many facts that might come up, and I'd rather enjoy me chance to be yer lover."

She pressed a kiss against his chest and then began to lower herself as she bent her knees. She kissed her way to where his cock jutted up from his belly. Closing her fingers around it, she stroked it, then licked the slit once more.

He groaned, restoring her confidence. She let it warm her and destroy the doubts that had snuck in to needle her. The next time she licked him, she drew her tongue all the way around the crown of his cock. He caught her head, his fingers threading through her hair. He thrust toward her, the jerk of his hips seeming compulsive, as though he had no control.

She liked that idea.

Let him be at her mercy for a change. She opened her mouth and let the head of his cock enter. He grunted, and the sounds pleased her; they meant more than polished words, for they were pure response. She pulled her head back then leaned forward to take more of his length inside her mouth.

"God, ye'll unman me!" He pulled free, earning a frustrated moan from her.

"Good!" She cupped the sacs hanging beneath his cock. "I believe it is far past time for ye to be the one being overwhelmed."

Gahan captured her hair and held her firmly until

she looked up at him. "Ye are nae a coward, Moira Fraser. Ye're a woman who is honest, and that I admire above all else."

No matter where she ended up in life, she was certain she would always remember the look of approval in his eyes. It was more than lust, more than desire.

But need was twisting inside her, so she resumed her assault on his member, sucking it deeply into her mouth and teasing the head with the tip of her tongue. It grew harder, the sac holding his seed tightening as the first drops eased from the slit on its head. But he pulled free, refusing to let her draw his full measure.

"I need to be inside ye, Moira." He scooped her off the floor and laid her on the rumpled length of his plaid. For a moment, he stared at her, the look of fierce possession on his face so intense she felt scorched.

But she reached for him, opening her arms in welcome. He covered her, stretching her arms above her head as she clasped him between her thighs.

"Ye're mine, Moira…*mine*," he breathed against her neck as he thrust deep inside her.

She lifted her hips to take him, groaning with delight. It shouldn't have felt so good, but it was pure rapture every time he pressed his length into her. There was only the rightness of the way they felt together, the building pleasure making ready to break inside of her.

When it burst, she cried out, tightening her hold around her lover. He strained toward her, thrusting his cock as deep as possible. Her breasts bounced with his motions until he stiffened and released his seed. She could feel the insides of her passage contracting around his staff, as if she were milking him. She couldn't move for a long time, her lungs laboring for breath and her heart pounding so hard it felt as though it might break through her chest.

None of it mattered. All she cared about was the feeling of Gahan's heart racing along with hers. He rolled off her and lay on the table, then gathered her close, covering her with his plaid.

At last she tried to rise, but he held her tight. She rubbed his chest, soaking up a last feel of him before gently pushing at him.

"I suppose ye are right, though I have no liking for it," he grumbled in response.

He let her rise. He swung his feet over the edge of the table and stood as she found her undergown. The side lacing allowed her to close it herself. Gahan frowned but grabbed his shirt and put it on too. He pleated his kilt then leaned back against the table to grasp the ends of the belt to buckle it around his waist.

"Do nae," Gahan warned her softly, menacingly.

She turned around and looked at him in confusion.

"Do nae look ashamed," he clarified as he shrugged into his doublet and worked the silver buttons closed. They drew her attention, reminding her of just who he was.

"I swear I'll sleep in yer bed tonight if ye do nae stop looking so guilty."

"Ye will nae." She lifted her chin and held his gaze. "And do nae bluster at me, Gahan Sutherland. Ye know as well as I the reasons we cannae do such a thing. Ye are nae a man who forsakes his duty. I could nae love a man who did nae have honor."

She realized what she'd said and gasped. "I did nae mean—"

"Aye, ye did." He moved toward her, and she retreated, shaking her head. She bumped into the wall, and he caged her there with a hand flattened on the wall on either side of her head. She didn't want to meet his gaze, didn't want to see confirmation of just how foolish she was.

"It humbles me, lass, for I have done little to deserve it."

There was sincerity in his voice. She looked up against her better judgment and found his eyes glassy with emotion. But it was too much; she knew she could never have him. She ducked beneath his arm.

"We must nae say such things." Tears burned her eyes, but she forbade herself to cry. There would be plenty of time for tears when she was back on Matheson land.

"Saer knows the truth of yer marriage."

She turned to look at him. "I know. He told me so. Do ye mean to drive me mad?"

"I mean to expose yer brother and Achaius for the liars they are," he insisted.

She turned around so he might lace her gown. Frustration was destroying the bliss of the moment. She drew in a deep breath and let it out as he finished closing her gown.

"What do ye mean by that sound, Moira?" he demanded softly.

She turned and met his challenge. But he didn't care for the calm acceptance on her face.

"What do ye expect to come of exposing them?

There is naught good about this entire situation. For all that Achaius is deceiving the world about our marriage, at least it gives me a place to go beyond Bari's reach. Expose him, and I will have to return to me brother's land."

"Ye'll come to me," he insisted.

"A Fraser inside Dunrobin? I think yer father will have something to say about that. If no, I am sure yer brother will, and it will nae be words of welcome."

He opened his mouth but shut it again. She shook her head. "As I said, naught good can come of this. That is why it's forbidden."

He reached for her, cupping her face, and she rubbed her cheek gently against his hand.

"Forbidden, and yet I crave it."

He wrapped his arms around her, holding her tightly for a long moment. "Just as ye crave it. I refuse to believe there is no way to have ye for me own."

"Yer mistress, perhaps." She gently pushed her way free. "Achaius is short in years. But I wonder, Gahan, do ye wish our children to be bastard-born?"

"Ye insult me to ask such a thing," he growled. "I would take ye to the church."

"Yer father would never allow it," she insisted firmly. "And he might easily disown ye, which is something I will nae take a chance upon."

"Are ye saying ye will nae wed me?"

She lost the battle to keep her tears from falling. Several trickled down her cheeks before she drew in a shaky breath to restore her composure.

"That is what I'm saying, Gahan. The cost would be too great for ye. It is more than the position ye enjoy. It would strike at the relationship ye have with yer sire, and I can see that is a dear thing to ye. I have no wish to be the woman who sours it. "

He didn't care for her answer. Rage flickered in his eyes, but a moment later he surprised her by grinning. "Ye do love me, Moira." He nodded, his expression full of confidence. "Ye do."

It was true. She did love him. The ride back to Dunrobin was too short because she needed to banish her emotions before others witnessed her eyes shining with unshed tears. But she could not pull her mare to a stop and linger, because Gahan had warned her he'd be leaving just long enough after her to throw off suspicion. She crossed into the castle and slid off the horse's back. The yard was still full of younger boys training with swords under the watchful eye of experienced men.

As she returned Athena to the stables, Moira tried to forbid herself to think about Gahan's promise to give her a place, but there seemed no way to evict the echoes of their conversation from her mind. Athena settled onto a perch and began to groom herself.

"Ye should have smothered the brat."

Moira spun around to find Bari glaring at her. She gasped as she realized what he'd said. "Ye cannae say such things."

He reached out and smacked her, the sound popping loudly in the mews.

"Ye do nae tell me what to say…half sister. It would have served them right to lose their blood, since they took Sandra from me."

The light of insanity flickered in his eyes. The sting on her cheek was nothing compared to the growing fear that he was losing all grip on reality.

"Bari, ye need to let go of yer hate. It is destroying ye," Moira said, trying to reason with him.

"I saw ye out, alone. I also saw that bastard riding out without even a single man at his back. There is only one reason he'd take such a risk." He raked her from head to toe with his wild glare. "Ye look like Gahan's whore now," he snarled.

She was pinned by the mews behind her. Bari pulled a small knife from the top of his boot and held it up.

"I should slice yer throat and leave ye here for yer lover to find."

He was insane enough to do it. "Enough, Bari," she said with more confidence than she felt. "Ye must make peace within yerself."

"What I need is vengeance for Sandra. She'll nae rest until I avenge her."

His eyes glowed strangely, the knife hovering threateningly, until someone caught his wrist from behind and yanked him away.

He sputtered, and the hawks all reacted to the sudden motion. They fluttered their wings and cried out as someone moved in front of Moira.

"Ye'll keep yer hands off what is mine, Bari Fraser."

Achaius emerged from the shadows of the mews, his retainers close. Two of them placed themselves between her and Bari.

Bari stood up, unrepentant. "She's Gahan Sutherland's whore." He pointed at the gown she wore. "She's wearing his clothing like she's proud of her ways. Ye should strangle her for adultery."

The birds had quieted down, and no one had come to investigate. Moira found herself searching for an escape route, but there was none.

"Gahan Sutherland?" Achaius questioned. "It was Lady Daphne who gave her the clothing. Having the future countess of Sutherland feeling kindly toward me wife might be an advantage someday."

"I saw her coming in from the woods, and Gahan left nae long after her. She's his whore," Bari accused.

Achaius looked at her, his retainers turning to flank him. She should have been frightened, but all that swept through her was relief.

"Ye see? She makes no excuses or denials." Bari spat on the ground in front of her. "Let me cut her throat and leave her here for that bastard to find."

"Now why would I let ye do such a thing?" Achaius asked gleefully.

Surprise flashed through her as Achaius turned to face Bari. "Since ye have no bride, no bastards, and no other kin, me wife is the heir to the Fraser clan. The issue from her womb will be the next laird."

"She will never inherit Fraser holdings," Bari growled.

Achaius stepped closer and lowered his voice. "Are ye sure, lad? Ye talk a great deal about feuding, and nae one bit about making sure ye have an heir. Ye have no cousins, no uncles, and no other siblings, only Moira, me properly wedded wife."

Bari's eyes widened. "Are ye playing me for a fool? Ye promised me ye'd join me in a feud against the Sutherlands. It was the only reason I gave ye land as dowry."

Achaius chuckled, the sound dry and brittle. "Marriage is for gain and babes. Yer sister is a Matheson now, and we protect what is ours."

"Does that mean ye are nae riding with me against the Sutherlands?" Bari demanded.

"Keep yer voice down," Achaius warned, "or ye'll get to see the room yer sister died in, I wager."

"Answer me," Bari hissed through clenched teeth.

Achaius ignored him and turned to look at Moira. "We'll be leaving now. I've had enough celebrating, Wife."

"I'll find someone else to join me," Bari threatened.

He shrugged. "Ride to yer death, lad. That will only leave yer clan to me." He turned to his men. "Saddle the horses. We're bound for Matheson land."

The Matheson retainers responded instantly. They began pulling their horses from the stables and saddling them. The Sutherland retainers watched curiously from their posts until Norris Sutherland appeared.

"It's been a fine visit, one I'll nae soon forget," Achaius declared loudly to Norris, "but the arrival of yer son has me thinking of planting me own seeds, as I told yer father already."

Norris nodded then looked toward the gate. The bells on the walls began to ring as Gahan returned to the fortress. Moira turned to watch him, her breath catching in her throat. He was magnificent. She stared at him, trying to memorize the details of his dark hair flowing back as he rode forward. The pommel of his sword gleamed behind his left shoulder, and his doublet sleeves were once more open and tied behind his back. He pulled up the stallion and took in the activity, his eyes darkening with fury.

"Glad I am to be able to say farewell to ye," Achaius said. He offered Gahan his hand. Gahan slid off his horse's back and reluctantly clasped the older man's wrist. Achaius nodded then turned to let his men help him mount.

"Forgive an old man for his whims, but I feel the need to be gone," Achaius announced.

Moira hesitated as her mare was brought forward.

What are ye going to do? Refuse to leave?

She'd always known it had to end. She drew in a deep breath and lifted her foot to mount. Gahan grasped her waist and lifted her onto the back of the mare.

"Thank ye…" Her words trailed off as she looked into Gahan's eyes one more time.

My lover's eyes…

Aye, she'd remember him that way. He withdrew his hand, and his captain stood near his back. Her throat was trying to swell shut, but she swallowed the lump.

"Good-bye, Gahan Sutherland," she said softly. "Please give Daphne me farewell."

Achaius didn't grant her any further time. He pointed toward the gates, and her mare was swept up in the flow of his retainers. They closed around her, shielding her from Bari and carrying her through the gates of Dunrobin.

Tears leaked from her eyes, and she didn't try to stop them. The wind whipped them away to hide her shame. She'd known it would end. But that made it no more easy to bear.

⤞⤝

He'd always loved Dunrobin. From the moment he'd been old enough to understand his father was the earl, Gahan had looked at the castle with longing eyes. When he was very young, his mother would cuddle him and tell him about his father. When she died, he struggled to ignore the barbs aimed at him because of the stigma of his birth. Dunrobin had represented home and everything dear. He'd bleed to protect it, and vowed to give his life if necessary.

But today, it felt empty.

The sun was setting, and it felt like every bit of breath was leaving his body. The Mathesons disappeared over the horizon, and he fought the urge to charge after them.

She'd said she wouldn't wed him. But only to protect him.

He ground his teeth with frustration, trying to think of a reason to go after her. But there was none. He watched as the Frasers finished saddling up as well and rode out toward their own land.

Cam stepped in front of him. "Yer father is asking for ye."

He wanted to refuse. But he knew he couldn't; that was not the way the world worked. Gahan reluctantly turned and entered the tower, making his way toward his father's private study. People cleared out of his way, offering him nods of respect. The gestures were yet another reminder of how the world worked. The Sutherland people didn't need him racing off to steal another man's wife. He had his duty to uphold the honor of the family. Only the English nobility expected their people to behave correctly while they did as they pleased. He was a Highlander.

But that did little to ease his frustration.

"Do nae tell me to be content with it, Father," Gahan said when he arrived.

Gahan paced back and forth in front of his father's desk. It felt like someone had cut something off him, living flesh severed from him while he was awake to feel the agony.

"What makes ye think I would say something such as that?"

Gahan froze, turning to look at his father. Instead of the stern look of disapproval he expected, his father appeared sympathetic.

"I know what loves feels like," Lytge said softly. "If ye recall, I gave ye me reasons for warning ye to stay away from the lass."

Gahan shook his head. "I am the greatest fool alive for nae admitting it to her."

It didn't seem possible that he'd heard Moira say she loved him but a few hours past. It felt like a huge chasm had opened up, uncrossable now that she was gone.

Someone rapped on the door.

"Come in," his father said.

Norris opened the door and tugged on his bonnet as he entered. He stepped aside to reveal a young boy wearing the Sutherland kilt. The boy pushed out his chin and reached up for the corner of his cap. Norris gently grasped the boy by the shoulder.

"This is young William. He was tending the mews today and has something to tell ye."

Norris eased the lad forward, and William stepped up after just the first nudge. He gulped down a deep breath before gathering the courage to speak directly to the earl.

"Bari Fraser was furious with his sister for nae killing the laird's new grandson when she had the chance to gain vengeance for Sandra's death," the boy said. "He wanted to cut his sister's throat, pulled a knife out to do the deed and all."

"He did what?" Gahan roared.

Norris held up a hand to quiet his brother. "There is more."

"It was Laird Matheson who protected her, but Bari Fraser claimed he'd seen ye in the woods with Lady Matheson and he knew for a fact ye were lovers. But Laird Matheson was nae angry. He told Laird Fraser that Lady Matheson was set to inherit the Fraser clan on account of the fact that Laird Fraser was talking about feuding with the Sutherlands."

"I knew it!" Gahan exclaimed.

"Did anyone else hear this, lad?" the earl asked.

William nodded. "There was three of us, but I'm the oldest, so I stepped forward."

"I need yer word that ye will keep silent," the earl insisted.

William nodded and tugged on the corner of his bonnet. "I will, and I'll make sure the other lads do too. We're Sutherland through and through."

The earl smiled. "That's right. A Sutherland is only as good as his word." He opened a small wooden chest on the desk and pulled three silver pennies from it. He pressed them down and tapped them with a fingertip. "Which is why I always take care of me people."

William looked at the silver with anticipation brightening his eyes, but he twisted the corner of his kilt instead of reaching for the pennies. "Yer gratitude is enough, Laird. Me father would ask where I got the penny, and I could nae lie to him."

The earl grinned. "Ye're a clever lad." He returned the pennies to the chest. William tried to hide his disappointment.

"You tend to the mews, correct? Are there any chicks ye favor?"

William's expression brightened. "Aye, Laird. I like them all, but there is one I think is the best of the lot from last spring."

"It likes ye, does it?"

William nodded.

"It is yers. Tell yer father ye earned the hawk's respect, and I saw fit to give it to ye. The other lads may take a hawk or a sheep for their diligence. That is nae a lie. Keeping yer word is being diligent to me."

"I thank ye, Laird, very much," William said eagerly. He tugged on his bonnet again, this time pulling so hard it was drooping over his eyebrow when he finished. Norris opened the door for him, and he scampered through.

"So ye have witnesses now," Saer MacLeod offered from where he stood in the corner. "But nae ones who would hold up if Lord Home became involved."

"That may be for the best," Lytge said. "As Daphne learned, the young king believes obedience to one's family is very important. Moira is wed to Achaius, and

I think the man is very clever, for he knows Bari is reckless enough to get himself killed before leaving an heir to the Fraser clan."

"I am going after Moira," Gahan informed his father. "Now that Achaius has revealed his plans to Bari, she is nae safe. Bari might try to get her out of the way to make sure he is the only one who can hold the Fraser land, or to ensure me blood does nae wear Fraser colors. It's true, the lass is me lover, but I wish she were me wife."

Everyone waited to see what the earl would say.

"I doubt ye will be welcomed through the gates of Matheson Tower now," Norris predicted.

The earl held up his hand when Gahan would have argued. "This will require more than yer passion, Son. I forbid ye to go to Matheson land. Is that clear?"

Every fiber of his being rebelled, but his father was steadfast.

"What do ye suggest?" It took more control than Gahan thought he had to ask the question. His father didn't answer. Instead, he began to tap the top of his desk with a fingertip.

Gahan knew the gesture. His father didn't have a solution. It was chilling, because there was a great deal of truth in what his sire had said. There was no way to force Achaius to relinquish Moira.

She was beyond his reach.

So the solution was clear. He'd have to find a way to make Achaius bring her to him.

⚜

"Enough! Yer sniveling brother is gone."

The retainer shoved Sandra's bag of food through

the opening in the door and closed it. She'd heard him leaving and knew it was true.

Bari was gone.

Her door had been guarded every day he'd been at Dunrobin, but now there was only the wind whistling through the open window. She walked to the cot and put on her undergown. Loneliness was a vicious thing, ripping into her self-confidence and leaving her prey to despair. Through the window, all she could see was the ocean. It was all she might ever see.

For the first few months, she'd laughed at Gahan Sutherland's inability to hang her. She'd thought him a weak fool. But now she wondered if he was in fact a far more sinister creature than she'd realized. Her imprisonment was a slow torment. Death would have been swift and taken her away from counting the days.

She trailed her fingers along her hands, appreciating how smooth her skin was. She was wasting her beauty inside the tower room. Was there no force in heaven or hell willing to help her?

She'd swear allegiance to the first one who appeared.

"Ye are hatching some plot."

Norris came through the secret passageway into Gahan's room an hour before daybreak. Gahan looked up for only a moment before resuming his preparations. His sword was almost ready, the blade shining from the oil he'd applied to the sharpening stone.

"And I want to know what it is," Norris continued.

"I will nae disobey Father," Gahan replied.

Norris crossed his arms over his chest. "That is nae an answer."

"I am leaving within the hour," he admitted.

Norris grunted. "As if I cannae see ye are making ready to depart. Where are ye going?"

Gahan held up the sword and inspected the blade with a critical eye. He made his brother wait while he slid it into its sheath and put the leather harness over his shoulder.

"Gahan? Do I really have to run to Father and tell on ye?"

Gahan shot his brother a deadly look. "Ye were willing to defy our sire to have Daphne, and I held me tongue."

Norris sighed. "That's true, but I was heading to Court, nae somewhere where it was likely I'd have me throat cut. Father forbid ye from Matheson land for good reason. I agree with him."

"I am nae going to Matheson land." He picked up his bonnet and adjusted his sword. "But I swear I am coming back with Moira, and I'd appreciate it if ye'd go back to bed. Go lie down next to the woman ye love and remember that nothing would have kept ye from having her."

"Aye," Norris agreed.

"And do nae insult me by worrying I'll break me word to Father."

Norris drew in a deep breath but let it out before nodding. He offered Gahan his hand then turned and disappeared into the secret passage. A moment later, Saer MacLeod moved into the main chamber from one of the small adjoining chambers. Cam followed, and Gahan nodded in approval as he watched the two men bring forth the means of getting Achaius out of his tower.

Sandra Fraser was paler but still a beauty—a deadly one, but Gahan was going to put her to good use. He wasn't breaking his word, but he was taking a chance with his father's good will.

For the first time in his life, he was willing to do so.

"So ye plan to use me as bait?" she questioned in a sultry voice.

"I do," Gahan informed her. "Consider it the cost of sparing yer life."

She fluttered her eyelashes. "I suppose that is a fair trade." She held up a single finger. "But I want yer word ye will keep yer promise to set me free even if Achaius does nae step into yer trap."

"As long as ye stay off Sutherland land, it is done."

"What of yer father?" Sandra asked.

"He left yer life in me hands." Gahan raked her with a hard look. "Do nae forget that, for I swear I will run ye through if ye try to wrong me."

It was a risky gamble, and he was sure many would argue the risk outweighed the gain.

Not to him. Regaining Moira was worth any risk.

Seven

For the first time, Moira found herself grateful that Achaius was a miser.

With spring breaking all around them, there was much to be done at Matheson Tower, and she threw herself into the work. But even exhaustion was not enough to keep her nights peaceful. Gahan inhabited her dreams: his touch, his voice, and even his kisses. She turned from one side to the other, seeking his embrace.

All she found was emptiness.

Matheson Tower needed cleaning, and it kept her busy for weeks. The maids were eager to please the new Lady Matheson, because Moira didn't place herself above them. They lined up to help her scrub the stone hallways with hard-bristled brushes and lye soap. They set up large cauldrons in the yard and kept fires burning under them to boil water. The ash was scooped up and used to make more soap.

She ordered the staff to bathe and set the cooper to making more tubs. He looked surprised, but went back to his shop to begin work.

Through it all, Achaius ignored her, which was a relief.

At least he didn't balk when the cooper delivered the tubs and wanted payment. The tubs were simply large half barrels sealed with pitch. But they held water, and that suited her needs. Within a day, the kitchens smelled better, and after three weeks, she no longer had to tell the staff to bathe. They did so happily.

But at the oddest times she would catch Achaius or his men watching her. If she ventured too close to the gate, someone would call her back into the keep and forget what they had wanted.

It might have been her imagination. More likely, they were just making sure she stayed where Achaius had control of her. Bari was forbidden on Matheson land now, which left her to make the best of her life, but it also meant the Matheson clan had not ridden out to feud. Moira didn't know what Bari had been up to in the past weeks, but it was a relief knowing that, so far, she had been able to keep her promise to her clanswoman to keep the peace.

Fann saw to her needs, following her about. The girl was bright, so Moira didn't protest.

Moira and her staff had just finished cleaning the hall when the bell in the church began to ring. Moira wiped the sweat from her brow and looked at Fann.

"We've visitors, someone important," Fann said.

Which meant it was Moira's duty to greet them. She untied her apron and tried to smooth her hair back into place. It was hopeless, and she sighed on the way to the doors of the keep. Achaius was already standing there, leaning on his cane as a dark-haired man rode through the gates.

For a moment, her heart leapt.

She longed so much for Gahan, she saw only what she wanted to see. When the man rode closer, however, there was no way she could continue deluding herself. He was well muscled and dark-haired, but his chin was smooth.

"That's Laird Grant's son," Achaius informed her. "Tell the cook to impress me at supper." He dismissed her with a wave of his hand as Kael dismounted and made his way up the stairs to clasp Achaius's hand.

"Kael Grant!" Achaius declared. "It is fine to see ye."

"And ye as well. This must be yer new bride," Kael said.

Moira stopped and turned back to face the man. Kael had a devil-may-care grin on his lips, and his dark eyes looked like they were sparkling with mischief. He was every inch a hardened Highlander, but there was something about him that suggested he enjoyed toying with others. She might label him an arrogant rogue, but there was a hint of something in his expression that made her realize he did not bluff. Ever.

"Aye, indeed," Achaius answered. "A fine bride, and I don't care if I'm bragging!"

Kael Grant moved closer to her, and he held out his hand. It was a common enough gesture, but she hesitated before placing her hand in his. It felt like the man was testing her. He raised her hand to his lips and gave her the briefest of grazes before releasing her.

"She's worth bragging about and, if I do say so, I believe ye have married the right Fraser sister." Kael tilted his head toward Achaius. "I think Saer MacLeod is mad to be wedding Sandra. I hear she tried to poison the Earl of Sutherland. But I suppose the man has his eyes on the heir to the Fraser land. I do nae think it is worth suffering a venomous bitch for a wife."

"Ye must have heard wrong." Achaius's tone was chilling. For the first time, all joviality was gone, and his expression was deadly. "Sandra Fraser is dead."

Kael looked surprised. "Nay, she is no. It seems none of the Sutherlands wanted to risk offending the young king by dispensing their own justice after Sandra tried to poison the earl, so they kept her at Dunrobin all this time. But now with the earl's grandson born, they want her gone, and Saer MacLeod agreed to take her. I'm on me way to witness the wedding but thought to stop and enjoy the evening with ye."

"I'm right glad ye did, me boy." The look in Achaius's eyes didn't match his tone. There was a cold, calculating glitter, one that made suspicion prickle up her nape. He caught her staring at him and waved her inside. She lowered herself and turned to go and find the cook.

She swore she felt Kael Grant watching her go.

❦

"When is this wedding?" Achaius said when he had recovered his cheerful mood. He was partaking of the supper the cook had somehow produced on short notice. Plates of cheeses added some lavishness to the common meal, and there were sugared orange peels Moira hadn't known were in the stores. Clearly the cook didn't consider it his duty to tell her where the costly items were.

"Soon," Kael replied. "Saer is so newly arrived from

the isles, he's making sure there are plenty of witnesses to his union. It's a smart move, and me father wants to know more about Sandra Fraser. He hears rumors she was falsely accused."

"I know she is guilty," Achaius insisted.

Kael raised an eyebrow. "Is that so?"

Achaius nodded. "The bitch needs to be hanged."

"Well, that is nae what is happening to her, and there was no trial. At least nae one the king would respect. Now that Saer has the lass, there is reason to doubt the entire tale."

Achaius took a swig from his mug and then another before returning it to the table. For a moment, his eyes became calculating and hard. But he masked it quickly and grinned.

"In that case, I'll be riding with ye in the morning, for I would like to know the truth."

Moira's belly knotted with unease. Her suspicions were finding more facts to support them.

"Ye've never been the type to ride all over the Highlands on errands of fancy." Kael spoke softly but with a tone that was solid steel. "Is yer reason for attending the wedding because Saer MacLeod is godfather to the Sutherland heir?"

Achaius could have argued, but it would have raised more questions. Kael Grant was no fool to be brushed off with a chuckle and a grin.

"Well, I was just talking before I finished thinking. Of course me idea was to take the lass to see her sister. Ye'll understand one day when ye are me age. Sometimes ye do nae make a lot of sense. But I knew what I meant. We'll be riding with ye."

Moira backed away and turned into the passageway that ran off from the side of the hall.

Sandra was alive?

She wanted to retch until Kael's words sank in. Half the news making its way through the Highlands was rumor and tall tales. But if Sandra was alive, it was possible she was not guilty of trying to kill the Earl of Sutherland. Which meant Gahan had lied to her. That hurt. Just the thought that Gahan had no honor caused her distress.

He kissed ye, when ye were set to wed another…

She swallowed the lump in her throat, but there was still bitterness in her mouth. It was true. She was seeing only what she wanted to see in Gahan. Their encounters had all been motivated by his need to keep her from doing something he didn't want to happen.

The knowledge stung. Tears filled her eyes, and she ventured into the darker passageways to hide them. Gahan was still all the things she loved, and yet she could not blind herself to the true nature of a Highland laird. He would protect his family's interests first. That was what she was to him—a means to an end.

It was better to know. So why did it hurt so much?

"Lady Matheson," Kael Grant greeted her at dawn. Moira lowered herself in respect, then reached under her mare to make sure the saddle strap was secure.

"Used to seeing to yer own needs, I see."

Once again, suspicion prickled along her nape. "Did ye nae do the same before mounting?"

"Aye, I did. 'Tis a foolish man who climbs into the saddle without checking."

Moira said nothing as she used a small box in the yard to help with mounting her horse.

"I hear ye are godmother to the Sutherland heir," Kael continued.

"She is indeed," Achaius answered for her as he appeared on the steps. He had on a doublet and a thick gold chain. For once his shirt wasn't stained with food, and his beard looked like it had been cleaned. "Me wife is a credit to the Mathesons."

The Matheson retainers brought his horse around and helped him into the saddle. He nudged his horse up to stand near Kael. Moira wasn't pressed to the back of the column this time. Two retainers flanked her as they rode through the gates and remained near her as they crossed the countryside.

It was very strange how their presence brought her no comfort at all.

MacLeod land

"At least *ye* are pleased," Saer MacLeod told Gahan.

"Ye grumble like an old woman," Gahan said.

Saer's eyes narrowed. Gahan got a glance of the hardened nature that had helped him survive as an outcast on the isles. "And ye are mooning like a love-sick calf," Saer said.

"I'm trying to regain the woman I want. Ye're helping me because ye'd do the same."

"I've nae met a woman I'd risk so much for, but

I admit I do nae like being told an old man can have what is mine," Saer confirmed. "Yet we are brothers, ye and I. Both bastard-born and scorned by the wives of our sires. A tower is naught but stones if there is no family inside it."

"How is yer bride today?" Gahan asked sarcastically.

"Very disappointed to be locked in another chamber," Saer admitted. "She's going to be trouble."

"Agreed. But she is the only thing that would draw Achaius out with Moira."

"And Bari Fraser to MacLeod land. Since Daphne is wed to yer brother, Bari knows he has no friends here. My loyalties are clear to one and all."

Gahan looked down at the Matheson and Grant retainers filling the yard of MacLeod Tower. He gripped the windowsill until his knuckles turned white as Moira appeared and dismounted. Running to her would be foolish...but he still struggled to control the impulse.

"It seems things have changed for Lady Matheson," Saer noted.

Instead of surrounding Achaius and leaving Moira to fend for herself, the Matheson retainers flanked her and made sure she followed Achaius inside the keep.

"Aye. That old man plays the jovial fool well, but he is truly a calculating knave," Gahan said.

"And he has every reason to wish ye dead," Saer remarked. "It's a dangerous game we've set into motion."

"Aye, but those tend to have the greatest rewards," Gahan said.

"Or costs."

Gahan couldn't argue with Saer. The man was

right, but he was also standing firm in his position in the ruse they were playing. "I will nae forget yer service, Saer."

"I admit I am enjoying this charade, because men like Bari and Achaius are the ones who use women like our mothers without any regard for their feelings. Moira is but a thing to them. I am going to enjoy watching their schemes crumble."

"It's a good thing ye have inherited a title in the Highlands, Saer." Gahan turned to leave the chamber. "With that sort of thinking, ye'll never make a good Englishman."

"Or an earl's son."

Gahan shrugged. "Do nae judge me father. I think he is allowing me to do this."

"Because yer brother has nae shown up?" Saer asked.

"He'll still arrive. Me sire cannae fail to take action or risk having it said Sandra was nae guilty."

"In that case, I hope Bari Fraser does nae keep us waiting."

❦

"Ye are nae sick," Norris observed.

Lytge chuckled and looked up from the desk in his sleeping chambers. "And ye must have suspected that yesterday."

Norris offered no answer but came into his father's private room, closing the distance so the retainers at the doors would not overhear them.

"I'm bored unto death," Lytge groused. "Only English lords are meant to take to their beds. I'm a Highlander and will die with the sun on me face."

"Then why are ye hiding up here?"

"Because I have to send ye after Gahan, but I need to give yer brother the chance to play his hand."

Norris nodded. "I thought so."

He sat down and began to shuffle a deck of playing cards. His father picked up the ones Norris dealt him and frowned over their edges at him.

"Ye will remind yer brother just how much I suffer for his cause."

Norris sorted through his hand. "Is that the only thing ye want me to discuss with him?"

"Are ye talking about Sandra Fraser?"

Norris nodded and put a card down then picked up a new one.

"We both gave Gahan the duty of dealing with her. That means we must abide by his actions." Lytge sighed. "I try to give both of ye the space to be men. It is nae always easy, but he has nae disobeyed me."

"Aye. He's on MacLeod land, and ye're right about Sandra Fraser. I told him I had no stomach for it, but I confess I am wondering just how he managed to get her compliance. Sandra is a cold-hearted female."

The wind blew in through the open shutters, bringing a warm touch of spring. The land was turning green as the new crops began to sprout. Norris played the hand, waiting for his father to make a move.

"Ye'll go tomorrow. After I show meself. Let those who are fool enough to think me feeble believe I was in bed and ye were unable to make a decision without me."

It was the sort of thing that kept the Sutherlands strong. No one really knew what any of them were thinking. Norris discovered himself quite pleased with it. True, he would have liked to be in the action, but maybe, just maybe, Gahan might be able to accomplish what all three of them really craved.

An end to the threat Bari Fraser represented.

≈

MacLeod land

"Ye made no mention of locking me up again."

Sandra paced back and forth when Gahan and Saer went to fetch her.

"Ye cannae expect freedom," Gahan said.

Sandra tossed her auburn hair and fluttered her eyelashes. "That's what ye promised me," she said in a soft, delicate voice. The woman appeared fragile and forlorn, but Gahan knew she was no victim. He had seen his father at death's door by her doing. The woman was a menace.

"Ye were promised freedom *from Dunrobin* in exchange for playing a happy bride-to-be," he said.

"Oh, aye." Sandra shifted her attention to Saer. She pouted. "It is going to be a bit of a chore. Ye are a savage."

Saer didn't take offense. He grinned at her. "One who will take delight in choking the life out of ye if ye try yer hand at betraying us. Among the savages on the isles, gender does nae protect the guilty from justice."

Sandra looked uncertain for a moment, but she controlled her expression quickly. She reached up to finger her unbound hair. It was brushed out and shimmering down her back. Fresh spring greens crowned her head in a delicate wreath. Her robes were of green and yellow, befitting a bride.

"I have dressed to please," she said.

"Aye, ye look the part," Gahan agreed. "Now make sure ye play it. One false word, and I'll do what me kin wanted me to do."

Sandra didn't look frightened or even worried. She brushed by him, fluttering her eyelashes and trailing her fingertips across his chest. "I told ye I would be of use to ye, Gahan Sutherland."

She treated Saer to the same then exited the chamber with a rustle of her skirts.

"That's an evil female," Saer said. "She'll nae do anything for us without trying to get what she wishes. It's clear she is guilty of trying to kill yer father."

"She is, and she's unrepentant. But something kept me from ordering her to be hanged."

"Now ye know what that was," Saer said. "Fate works her will on us all."

Saer followed Sandra down the stairs, leaving Gahan to ponder what he'd said. Was Sandra alive because fate was intervening? That seemed rather far-fetched. He'd always lived his life by the understanding that he made his way in the world through his actions and will.

Tonight would be no different. He descended to the chamber below where Cam was waiting. Steam rose from a basin, and Cam was making sure a blade was sharp. Gahan sat down and let his half brother shave him clean. Next, Cam worked on his hair. Once he was satisfied, Gahan stood up and stripped out of his Sutherland plaid. For the first time in his life, he put on a kilt from a clan other than his father's.

There were men who would call him a dishonorable wretch for doing it. He didn't care. Determination was blazing in his gut. The means didn't concern him, only the victory.

∽✦∾

"My sweet little sister."

Moira stood stunned in the Great Hall of MacLeod Tower. Sandra swept toward her with a bright smile on her lips. Gooseflesh rose on Moira's arms; it was like a ghost had materialized. Even knowing she was going to see Sandra hadn't really driven home the fact that she was alive.

Sandra hugged her while Moira remained caught in her shock.

"Ye clean up decently after all. Bari was wise to see the possibility," Sandra whispered in her ear before backing away to bestow a bright smile on Achaius. "Ye must be me brother-by-marriage." She lowered herself prettily.

Saer MacLeod held out his hand, and Sandra went toward him. The head table was soon full, and the meal began. There was music, and Sandra made a charming picture as she smiled sweetly and praised the musicians. She reached for Saer's hand from time to time, stroking one fingertip along the top of his hand. The intimate gesture wasn't lost on anyone.

But the bells on the tower walls began to ring. Saer held up his hand for silence, and two retainers ran down the center aisle.

"Frasers are at the gate, demanding entrance, Laird."

"Me brother!" Sandra exclaimed. "How lovely. Ye would nae make him spend the night outside the gate."

Saer MacLeod looked like he was contemplating just that, but he relented. "Allow Laird Fraser in with his men. No swords."

"What Highlander worth his plaid gives up his sword?" Sandra demanded.

Saer shot her a hard look. "Anyone who wants to enter me tower."

They heard the groaning of the gate as it was lifted. It took only a few moments before Bari was striding into the hall. He was covered in dirt, and his chin sported a two-day's growth of beard. He froze at the entrance of the hall, staring at Sandra for a long moment. She pushed her chair back and ran to meet him. Bari hugged her close, but Saer followed his bride and offered Bari his hand.

Bari clearly wasn't pleased having his reunion with Sandra interrupted. But he clasped the wrist offered to him.

"I'm happy to see ye will be able to attend our wedding tomorrow, Laird Fraser."

"Thank Christ ye are nae wed yet."

Saer stepped back. "Did ye come here to object?"

"Of course I did!" Bari shouted. "How long have ye known me sister was alive?"

"I never knew she was dead," Saer replied.

Bari was taken aback. He looked like he wanted to argue, but held his tongue. "I suppose that's true."

"Ye suppose?" Saer asked. "Ye can take yerself out the gate I raised for ye if ye plan to insult me by questioning me word."

Bari hurried to smooth over his host's ruffled feathers. "I do nae doubt yer word. I meant I had forgotten how newly arrived ye are here."

"It's been a year, man."

"An entire year," Sandra confirmed. Her gaze locked with Bari's, and his eyes narrowed.

"Mind yer outbursts, and we'll get on well enough." Saer turned to move back to the head table.

"Laird MacLeod, we have no formal agreement for me sister, and I have other offers for her. I ask to depart with her," Bari said.

Saer turned to face off with Bari. He stood half a foot taller than her brother and looked far harder. " I invited ye here for a wedding because she is yer sister. If ye are nae here for the celebration, ye made a long trip for naught. No one will be telling me what to do on me own land."

There were several answering grunts from the MacLeod retainers.

"Ye're wedding her without a dowry?" Bari inquired suspiciously.

"She's heir to the Fraser clan. And I hear rumors ye're making ready to feud with the Sutherlands. Since ye have done naught to produce an heir of your own, once ye're gone, our son will inherit everything." Saer captured Sandra's wrist and pulled her along with him toward the table. "That's gain enough for me."

"That was promised to me when I wed Moira," Achaius said through gritted teeth. Everyone turned to look at Achaius. The old man was furious.

"Sandra is the elder sister," Saer replied. "Who told ye she was dead?"

"Those bastard Sutherlands," Bari raged.

Saer slammed a fist on the table.

"The Sutherlands are me overlord. No man shall sully their name beneath me roof." He turned to face Achaius. "It does nae matter what ye thought. Sandra is the elder sister. Her blood inherits," Saer stated. "The evening is ended."

The musicians stood and lowered themselves, then left. The men and women who had been sitting at the lower tables began to leave the hall. Maids started clearing the tables and pinching out the candles. The hall was no longer bright, merely light enough so cleaning might be done.

Saer left, taking Sandra with him. She cast a long look back at her brother before disappearing into the passageway.

"Take yer mistress upstairs," Achaius ordered two of his men.

"I'll take her," Kael Grant offered in a low tone. "I would nae see ye leave yer back unguarded with the way young Fraser is glaring at ye."

"Ye have me thanks," Achaius said.

Kael pulled Moira's chair back for her. One look at his face made it clear staying wasn't an option. Her temper heated in response to the expectation in his eyes.

Let them fight. She was sick of their pettiness.

At least the hallways were quiet, but very few lanterns were left burning. The MacLeods were still recovering from being raided after their last laird followed the defeated King James III at the battle of Sauchieburn against his son. It had divided Scotland, which made it vital for men like the Earl of Sutherland to maintain alliances.

❦

Gahan waited for Moira to pass him by. The passage-ways were cloaked in deep shadows, granting him all the shelter he needed. Kael slowed his step, allowing her to lengthen the space between them. Once Moira's foot landed on the first step, Kael offered Gahan his hand. Gahan clasped his wrist before changing places with him. Moira never looked behind her and Gahan kept his chin down. He was taller than Kael but in the darkened stairway, he hoped the retainers wouldn't look too closely.

❦

Two Matheson retainers stood outside the door of the chamber Saer's head of house had shown her to for the night. They tugged on the corner of their caps for Kael. But they left quickly when they realized their laird wasn't with Moira. She turned and lowered herself.

"Thank ye—" The words froze on her lips when she looked at the face of the man beside her. He swept her inside the room and shut the door as she struggled to believe what was right in front of her.

"Ye shaved yer beard." He shrugged as she continued to look him over. "And ye're wearing the wrong colors, Gahan Sutherland."

"So are ye, Moira, for ye are nae Lady Matheson."

She began to reach for him but pulled her hand back. "Why are ye here?"

His gaze cut through the doubts clouding her thinking.

"I'm here for ye, Moira. Do nae think ye can tell me ye love me and then expect never to see me again."

"Ye would nae be the first man who cared little for affection from a woman ye've already had."

He grasped her wrist and tugged her into his embrace. "I do nae think a lifetime will be long enough for me to say I've had me fill of ye. Do ye think I'd wear the colors of another clan for any reason beyond love?"

She sighed, because it really felt like she belonged there in his arms. Tears flooded her eyes, and her knees felt weak. She flattened her hands against his chest and smoothed her fingers over the ridges of muscles. She felt his heart beat and buried her face against his chest to muffle a sob.

He held her head and kissed it. He tightened his arms around her as though he might never let her go.

"But...it's impossible."

"Nay, it is nae. Defeat is nae a word I know."

He stroked her cheek then lowered his face to seal her lips with his. It was a sweet meeting of mouths, a slow reunion that stole her breath. He teased her lips, tracing their delicate surfaces with his lips, then began using his tongue to taste her. She reached for him, needing to hold him. The kiss changed as she moved, passion taking root inside her. It was blistering hot and sprang up in an inferno that could not be tamed.

But she didn't want to control it. All she wanted was Gahan.

"I cannae be near ye without wanting ye," he whispered.

They weren't polished words, but she found them more complimentary than any she'd heard. The rough timbre of his voice betrayed a need that matched the one eating at her. She wanted to steal the moment. Ensure it was not wasted. She reached down, rubbing her hand along his thigh to the hem of his kilt. Her fingertips found bare skin, and she drew her hand up and along the inside of his thigh.

"Moira…"

She lifted her chin. "Ye cannae expect me to temper me passion when all we have ever had is stolen moments."

"A fact I plan to change."

She stopped just short of touching the sac that hung beneath his member. "I see…Should I behave meself?"

"I hope not." His teeth were bared, and his lips pulled back farther when she stroked the skin enclosing his seed. "I think I'd beg ye nae to."

"Ye are nae a man who begs."

"I'm willing to make an exception for ye."

She made it to his staff and drew her fingers up its length. He closed his eyes for a moment, pleasure taking command of his features. It was a savage sort of delight, primal and hard. Yet it stroked the part of her that enjoyed his touch. The creature she'd never suspected lived inside her, just waiting for the right touch to awaken it.

She was fully aroused now, the flames of passion burning hotter. He pressed a kiss against her neck and then another, then groaned.

"I promise, the next time I have ye, nothing will tear me away."

He lifted her up and pinned her against the wall. She clasped his hips and pulled him toward her. There was no thinking, no contemplating, no intrusion from her common sense at all.

There was only Gahan. It felt like it had been months since she'd had him. Her body filled with delight and rushed toward climax. It was over too soon, frustrating both of them. Gahan let her down, turning her around and hugging her tight. He leaned against the wall, and she found his embrace far preferable to the bed waiting inside the chamber. The bed would be cold and lonely. The shadows offered her the warm embrace of her lover. Yet it was dangerous.

"Ye must go." She tried to push the arm around her waist aside. "I still have a husband."

"Do nae call him that. He never consummated the union. This is the Highlands," Gahan insisted. "No man takes a wife he cannae use."

It was blunt, but she appreciated the sound of it.

Ye're just hearing what ye want to…

And believing such things might get Gahan killed.

"He will never admit to it, and his men will run ye through if ye are discovered here."

His arms tightened for a moment, then he kissed the top of her head and inhaled the scent of her hair. In spite of the satisfaction still glowing in her belly, she felt the stir of renewed need. He released her.

"Ye're right, but I plan to put an end to this tonight." He moved over to a table and picked up a sack. "These are for ye."

He pulled a pair of boots from the bag and set them on the table.

"Achaius will become suspicious if I wear them."

Gahan's eyes narrowed. "I doubt it. The man is below stairs, no doubt haggling over the shade of yer inheritance, like a head of cattle. He spares no thought to yer personal comfort."

"It is so in most marriages."

Gahan tipped one boot toward her to reveal a sheath sewn into its side. He pulled on a piece of antler, which looked the same as the other buttons used to close the boot, and drew a thin dagger from it.

"Be careful when ye push it into place. The blade is sharp and strong." He handed them to her. "Put them on and do nae take them off."

"Ye want me to sleep in them?" She was already sitting down on a stool, eager to have warm toes. The boots were made of thick, soft leather. They'd cover her ankles, and had been oiled to make them waterproof. Since her father's death, she had not worn anything so fine.

"No one is going to sleep tonight," Gahan said grimly. "Murder is on the mind of more than one man inside this keep, and I want to know ye have some means of protecting yerself."

He watched her lace the first boot closed. She grasped the antler horn handle and pulled it free. The candlelight flickered on the blade glimmering with folds that looked like small stars.

"This is Damascus steel. It's the only steel strong enough to be forged this thin and nae break," Gahan told her.

"It is too expensive a gift for me," Moira said. She

pushed it back into the sheath and reached for the knot she'd tied off the lace with.

Gahan grasped her chin to bring her gaze to his. His eyes flashed with determination. "Ye are worth it, Moira. Sandra is an accomplished assassin. Do nae trust her or let her too close. If ye even suspect she is acting strangely, put that blade through her throat. I wish I could keep ye guarded, but—"

"But I wed Achaius." She stood and stroked the side of his face. "I thought it would bring peace. The women on Fraser land, they begged me to try and make him happy so he'd nae be in the mood to join with Bari in his feud."

"I'd never respected ye so much as when I watched ye walk to the church." Pain filled his eyes, but also admiration. "Ye were as strong as any man I've seen going into battle." He drew in a deep breath. "Yet the battle has nae yet been fought. Wear the boots and do nae trust anyone. I am going to make sure Bari is pushed past his endurance. I've had enough of this shadow fighting."

He turned, the longer pleats of his kilt flaring out in the back.

"I trust ye."

He turned and smiled at her. "And I love ye."

She held her breath as he opened the door and left.

Her face split with a smile so big the corners of her mouth felt like they were being stretched. She hugged herself and turned in a circle, because she just couldn't stay still. Her skirts flared out and settled down as she sat down to put on her second boot.

The smile melted as she listened to the silence of the

chamber. So much was unsettled, and her future lay in the outcome. Once she put on the second boot, she stood up and began inspecting the chambers. There was a sense of unease drifting on the night air. It sent a tingle down her neck and made time feel like it was frozen. But no matter how much dread filled her, she found herself happy to be facing the moment of truth at last.

She just prayed fate decided to be kind for a change.

"Are ye spending the night with me?" Sandra purred at Saer.

"Did ye think ye'd be allowed privacy with yer brother here? Are ye hoping he'll find a way to free ye?"

She lifted the wreath of greens from her head and set it aside. With a delicate shrug of her shoulders, she trailed a finger over the swell of one breast.

"I assure ye, privacy is the last thing I crave." Sandra offered him an inviting look. "I have had a year of me own company and find myself bored with privacy."

Saer pushed away from the wall he'd been leaning on. Sandra's eyes brightened with impending victory, but he lifted his hand and gestured someone forward.

"Angus will be happy to keep ye company. I cannae leave men at the door, else risk ruining the illusion ye are happy to be me bride. Yer guard will be inside."

The man who moved into the light cast by the candles was a hard creature. Sandra recoiled from his bulk. He wore a half sheepskin on his back like a savage, and two scars ran down his right cheek.

"She'll do her best to lure ye close, but I suggest

ye keep yer cock away from her, else ye might find
yerself dead."

Angus grinned. "She'd nae be the first to try their
hand at ending me days. But unlike the Sutherlands,
I never leave one alive who has done me a wrong."

Sandra sat back down with a pout on her lips.

What sent a chill down his back was the look of
determination in her eyes. The woman was evil, no
matter how fair her features and form. Angus pulled
a dagger from one of his sheaths and fingered the
blade suggestively.

Sandra turned to contemplate her reflection. "Send
a maid up with some wine, since ye've made it clear I
shall have no other entertainment."

"Ye are nae here to be pampered," Saer replied.

She shot him a hard look. "I doubt Angus is accomplished in helping ladies disrobe. How much did this
gown cost ye? It would be a shame if it was ruined
when I tried to take it off. Considering the state of yer
coffers, it would be very sad."

"I'll send a maid."

Saer turned and left, reaching down to pat the side
of his boot to make sure his own dagger was in place.

It was going to be a bloody night; he was sure
of it. Now that Gahan had played his hand, Bari
and Achaius had only until dawn to try and prevent
Sandra's wedding.

❧

Achaius stumbled into the chamber, his steps scuffing
the floor in his haste. He spotted her near one of the
windows and pointed his cane at her. "The maid has

claimed ye have nae bled since we returned from Dunrobin. Ye're useless to me without a child."

Rage edged his words, but Moira wasn't afraid of him. She lifted her chin and stared straight at him. Knowing Gahan was near made her bold, or maybe just desperate. All she knew for sure was she couldn't continue the charade that was her marriage.

"How could I be with child when ye have never lain with me?" Moira said angrily, her patience exhausted.

"Because Gahan Sutherland is yer lover," he shot back, jabbing his cane in her direction. "Do nae think I do nae know he's been sniffing after ye from the moment he laid eyes upon ye. Why do ye think I made the trip to Dunrobin? I wanted to make sure he had the chance to toss yer skirts."

He was coming closer, working his way across the floor with his tirade. "Ye're as calculating as Bari," she accused. The wall behind her bothered her immensely. She edged away from him, making sure to keep out of his reach.

"It's me position in life to make sure I leave me clan better off than it was when I became laird! Nae that I would expect any woman to understand the way of the world." He sniffed. "Yer value is between yer thighs and in yer belly. Now did ye fuck him or nae? Ye'd better nae be a useless virgin still, because the only thing I need you for is a Fraser-born heir."

Moira gaped at Achaius. Could she be pregnant with Gahan's child? Now that she thought about it, her monthly courses *had* stopped, but she'd been so preoccupied with trying to put all thoughts of Gahan out of her mind by putting Matheson Tower to rights that she hadn't noticed till now. Moira unconsciously put a protective hand to her belly. Achaius's eyes widened.

"That's all the proof I need. Now I just have to wait to claim the brat as our son, and I won't have need of ye anymore." Achaius cackled and then started coughing, the fit causing him to lean on his cane.

Fear knotted in her belly. She didn't know what to do, only that she had to find Gahan. Moira bolted to the door, throwing it open and almost barreling into the Matheson retainers who turned to stare at her. They were barring her path.

"Me husband has instructed me to go to the kitchen to fetch something to ease his cough," she said, trying to appear as calm as possible. She stepped forward, making the men choose to either let her collide with them or move out of her way. They moved aside, and she hurried down the steps before Achaius recovered.

Her freedom was going to be short. She made it to the bottom floor of the keep and looked around. Everything was cast in shadow. The wind was howling outside, making the candle flames dance and blowing some of them out.

It was the sort of time when evil spirits rose up to do their work.

She shook her head, forcing herself not to get caught up in superstition. The only evil at work was that of greedy men.

And women like Sandra.

Heavy steps came from the stairs, and she picked up her skirts to run. She didn't know where Gahan was, but she couldn't stay where the Matheson retainers might find her. The hall would be full of people, and they would likely return her to her husband, so she turned and ducked into the narrow passageway that served as a link between the hall and the kitchens.

The main kitchens were outside to protect the keep from fire. The night air was bracing as she made her way along the outside of the building. She didn't dare go inside the kitchen either, for the boys who served the keep would be sleeping there. In a castle full of people, she was very much alone. Finding those she might trust was almost impossible.

But she had to or lose everything.

❧

"Get after her!"

Achaius didn't much care for the bewildered look his men sent him. He raised his cane and brandished it at them.

"Now, ye sons of whores! Fetch me wife back!"

They frowned then turned and ran down the stairway after his wife.

His.

No one was going to ruin his plans. Certainly not her devil of a sister.

The empty doorway offered him an opportunity. He looked down the stairway and listened for a long moment before heading up the stairs. Everyone thought him a feeble old man, so they didn't bother to mask what they were about when he might be watching. He climbed to the third floor and pushed the door open.

Sandra Fraser was preening in front of a mirror, with a maid beside her. She let out a screech when she saw him, but he'd already shoved the door shut.

"Now there, lass, there's no need to be so skittish." Achaius smiled jovially at the huge man standing near the door. "Although I'll admit there is part of me that longs for the days when I could rouse a wench so!"

Sandra dug her hands into the skirts of the maid, dragging the girl across the room like a shield. "Send him away! He'll kill me." Sandra looked out the open window, searching for anything to jump down onto.

"*Kill ye?* An old man like me?" Achaius replied. He tipped back his head and laughed. He looked at Angus and grinned as he shuffled closer to the man. "Careful, lass, me pride shall burst from all yer praise."

Angus grinned, dropping his guard. He looked toward Sandra. "Stop yer—"

His last word was only a gurgle. His huge body jerked several times as he looked back at Achaius.

"Ye should have listened to her, lad."

Angus fell forward, blood spilling down his chest. His lips moved like a freshly caught fish for a moment as he tried to draw breath.

"No!" Sandra screamed. The maid was whimpering as she tried to fight her way free of Sandra's grasp.

Achaius raised the dagger and plunged toward his target. He had one brief moment of victory as he gained a hold on Sandra's shoulder. He gripped the fabric of her gown and raised the dagger high, but she yanked away from him. He kept his grip on the fabric of her gown, but the window shutters behind her were open. The violence of their struggle sent all three of them tumbling down the outside of the tower. They bounced onto the roof of the stable.

❧

At least she wouldn't die in the top chamber of Dunrobin Castle.

Sandra floated in a haze of dream fragments as she toyed with just going back to sleep. But the scent of smoke teased her nose. There was a crackle as something caught fire, and she jerked upward, forcing herself to wake.

Were the Sutherlands burning her?

Sandra opened her eyes and saw that the candle near her mirror had been knocked through the window with her. She snuffed it out before taking notice of where she was. Clouds covered the moon, making the night black. The maid lay in a tangle of arms and legs, her neck at an odd angle, her eyes staring sightlessly into the night sky. What little light there was glistened off the wet blade of the dagger still gripped in Achaius's hand. He was half on top of the maid, his body still.

Sandra listened, waiting for someone to approach or notice her. It was a thatch roof she was lying on, the straw still wet in the middle, which accounted for why she wasn't engulfed in flames. But only the wind blew, making the small area that had been on fire glow red. She smiled and added more thatch to the embers. She pulled the dagger from Achaius's hand and tucked it into her garter. Smoke rose from the thatch, and a flame erupted. She nudged it toward the edge of Achaius's kilt and watched it catch. She moved more toward the maid and made sure her gowns were lit before moving along the wall toward the dark end of the yard. The thatch was sharp, cutting her hands, but she climbed to the edge and slid down the pole at the corner. When she touched the ground, she smelled the scent of fresh horse manure. There was a soft nicker from one of the animals, and she back away before it smelled the smoke.

The fire grew, giving her the chance to escape. By the time someone cried the alarm, both bodies would be completely engulfed in flames. The horses began to scream with panic, rearing up to fight their way free of the stable.

At last, freedom was hers.

❧

Moira tried to force herself to see through the darkness. She couldn't go back, so she kept going, sticking close to the wall to let the shadows shield her. The Great Hall had light, but she hesitated, stopping short of the doorway, because everyone beyond was only a dark shape.

"Who's there? Show yerself."

Moira hesitated in the shadows because she was sure her mind was hearing only what she wanted.

Cam added his command to Gahan's. "Come into the light now."

"Thank Christ," she breathed as she moved closer to the doorway that opened into the hall. She inched into the light, allowing only enough for Gahan to recognize her.

Gahan stood up and joined her. "Why are ye here?"

"Achaius…he…he thinks to lock me away, in the hope I am with child, but he said he'd make sure I did nae survive the birth." She looked behind her. "And the Matheson retainers are looking for me."

Cam had come close to shield his brother's back. The wind was howling, making the window shutters rattle. Listening for footsteps was difficult. What they heard was far worse.

"Fire!"

❧

Every castle lived in fear of fire.

With the call of alarm, everyone left their beds to fight the threat.

The stableboys woke and grabbed the buckets that were kept near the stable doors in case of fire. The wind was whipping the flames high. The entire top of the stable was burning. Men rushed to pull the frightened horses out. The animals were in a panic, and soon the yard was full of snorting horses and cursing men.

Sandra pressed back into the darkness as she watched those arriving to fight the fire. She was so close, and yet still too far away from freedom. Since the maid had been one of many, the fire might just give her the opportunity she needed. But the gate was still down, trapping her inside the MacLeod castle grounds.

Bari came into view, watching the firefighting efforts from the yard. It took all her courage to walk toward him. She was so close, yet it would take only one person to recognize her. She tried to pick a moment when everyone was focused on the fire and the bodies.

"Looks like Laird Matheson and Sandra Fraser," one retainer shouted.

Sandra trembled with joy as the MacLeod retainers looked at the burning roof out of the window she'd fallen through. She made it to her brother's side as he looked over to investigate who was near.

Bari gaped at her then clamped his mouth shut, biting back the words he wanted to say.

He gripped her wrist and pulled her into the second keep. "Get up to me chamber and put on me other kilt. Bind yer breasts and hide yer hair so ye can ride out with me retainers."

He looked at his second-in-command. "Rouse the men. We are leaving."

He cupped the side of her face, his hand trembling with his happiness. A moment later, he was back in the yard, shouting her name.

"Sandra? Sandra? Where the hell is me sister, Saer MacLeod!"

❦

Saer wanted to smash his fist into someone's face.

It would certainly be easier than trying to settle the arguing lairds around him.

Bari Fraser was cursing as he ordered his men to take the body of his sister, and the Matheson retainers were demanding information. Saer rubbed a hand down his face.

"Ah, the passion of Highlanders," Kael Grant observed. "And they call ye the savage. It looks like that old man was more bloodthirsty than ye."

"Enough!" Gahan roared.

Silence fell over the assembled crowd, but only for a moment.

"What in the hell are ye doing here?" Bari Fraser demanded.

"I brought yer sister," Gahan informed him. "Me father left her fate to me."

"She's dead now," Bari growled, pointing at the body wrapped in Fraser plaid lying at his feet.

"As is our laird!" the Matheson retainers howled.

"There is a dead retainer in the chamber Sandra was in. Laird Matheson is the one who killed him to get to Sandra. Yer laird deserves the death he got," Gahan said. "Laird Matheson was clearly intent on making sure Sandra received the death she'd earned by trying to poison me father, as I heard him swear he'd do before he wed Moira Fraser."

There was grumbling from the Matheson men, but Gahan cut through their objections. "It's that way, or I have to consider he was trying to insure his wife was the clear heir to the Fraser clan, and he was willing to commit murder to see it done. The Church will likely excommunicate him. Which explanation do ye prefer?"

The Mathesons quieted down and turned to wrapping their laird's body in a plaid.

Moira found herself doubting what she saw. Achaius's body was charred, but his signet ring had been on the corpse. His captain held it now as the Matheson retainers began to saddle the skittish horses. He looked at Moira for a long moment, clearly unsure what to do.

"Lady Matheson will be staying here," Gahan said.

The Mathesons didn't like Gahan's announcement. They stopped what they were doing and glared at him.

"She needs to bury her husband," the Matheson captain insisted. "And our laird said she might be carrying a Matheson in her belly."

"The marriage was never consummated," Gahan declared.

It should have shamed Moira; instead, relief flowed through her. Everyone looked at her, and all she felt was a sense of freedom. "It's true. He soiled the sheet to cover the fact that age had stolen his vigor."

The Mathesons all nodded, most of them looking relieved to know they would not have to take her home with them. Achaius's sons wouldn't be interested in sharing their inheritance with her, and neither did any of the clan's retainers. It would mean less for them.

They finished saddling their horses, then raised their laird up on top of his horse. They left Moira nothing, taking her mare when they rode out of the MacLeod keep.

She'd never been so happy.

"At least I'll be getting yer dowry back," Bari declared. "Mount up, Moira, we are taking Sandra home."

So quickly, she was terrified once more. The law favored Bari in every way.

"Since I was promised a Fraser sister, this one will stay to see if I like her," Saer MacLeod said.

"Ye cannae do that," Bari argued. "I promised ye naught."

"I'll keep whatever woman I please. I'm a savage man," Saer responded menacingly. "I suggest ye leave me castle before I decide to keep ye and ransom ye back to yer clan."

Bari looked to Kael Grant. "Do ye see that yer overlord's son is allowing this?"

Gahan remained impassive. Kael hooked his hands into his belt. "He also allowed ye to make peace with his father, when there is nae a single laird in this yard who believes ye knew nothing of Sandra's doings."

"Take yer sister's body and go, Bari," Gahan said. "And if ye still want a feud, I'll be happy to meet ye on the field, but ye'll find it hard to get another clan to ride beside ye now."

"Something Gahan will nae have difficulty with," Saer said. "The MacLeod stand with Sutherland."

"My feelings exactly," Kael added. "So do the Grant."

Bari stiffened, but he turned and left without another word.

⁂

It seemed unreal.

Moira watched the Frasers leave until even the sounds of the horses' hooves had faded. The gate lowered, and the MacLeods did their best to settle back down for the remaining hours of the night. The yard inside the walls of MacLeod Tower was dark and quiet with only the sound of the blowing wind.

"I've waited a long time to do this," Gahan said softly from behind her.

She looked at him as Saer and Kael also waited for him to make his meaning clear.

He closed the distance between them, reaching up to tug on the corner of his bonnet, and offered her a perfect bow. "I've waited for the chance to carry ye off to me bed, in front of everyone else."

He scooped her off her feet and cradled her against his chest. Saer snorted with amusement as Kael waved at them. Gahan carried her with ease through the yard, into the keep, and up to his chamber at the top of the second tower. It wasn't a huge room, but it was perfect. Gahan lowered her to the bed and lifted her hand to his lips.

She laughed softly. "Is that nae a bit innocent?"

He stood up and took his sword off. He placed it near the bed before working to remove his boots. She began to do the same, the excitement of the evening wearing off and leaving her exhausted. It felt like she'd been on edge for weeks and was only now being allowed the opportunity to relax.

"I believe I want to court ye, Moira Fraser." He left his kilt on a table and joined her in the bed.

He cuddled her close, pressing her head onto his shoulder. She should have answered him, but she was too tired to make her lips work. The only sound she seemed capable of uttering was a soft, contented sigh.

❧

Bari pulled up once the horizon began turning pink. His men were grumpy and displeased with the turn of events. No Highlander enjoyed defeat, even a verbal one.

"We've come away with the prize, lads."

Doubting expressions were his reward. Bari grinned, and Sandra pulled the bonnet off her head.

"Me sister, Sandra, reclaimed from the bastard Sutherlands at last."

Dawn washed over her face as his retainers nodded

with approval. Grins split their lips as they began to laugh. Bari joined his men, their amusement ringing out loud and clear.

"And do nae ye fear, lads. I will nae take the slight Gahan Sutherland has dealt me without retribution."

He kicked his horse into action, missing the disgruntled looks behind him. The Fraser retainers looked among one another, shaking their heads before following their laird.

There was little else they could do, even if they were tired of his quest for vengeance.

The MacLeod head of house wrung her apron. The fabric was creased in several places, betraying her rising level of agitation. She hurried through the hallways and ended up in the kitchens once more, a deep frown creasing her brow. She took a deep breath before heading into the hall.

The supper merriment was dying down now, but the laird was still at the table with Gahan Sutherland and Moira Fraser. Kael Grant sat there as well, enjoying warm cider.

"Laird." She hesitated as all three men looked at her. "Laird MacLeod," she specified.

"Aye?" Saer inquired.

She wrung her apron tightly, biting her lower lip until she found the words she needed to say. "Young Anna is missing. I've checked with everyone, and even sent to the village to see if her family knows where she be."

"It is spring," Saer remarked. "Perhaps she wed?"

The head of house shook her head. "See, there

is the part that has me worried. She's promised to a young lad, and he has no idea where she be. There is naught missing from her bunk either. But last night, the cook sent her up to Sandra Fraser with wine. No one saw her leave the tower chamber."

Tension filled the room instantly.

"Did anyone see the body Bari claimed as his sister?" Gahan demanded.

"It was charred, the hair gone," Saer said. "But in the dark, I cannae swear it was Sandra."

Gahan stood up. "If Sandra is alive, she will cause trouble." He pulled Moira's chair back. "I promised ye a courtship, lass, but I need to break that promise. We must return to Sutherland."

Moira nodded as a knot formed in her belly.

Part of her doubted anything could protect them from Sandra's evil. Not even the security of the Highland fortress.

⤜⤝

Seabhac Tower, Fraser land

Sandra trailed her fingers along several of the under-gowns laid out on her bed. She let out a little sigh as she felt the silk.

The Sutherlands would pay for leaving her to rot in their tower. *Gahan* would pay.

"The blue one."

She waited as Alba hurried to please her by bringing the undergown to her. Two other maids stood nearby. They didn't look at her but kept their eyes lowered until she decided what she wanted.

It had been too long since she had been cared for as she should be.

"The russet overgown."

The maids had it in hand instantly. They dressed her and set her hair, then lowered themselves and scurried out of the chamber.

Sandra made her way down the steps, enjoying every single one of them. The servants stared at her when they saw her before hurrying to lower themselves. She walked through the Great Hall, soaking up the sight of it, then continued on to her brother's private war room.

There were pikes resting in weapons racks, and armor on the wall. Costly helmets were stored on wooden heads, their surfaces shining from recent oiling. It was the section of the castle dominated by men, but that didn't stop her. She walked toward the sound of her brother and his captains, intruding where other females would not have ventured. The room was full, all ten captains attending her brother.

"We are nae going to feud," she announced.

Bari glared at her over the large table in the center of the room. A map was spread out over it.

"I'll have me vengeance, Sandra. The Frasers will have their due."

Sandra nodded. "Oh, aye. We shall have our due, but I crave the blood of Lytge himself for letting his sons imprison me. We shall have that only if we go to the king."

Bari looked at the map, studying the land formations that aided the Dunrobin defenses. "The king is a boy."

"Exactly, but one who wishes to become a man," Sandra purred. "He does nae like to hear that his earls believe themselves above his law."

Bari's captains began to sit back, losing interest in a campaign that would cost lives when there was apparently an alternative. Bari was torn as well. Sandra saw the weakness in their eyes and seized on it.

"We shall go to Court and plead our case. It will be simple to prove my innocence."

"What of the evidence and testimony against you?"

"What of it? They did nae hang me. We will say they planned to prod ye into a feud and then have Saer MacLeod wed me to gain the Fraser clan's land." Sandra opened her eyes innocently. "Are there nae witnesses to the fact that Gahan Sutherland brought me to Saer MacLeod, his brother-by-marriage? And poor Laird Matheson fell to his death before he might have a child with Moira, and now Saer MacLeod has claimed her since they believe me dead."

The Fraser captains grinned, and Bari nodded approvingly. "Ye were born the wrong sex, Sandra, for ye have the cunning of a man."

"I enjoy me sex very well," Sandra replied. "And I think it will help me seduce the king into helping us gain vengeance against Lytge Sutherland."

"What about his sons?"

"They will suffer when their father is executed for overstepping his authority."

It was a perfect little plan. For sure, there were those who might call it a plot, but Sandra didn't care. She craved victory, and it was going to be hers. Very soon.

❧

Bari Fraser felt his sister watching his every move as he wrote the note, but he had to keep his attention on his quill. The script needed to be tiny to fit into the pouch on a hawk's leg. He put as much detail as he might into it, then blew across it to dry the ink. Sandra smiled, pleasure sparkling in her eyes. She was sorting through the letters on his desk as she'd done in the past. Reading the information meant for his eyes alone.

"This will nae gain us the Sutherland retainers. Which was why ye set yer sight on Norris in the first place. He's wed with a son now."

She pouted. "That is a shame, but at least we shall have the most gain while the Sutherlands suffer. I shall find a new groom to bring ye retainers."

"Ye're vicious, Sandra."

She lowered herself in front of him before opening the door of his study for him. "How kind of ye to praise me, Brother. Do nae worry. I hear the Earl of Ross is at Court. I'll have an earl for husband yet."

He passed her and chuckled. "I believe ye just might."

And he was going to make sure of it. He made his way to the mews, almost shouting for Moira before recalling that she was not there to serve him.

He wanted to make sure the Sutherlands would not benefit from her, but for the moment, he didn't know how.

He slipped the message into the hawk's pouch and set it loose. The raptor took to the sky eagerly and headed toward Edinburgh.

Eight

THE ROADS WERE EASIER TO TRAVEL NOW THAT THE snow was gone. They made good time, riding north toward Dunrobin. The Sutherland retainers rode in two columns, with Gahan riding near the front. One of the lead horses held the standard of the Sutherland clan, the blue banner whipping in the wind to announce the presence of one of the sons of the earl in their ranks. It was a warning against anyone who might have attacked them. Since Gahan was the son of a nobleman, the penalty for attacking him would be death.

But it would also tell Bari where they were.

Moira scanned the hills and forest as they passed them. Dread roiled in her belly, like a premonition of impending doom. Bari wasn't going to rest, especially with Sandra back by his side. She was sure of it.

Just before sunset, Gahan held up his hand. He listened and looked at the sky. A shrill cry came, and then another as a hawk circled them. One of the hawks the retainers carried cried out, calling to the one in the air. A moment later, the newcomer landed on the arm of the same retainer.

"Ye train mated pairs," Moira remarked. "Clever."

"It's the only way to ensure a hawk will find me on the road," Gahan said.

It was more than clever; it was actually quite brilliant. Most hawks mated for life. They had a keen sense of sight and could spot their mate from the air. If the birds were trained to fly to Dunrobin, as this one was, it would see its mate and stop on the way.

Gahan removed the message and let the hawk greet its mate. Cam opened a pouch hanging on the side of his saddle and produced a thin slice of meat for the raptor.

"That fucking bitch," Gahan swore. He handed the scrap of parchment over to Cam and turned to speak to Moira.

"Yer sister Sandra is on her way to the king to cry for justice. They stopped on Cameron land."

"They clearly do nae understand that Bjorn Lindsey is friendly with yer father," Cam added.

"Bari Fraser does nae care much for what others think when it conflicts with his own whims," Moira informed them.

For a moment, Cam and Gahan stared at her. The other men watched for their reactions. She held her head steady, making it known which side she was on. Highlanders didn't respect anyone who wouldn't choose a side.

"Ye might think me harsh to speak against me blood, but I believe Bari is mad, and Sandra has always been touched by an evil nature."

"She is that, sure enough," Gahan confirmed. "We must go to Court. They will blacken me father's name and twist the facts, I'm sure of it."

His voice carried with it the ring of authority. His men didn't hesitate to turn their horses around; none of them looked over their shoulders either. Their dedication to their clan was glittering in their eyes. But Moira found herself captivated by their leader. Gahan was worthy of his men's respect and allegiance. He was everything she'd always longed for in her brother and found herself disappointed by Bari's lack of honor.

He locked his dark gaze with hers, and there was no apology there for what he felt he must do. Instead, she saw his determination, and she rose to the challenge. Straightening up, she pointed her mare toward Edinburgh.

His lips twitched, appreciation softening his features for a moment. "Ye are going to wed me, Moira Fraser."

"Is that a fact?" She couldn't help arguing with him. "Ye're an arrogant one. Perhaps I shall be a merry widow."

He tilted his head to the side and smirked at her. "I'm a Highlander." He leaned close to her, his breath teasing the side of her neck for a moment. "And ye have a craving for me, lass, one I plan to feed."

He was away before she could draw in enough breath to argue. A shiver rippled down her body as the skin on her nape cooled. The man heated her blood. She did crave him.

But that just might be her damnation, she feared. Because the king was in Edinburgh, and Gahan would be subject to his rule. Everything she admired about him might just be used against them, because he'd do his duty, as surely as she had done hers.

The road was long, but it flew by far too fast, and the future was so uncertain.

Norris looked up as a boy came running into the Great Hall. He was halfway down the aisle before he paused and tugged on his bonnet. But he began running again and made it to the steps in front of the high table.

"A pair of hawks just arrived."

It was just past noon, which made Norris frown. The birds had to have been sent the night before and taken shelter during the dark hours.

The lad came up the steps and handed him the tiny rolled parchment. Norris read it twice before getting up to find his father.

"I should have hanged that bitch," Lytge spat. He stood up and looked more full of energy than he had in some time. "She's going to twist up the entire sordid mess. We can count on that. She has a talent for beguiling. Get me horse ready, I'm heading to Edinburgh."

Norris almost argued but shut his mouth. His father didn't miss it, either. He chuckled as he turned to stare at him.

"That's right, me boy. Ye know what I look like when I've set me mind to something."

Norris offered his father a grin. "I was thinking it was going to be very fine entertainment, watching ye face off with the Frasers once and for all."

"Aye, it will be the final battle."

His father didn't move very quickly toward the door. Age had taken its toll on him, but his face was set with determination. Norris followed him proudly. They were Sutherlands, and if they had their way, the Frasers were going to get the battle they'd wanted.

But no battle was certain. With a young king, nothing was for sure. They just might be riding to their deaths.

❦

The Court of Scotland was full. Gahan scanned it twice before entering.

The king was approaching his eighteenth birthday, and it looked like all the crowned heads of Europe wanted to keep an eye on him. There were ambassadors and their entourages. Many of them carried portraits of their princesses, hoping to catch the young monarch's eye. James IV would have to wed, and the choice of bride would be a critical one.

There were also many daughters of Scotland's nobles. They wore the newest fashion of skirts and bodice instead of long gowns. Their cheeks were darkened with rouge, and their lips painted. The men wore English-fashioned doublets with their kilts, many of them decorated with trim and skirting at the waist. Gahan preferred his wool doublet, and being in the Highlands, it served him well.

Their arrival was cause for silence. The horde waiting to be admitted into the inner rooms of the palace parted as Gahan Sutherland and his party marched toward the doors being guarded by royal retainers. Moira was flanked by Gahan's men, and she set her teeth into her lower lip as they neared the doors. Gahan didn't look like he was in the mood to be deterred, and the royal guards were holding iron-tipped pikes.

"I have no quarrel with ye," Gahan informed the retainers respectfully. "But I'm here to stop a venomous snake from spitting her poison in the king's ear, and I plan to be heard."

The retainers held their position for a long moment before one of them pulled his pike back. His comrade looked at him in confusion.

"The Sutherlands fought well at Sauchieburn for the king," the guard said.

The second pike was pulled back, and their party swept into the inner court of James IV of Scotland. Here there was music and more ambassadors waiting to be seen. At the far end of the room was a set of double doors that were firmly closed, the seal of the king carved on them. Six retainers stood guard.

Gahan was not a man used to waiting, but Court was a place where everyone waited on the will of the king.

It was also a place where informants waited in the shadows. Moira could see them whispering near the walls. It wasn't warm enough to need a fan, but ladies lifted theirs and hid their lips as they spoke. She shivered, the knot of dread in her belly burning. The king's father had been a tyrant who faced a rebellion at the battle of Sauchieburn because half his nobles were unwilling to follow him. The Sutherlands had followed the young Scottish prince, but it was well known he harbored guilt over helping to kill his father.

That guilt might manifest itself as a harsh ruling against them if the king believed Sandra's story.

The doors suddenly opened, and a herald struck the floor with his staff.

"Gahan Sutherland. Enter."

"It looks like we won't be standing around after all," Cam remarked.

"What it means is that bitch has already made it to the king's side," Gahan said grimly as he began to move forward.

The guards allowed only Gahan, Cam, and Moira inside. The Sutherland retainers didn't take kindly to being denied access to their laird, but Gahan turned and silenced them.

The doors shut with a sound that made Moira's heart quicken.

"It seems you were rash to say the Sutherlands would not appear before me, Laird Fraser."

The young king was a healthy man. He had auburn-brown hair and a sturdy frame. He wasn't as tall as Gahan, but he was not a short man. James IV sat on a throne set on a canopied dais. Behind him was a tapestry with the Stuart arms woven into it. He wore no crown. His clothing was fine but not overly embellished. He seemed a man of action more than a pampered prince.

Bari was attired in a very fine doublet adorned with gold pieces sewn into the fabric. The three feathers on his bonnet, which declared him a laird, were fastened with a ruby brooch. Sandra looked like a princess. Her skirts were made of velvet and trimmed with silver bobbin lace. The tight bodice of the dress pressed her breasts up into a tempting display that she made sure was angled toward the king. Her hair was covered with a pearled snood, and she had a golden necklace around her neck.

"That's his bastard," Bari spat. "Which is a further insult to Yer Majesty."

Gahan stopped and lowered himself before the king. Moira and Cam followed his lead.

"I disagree, Laird Fraser," the king replied. "It is well known that the earl acknowledges both his sons. I respect him more for acknowledging his sins."

"Aye, Yer Majesty, because the Sutherlands plan to make sure they rule in the Highlands," Sandra insisted. "Gahan Sutherland locked me in a tower for over a year and then took me to his brother-by-marriage, planning to marry me off to control the Fraser clan. All this after he picked a fight with me brother and killed him." Tears glistened in her eyes, completing the look of helplessness.

"As ye can see, Yer Majesty, he boldly appears before ye with me half sister." Bari pointed at Moira. "The Sutherlands intend to destroy the Frasers and claim the lairdship for this bastard."

Gahan sliced through Bari's accusations. "Ye ramble like a madman." He aimed a level gaze at the king. "I'd take offense, Yer Majesty, but there is no reasoning with a lunatic."

"Laird Fraser's arguments *are* curiously passionate," the king concurred.

Bari's complexion darkened. "Because the Sutherlands have tried to destroy me entire family! I came to ye for justice! The sort that I understood ye knew the value of. Nae even a week past, Gahan Sutherland, Saer MacLeod, and Kael Grant all threatened to feud with me if I did nae allow them to keep Moira."

"Is that true, Gahan Sutherland?" the king asked quietly. There was no missing the tight set to his features. "For I see Moira Fraser is in your company, and her brother claims Saer MacLeod was keeping her because Sandra was believed dead."

"It *is* true!" Bari raged.

The king's voice rose. "I will hear your answer."

"We believed Sandra Fraser dead, Yer Majesty, and aye, Saer MacLeod did say he was keeping Moira," Gahan said. "But I am the one who will wed her."

"She is me sister!" Bari interrupted again. "I forbid it."

Bari reached for her, but Cam stepped into his path. Bari turned back to face the king. "Ye see how arrogant they are? In the Highlands, the Sutherlands rule like kings! They stop at nothing to get what they want, even stealing me own blood—Fraser blood."

"Enough!" the king declared. "You tell a good tale, Laird Fraser, but there are always two sides to a coin. I would be no better than my sire if I judged this case without hearing from the earl."

"He'll tell ye naught but lies," Sandra implored. "There was nae a single soul who would help me whilst I was imprisoned in that tower." She whimpered and pointed an accusing finger at Gahan. "He even gave me poison, hoping I'd damn meself to eternal hell."

"Poison for a poisoner," Gahan reasoned. "Ye nearly killed me father and had Daphne MacLeod hanged for yer crime. I should have hanged ye to put an end to the trouble ye cause."

"Why did you not do so?" the king asked in a somber tone.

"Because he knew she was innocent," Bari snarled.

"Speak again without permission, and I shall have you removed," the king snapped. "Why did you spare her life, Gahan Sutherland?"

"It's the truth that I had no stomach for killing a woman. Neither did me brother or father. It is nae a Highlander's way."

The king fingered the lion-claw armrest of his throne for a long moment. "That is something I understand well, yet executions are sometimes needed."

Sandra gasped. "I am innocent! It was all a ploy to gain Daphne MacLeod's dowry and keep me from wedding another! Norris Sutherland is so greedy, he had me locked away until he could get rid of his wife without suspicion. He locked her out of her chambers, and she had to give birth in a stairway! He told me all about how he hoped she'd die!"

"That is nae true!" Moira argued. "She was in the stairway of my room by her own actions. Norris was very upset by it."

Sandra faced her. "Oh, little sister! Do nae believe them! Come home before it is too late." She knelt in front of the king. "I beg ye, return me sister to us."

"Over me dead body," Gahan growled. "Yer idea of affection was to wed her to Achaius Matheson, a man old enough to be her grandfather."

Bari defended himself. "It was a solid match, and now she is widowed, her husband dead after ye pushed him out of a tower on MacLeod land so ye might have Moira."

"It would have served me purposes as ye describe them to leave Moira wed to an impotent old man while I bred Sandra and then killed ye. There is the difficulty with yer lies, they do nae make any sense."

"Achaius was nae impotent," Bari insisted.

"He was," Gahan declared. "He never consummated his union. If I were the arrogant, greedy man ye are painting me, I'd nae admit yer sister was a maiden when she came to me bed. I'd be looking to collect her widow's portion from the Mathesons, but I am here to speak the truth. Unlike ye."

"Ye…ye bastard!" Bari raged. "How dare ye touch me sister!"

"How dare ye bind her to an old man?" Gahan countered.

"Adultery is a grave sin." The king's voice was edged in authority. Moira felt her belly tighten as the air froze in her lungs. She and Gahan had broken a commandment. The circumstance did not matter.

"Yes it is, Yer Majesty," Gahan agreed. "But an unconsummated marriage is nae a holy union. The sin I am guilty of is needing to wed the lass. Something I am eager to do."

"Did Laird Matheson bed you?" the king asked her directly. The bluntness of the question made her cheeks burn.

Moira shook her head.

"I saw the soiled sheet," Bari protested.

"An old man's attempt to protect his pride," Gahan said. "I'd prefer nae to speak of it. He is gone now, and there is naught to be gained by trampling his name."

Sandra spoke up. "Perhaps Moira soiled the sheet to hide the fact that she is yer lover."

Gahan surprised them by laughing. "Then why would I have taken ye to Saer MacLeod? Would it nae have made more sense to smother ye while no one knew ye were still among the living? I'd keep Moira and her widow's thirds, for there would be no one to force me to tell the truth. Me actions do nae match the evil portrait ye are painting, Sandra Fraser."

"No, they do not," the king agreed. "You shall all stay until I can summon the Earl of Sutherland to account for these accusations."

"He'll tell ye more lies," Bari insisted.

The king was growing impatient. "He is a noble of this realm and will not suffer being called a liar without proof. You are his vassal, Laird Fraser, and will mind your tongue, or I will have you shut away until I am ready to judge this matter."

"I believe me father is already on his way," Gahan said. "I sent a hawk yesterday, and me father is a loyal subject."

"Good. You will all remain here at Court. Lady Matheson will be kept in my custody."

"Yer Majesty—" Gahan protested.

"Save your breath," he interrupted. "I am no longer the boy you fought beside at Sauchieburn. I see in your eyes the desire you have for her. As she is a new widow, it will breed discontent to have the pair of you seen together. Laird Matheson's sons are both here and looking for any reason to discredit me. You are also both guilty of fornication at the least and adultery at worst. Lady Matheson will be taken into my personal apartments until this matter is decided."

❧

It was the horror she'd feared. Gahan was furious, rage flickering in his eyes. As much as she detested being parted from him, she wanted even less to see him destroy himself for her sake.

He drew in a stiff breath, fighting the urge to argue. He crossed his arms over his chest, looking immovable and imposing, the muscles in his jaw and neck cording due to his restraint, but he nodded.

The king gestured to the retainers behind him. They came around the raised platform and flanked her. For all the sense her actions made to her mind, her heart rebelled. It felt like she was being torn away from Gahan. She reached for him, unable to stop herself. Gahan caught her up in an embrace that threatened to crack her ribs.

She held him tight for a moment before forcing herself to push him away. It should have shamed her to have the king witness such a display of affection.

But she didn't care.

Everyone dear to her watched her leave in the company of the king's men. She felt Gahan watching her until she passed through a side entrance of the king's receiving room. The passageway was meant for the king. The walls were plastered and painted. Even the ceiling was decorated with paintings of clouds and cherubs. But none of it pleased her. No, as she was escorted away by the king's men, she very much feared she'd experienced the last perfect moments of her life.

Once again, Bari was making sure she served his interests no matter the cost.

※

Lord Home waited until the room was clear before appearing before the king.

"Very interesting."

James looked at his mentor and head counselor. In many ways, he was more of a father than his own sire had ever been. "Do you think the Earl of Sutherland will appear?"

Lord Home thought for a moment before giving a single nod of his head. "The Sutherlands have been strong because of their close family ties. The earl seems to command such from his vassal lairds as well."

"With the exception of Laird Fraser."

"Aye, Yer Majesty," Lord Home said. "Yet his sister is a conniving one. I've heard that from others. There are rumors she forged a letter in my name and has a seal."

"That is a grave charge."

"It is indeed," Lord Home agreed. "I thought her dead, so I did not pursue the matter."

"And now?" the king inquired.

"Now?" Lord Home smiled unpleasantly. "Now we shall give her enough rope to hang herself with or expose the others in this mess. They will all testify against one another. Only actions will prove who is telling the truth."

"What is your plan?"

"It's simple, really. Since you had the good sense to secure Lady Matheson, I believe she is the key."

"Gahan Sutherland claims to love her."

"An interesting claim, but his brother wed for affection as well. It might be a condition of the Highlands." Lord Home pondered. "It will prove the key to solving this puzzle."

"How so?" James questioned.

"We shall see who attempts to bribe their way to Lady Matheson, and then we shall know who is not as loyal to your will as they just so passionately claimed. That will be the guilty man."

The king's eyes widened. "Indeed, it will prove the matter."

❧

"This is hell," Saer MacLeod declared when Gahan returned to the main hall. The new MacLeod laird looked completely ill at ease among the pomp and ceremony of the Court.

"Ye will nae find a den of worse cutthroats this side of the English border," Kael Grant confirmed as he joined them. He offered Gahan his hand and clasped his wrist in greeting.

"The king took Moira into his private apartments."

No one missed the deadly timbre in Gahan's tone. They all wore dark frowns as the courtiers nearby looked on.

"What in the name of Christ?" Kael Grant suddenly exclaimed. He turned and strode toward a raven-haired woman. He spun her around, earning a cutting look from her before she recognized him.

"Ye are supposed to be with Cousin Ruth, Nareen."

Nareen Grant had emerald green eyes that sparkled

with rage. She lowered herself prettily then rose back up and turned her back on her brother. Her skirts swished as she made a rapid path toward the doorway.

Kael gave chase, and Gahan followed. Kael reached for her arm again, but she turned and sent him a cutting glance while pointing toward the gardens. They both followed her, and she did not stop until she was well away from the palace.

"Now, explain why ye are here," Kael demanded.

"Because dear, sweet Cousin Ruth is a conniving bitch," Nareen informed her sibling with a smile on her face in case anyone was watching from across the green. "Ye never checked up on me after banishing me to the lowlands, sweet Brother. I had to see to myself."

"I would have known if she sent ye to Court," Kael insisted.

"She didn't. At least here, I have some protection," Nareen whispered. "Ruth is a madam. She has several young charges and will let them be used for the right amount of gold. Laird Ross stopped in one night, and I begged him to let me serve his daughter as a personal attendant. It was the only way to escape before Ruth sold me."

Kael Grant was enraged, his face turning red. "I will choke the life out of that bitch. She was to instruct ye on the running of a large estate."

Nareen laughed. "I do nae regret it, nae even now, Brother. Ye men are too arrogant by far. Ye look on women as naught but things to be used for yer amusement. It does nae matter a bit. I am clever enough to see to meself."

"Ye should nae have had to," Kael declared in a

hollow tone. "I never thought me own kin would prove to be untrustworthy."

"Trusting others, even kin, always makes ye vulnerable."

For a moment, Nareen's green eyes glistened with unshed tears. The fear and horror she'd faced was there, but she masked it quickly when she realized Saer and Gahan had also followed them. She looked at Gahan and smiled, the curving of her lips transforming her face into a radiant vision of beauty.

"I hear ye declared yer love for Moira Fraser before the king."

Surprise registered on all their faces, earning a soft, delicate laugh from her. "Naught is secret for long here at Court. The king has had her taken to the pink room. If ye have coin for bribing, I can sneak ye in there tonight."

Gahan stiffened. "Do nae toy with me, lass."

Nareen offered him a confident look. "Ye may have almost anything ye wish here for the right price. Attending Court is costly, and there are many who would let ye see the woman ye love for a few pieces of gold. They care only that ye leave her where the king has put her. No one will help ye free her."

"The truth will." Gahan didn't care for the way Nareen received his comment. There was a look of sympathy in her emerald eyes, one that looked very much like experience.

He opened his purse and pressed several gold pieces into her hand. "Ye have me gratitude."

Kael caught his shoulder. "Are ye sure that is wise?"

"The king did nae say I could nae see her."

And wise or not, the separation was eating a hole in him.

❧

The room she was shown to was a grand one.

Moira stood still for a long time, staring at her surroundings. The wood floor was polished and smooth, the varnish gleaming. The hearth had a pile of thick logs next to it, and a brass screen to keep sparks from jumping out onto the wooden floor. Several large windows let in the afternoon sunlight. She counted twenty-four panes of glass in each window, held together with iron to form each window frame. She reached out to trace one of the iron pieces, smiling at how smooth it was. Instead of shutters, there were thick draperies to cover the windows at night. There was enough fabric for several dresses. The expense defied her sense of logic. To spend so much coin on something that was only pretty offended her sense of duty to her clan. A castle was built for the protection of everyone.

Only a palace had such things.

There was a table near the hearth covered by a thick, colorful tapestry. Silver candleholders stood ready for sunset, set with beeswax candles. Two large chairs with seat cushions waited, but she turned to look at the bed next. Its canopy was huge. Long lengths of scarlet velvet ran down each of the four poles at its corners. At night they would be closed to keep the bed warm. The velvet was finer than any dress she had ever worn. She touched it gently, marveling at its silky softness. Like a baby's cheek.

Yet she discovered herself disenchanted with it all. They were naught but things, and they offered her no comfort. She craved the man who had so boldly declared he loved her. She would cherish that moment forever.

Moira turned in a circle but still felt misplaced. Tears irritated her eyes and she blinked them away, because she was no child and would not weep. Besides, weeping meant abandoning hope. She wouldn't do that, not until there was no longer even the possibility that she might see Gahan again.

The king had not appeared unjust. Yet she still rebelled against his having so much power. She reminded herself that God had put him on the throne. At least the Church would tell her that. Everyone was in their position due to divine intervention.

Was that why she'd woken up a maiden after her wedding?

At least it was cause for hope, a small notion that allowed her to believe heaven wanted her to be happy.

Her kin certainly didn't.

∽

Saer MacLeod stepped into Gahan's path when Kael moved off with his sister.

"Are ye sure ye can trust that lass?" he asked solemnly. "She has anger trapped inside her."

"Aye, but she was always a trustworthy woman."

"She feels betrayed," Saer observed. "That can change a person."

"I have no choice," Gahan replied. "I'll nae let Moira spend the night without me protection. Bari and his sister are accomplished assassins."

"They are black-hearted," Saer agreed. But he was more concerned with Nareen Grant. She was a handsome woman. Her emerald eyes were captivating, and she moved like she enjoyed her body.

That idea made his blood stir.

As laird, he would have to wed, and there had already been a few offers sent his way. But his time on the isles had given him a taste for females who enjoyed the pleasures of the flesh without pretense. Just thinking about a proper bride left him cold.

Nareen Grant was not proper.

She was inventive and a survivor. Kael was furious and rightly so, for a brother was expected to protect his female siblings. Yet Saer discovered himself pleased to see that Nareen had withstood the test.

Aye, he was a survivor, but so was she. Maybe there was a woman in the Highlands he could want enough to wed.

❧

Someone knocked on the door. Moira had time only to turn around before the royal retainers standing outside pushed the doors inward.

Two large men carried a silver tub between them. The back of it was higher than the foot, making it look like a slipper. A line of boys followed, each of them wearing a yoke with buckets of water attached to each end. Two older maids lowered themselves before directing the men on how to set up the tub.

"The king has told us to make ye welcome, Lady Matheson, and to see to yer comfort," one of the maids said.

They deposited the tub with a soft thud. There was a rush of water as the boys gladly poured their burdens into it. The second maid was using a long poker to stir up the coals in the hearth before she set new wood. There was a pop and crackle as it caught.

"We've got fresh water for yer bath, and the kitchens will be sending the hot water in but a moment."

Two more maids appeared with their arms full of clothing. They lowered themselves at the doorway before moving to the table and spreading out the gowns they'd brought.

"There is silk and velvet and the softest linen chemises ye ever felt."

Moira listened to the women chatter. There was an air of celebration about them, and it drove the dread from the chamber.

At least it made it less noticeable.

The bath was warm and cleaned away the dust from the road. The chemise she put on was soft, and she enjoyed it as she sat near the fire to dry her hair. But Moira refused to put on any of the dresses.

"Whyever not, dear?" the maid asked.

"Those are meant to be worn outside this chamber," Moira explained.

"Aye, ye're right about that. No need to lace ye in if ye will only need help getting free of it to enjoy the bed. But ye need a bit more than that chemise for the moment."

The woman winked before laying a dressing robe across her shoulders, and then she hurried back to the doors and opened them.

Moira's jaw dropped open as Gahan strode boldly

into the room. He swept her with his dark gaze before stepping out of the doorway to allow Cam and several other retainers carrying platters of food to enter.

Enjoy the bed…

Her cheeks burned scarlet, and she gripped the dressing robe tightly, but none of the men looked at her. Cam tugged on his bonnet then withdrew outside the doors. The king's retainers closed them firmly, leaving her facing Gahan.

Gahan took full advantage of her surprise and plucked up the dressing robe before she recovered her wits.

"What are ye doing here?" She jumped to her feet, earning a grin from him.

"Bribing the royal guards to let me in. Their orders are to make sure ye stay, so they took me gold happily." His dark gaze settled on her breasts. "I knew I was going to enjoy that chemise on ye. With the fire behind ye, it's transparent."

Her cheeks felt on fire, but she rose to the challenge—oh, it was a challenge, sure enough. The man in front of her was pure Highlander, and he was daring her to enjoy being his woman.

She moved slowly, her hips swaying without conscious thought. Instinct took command of her actions as her blood began to race. She moved toward him, enjoying the way his eyes focused on her.

"Ye have me at a disadvantage…" She trailed her fingers along his chin, loving the feel of his beard. "I was nae expecting company."

He cupped the side of her face, his fingers gently slipping across her skin. It was so delicate, yet the touch made her shudder.

"Ye should have more faith in me." His tone was low and edged with determination. He slid his hand into her hair and gripped it gently. "I will seek ye out, no matter where ye be, Moira, for ye are mine, and ye are going to be me wife."

He kissed her, sealing her response beneath his lips. There were reasons why she needed to argue. But his kiss burned all of them away. She didn't want to think. And yet she couldn't be overwhelmed either. It was almost insane to allow herself to be swept into a mindless state in so dangerous a place.

She slid her hands along his face and trailed kisses across his jawline. He made a low sound of enjoyment as she kissed the warm skin of his neck and then moved lower.

"I have nae had any practice in being a wife." She untied the laces to his collar. "For example, I have never scrubbed a back."

"I am fresh from the tub, lass, so that will nae need doing." He pulled his sword off his back and leaned it up against the wall by the bed. But he sat down on one of the chairs and extended his foot toward her.

"But ye could show me how well ye disrobe me." There was a wicked promise in his tone. "I believe it's a skill ye'll have need of. Very often."

She grasped the ends of the tie that held his boots closed and loosened the knot. As she leaned forward to work the tie along the antler horn buttons, he took the opportunity to look down her chemise.

"Ye have the sweetest pink nipples."

She straightened but realized she was ruining the game. There was a sense of control when she held his attention. It was something she'd heard whispers of—that time when a woman enchanted a man in lovemaking.

She took her time with the second boot, drawing a long chuckle from Gahan.

"Ye are toying with me, Moira."

She set the boot next to its twin and placed her hands on his bare knees. The fabric of the chemise pulled tight across her breasts, showing him her curves but not allowing him to see down the neckline anymore. She leaned closer and kissed him. Pressing her lips against his, she tasted the soft skin in a delicate motion. When she pulled back, she rubbed his knees and slid her hands up, beneath the edge of his kilt.

"Are ye going to order me to behave?" She pulled her hands back down to his knees and then stroked up farther. "Of course ye are nae me husband, and I find being a widow quite merry."

One dark eyebrow rose. "Merry?"

He stood and scooped her off her feet. In another moment, he was spinning around with her held tight against his chest. The blood rushed past her ears, making a roaring sound as her body tightened with excitement. He finally stopped and tossed her onto the bed.

"Would ye be merry if I left ye to yer widow's bed?"

She rolled over and flung her hair back. She laughed, and the sound surprised her, because it was husky and sultry. On all fours she faced him, feeling more alive than she could ever recall.

"A merry widow can play the games of a lover."

"So can husband and wife, Moira."

He opened his belt and caught his kilt before it slipped down to the floor. He tossed it onto the table with a practiced motion.

"Neither of us knows what marriage truly is," she said as she sat back on her heels. "Yet I know I want no more of the falseness that was my last marriage."

He pulled his shirt up and over his head, baring his body to her. His chest was covered in dark hair, the muscles hard and defined. His chest tapered down into a lean waist and hips. His cock stood out proudly, the head ruby red. Her cheeks flushed, but she realized it wasn't with shame, it was with anticipation.

She was exactly where she wanted to be.

He started to move toward her, but she held up her hand. He froze, waiting on her whim. There was something in his eyes that pleased her, a flicker of expectation that filled her with confidence. He was waiting for her to please him. Not because he demanded it of her, but because she wanted to be his lover.

She eased up her chemise, baring her thighs. His dark gaze settled on the naked skin, his lips thinning as she tugged the fabric higher. Her heart was beating hard but not racing. It felt deeper, more sensual than any experience she'd ever had. She paused with the fabric just covering her mons.

"Now I know ye're teasing me," he groaned.

"Aye," she admitted before raising the chemise all the way up and letting it fall to the surface of the bed. "But only because I want to be yer lover, nae just yer conquest."

"Those can be one and the same, lass."

His voice was so deep it almost sounded like he

was purring. A promise was brewing in his eyes, and need began to twist her insides. He moved toward her, placing his hands on her thighs and stroking her the same way she had him. She gasped, the contact between their flesh sending ripples of awareness through her.

"A lover returns the favors given…" He leaned down and kissed one puckered nipple. Sensation jolted her as he crawled farther up the bed.

She had to lean back, far back until she was lying on the bed. A pleased grin split his lips and he captured the same nipple and sucked it hungrily. She'd never realized a man's mouth might be so warm. It was searing and set her insides to boiling. Her clit was throbbing for attention, desire ripping through the teasing mood she'd been in. She reached for him, but he lifted away from her, his eyes burning.

"Nae just yet, lass…" He gripped her knees and spread her thighs. "I seem to recall ye tormenting me with yer sweet lips."

He was going to make her wait for it though. First, he stroked her, cupping her breasts and petting her belly with motions so slow she found it hard to remain still. Every inch of her skin began clamoring for contact. She didn't want to keep her eyes open either. It was like her sight interfered with her body feeling everything it might. She closed her eyes and arched into his touch, a tiny moan escaping her lips when he stopped just above her mons. He rubbed her belly, making a small circle that drove her mad with frustration. Anticipation was heightening all of her senses, intensifying every single touch.

"Ye are beautiful, Moira." He leaned down and kissed her belly. "I do nae think I have told ye how fair ye are."

She opened her eyes and gasped when she watched him shift his attention to her mons. He toyed with her curls for a moment before leaning down to kiss her clitoris.

"Holy mother of Christ!" she swore as she jerked. She didn't really gain any distance, because the hand he had resting on her belly pressed her down to the surface of the bed.

"Now who is bringing Christ into inappropriate moments?" he teased her.

"Well, I did nae expect ye to kiss me...there."

He settled his thumb on the spot he'd kissed, working it back and forth until the folds of her slit parted to allow him to touch her clitoris.

"Ye licked me cock." There wasn't a hint of shame in his tone. No, in fact there was the definite ring of promise.

"Ye cannae mean to..." Her mouth went dry, and her tongue refused to finish her thought.

"I swear there is nothing that could tear me away."

Her eyes remained wide as he lowered his head and made good on his promise. She bucked again, the level of heat almost too much to bear. It was searing and intense. She'd never felt so much sensation, except for when he was inside her. She craved the man in an unnatural manner. She clawed at the bedding, searching for something to hold onto as it felt like the world was spinning out of control. She arched up to press herself against his mouth, seeking enough pressure to unleash the explosion she felt brewing in her depths.

But he denied her. Instead he lapped her gently, flicking her clitoris with the tip of his tongue before trailing it through the center of her slit to the opening of her body.

"Ye are sweeter than cream…"

Every inch of her skin felt like it was on fire; perspiration even moistened her hair. He licked his way back to the top of her slit, this time closing his lips around the little button nestled there. It was almost enough…And yet release remained maddeningly out of reach. She growled as her frustration reached the point where she was sure to go mad.

"Stop toying with me, Gahan!" she panted.

"And do what instead?" His voice was hard with demand. She locked gazes with him, seeing the man she'd battled against the first few times they'd met. "Do ye want me to tumble ye quickly and leave before we're discovered?" He rose above her, crawling up the bed and trapping her with his huge body. "Or do ye want something more?" He settled himself between her thighs, the head of his cock slipping easily between her slick folds.

She held him, clamping her thighs around his hips as she gripped his shoulders. But he didn't thrust into her, didn't fill the emptiness threatening to make her scream.

"Swear ye'll wed me, Moira."

She slapped his shoulder and snarled. "Blackguard! To demand such a thing once ye've made it near impossible for me to think."

"Oh, I demand it, lass." His voice was hard, like

his body. He thrust into her, filling her passage with a quick motion that sent the air rushing out of her lungs. "I want to demand ye welcome me into yer bed, every night as ye are now."

He pulled free and thrust in again, quickly. The bed rocked with the force of his motion, and she raised her hips to take it.

"I demand that ye let the world know I am what ye crave…" The bed ropes creaked as he continued to ride her with a hard pace. "I demand ye never let yerself be at the mercy of that half brother of yers…"

Pleasure was tearing through her, but so was the need to make her own demands heard. She lodged her feet on the surface of the bed and heaved. She shoved him over onto his back and rose above him. He growled with satisfaction as he lifted her above his cock and impaled her on it.

"Well…I demand that ye stop risking yer position," she said.

He guided her up and down. It didn't take long for her to learn the rhythm. She was suddenly in complete control of their pace, yet still at the mercy of her desire. They were both caught in the same web.

"Me position means naught if it makes me a coward. I'll speak up and face the consequences me words bring."

He bucked beneath her and flipped her back over. His pace quickened, giving her the final amount of friction she needed to explode in rapture. She forgot to breathe and didn't care that her lungs burned. She was caught in the moment of twisting, wringing pleasure that touched every fiber of her being. Gahan ground his length into her, and she heard him snarl as his seed erupted into her womb. It was searing hot, setting off another wave of delight.

The bed became a trusted ally against the fatigue that settled over her. Her muscles were lax and exhausted. Her heart still pounded in hard motions even as it slowed. She felt light-headed, and her eyes closed as the room spun in a lazy circle. And she did not care. Not a bit.

Gahan gathered her close, rolling over onto his back and placing her head on his shoulder. She listened to the sound of his heartbeat as she savored the moment.

"Ye'll wed me, Moira."

He stroked her shoulder and hugged her tight. For the moment, everything was perfect.

⁂

Sunlight streamed through the windows, since the shutters had never been shut. Moira stretched, sighing.

"I am going to enjoy being wed to ye, lass."

Her eyes opened wide, and she sat up. The bedding slipped down her body, allowing the morning air to tease her bare breasts. Gahan's eyes settled on her puckering nipples.

"I'm going to enjoy it very, very much."

"Ye are still here."

Gahan was already on his feet and wearing his shirt. He was enjoying a thick slice of bread and cheese left from the meal they'd never touched.

"Gahan, ye must nae place yerself at risk for me."

One of his dark eyebrows rose. "Ye are in more danger of being gossiped about by being seen with me, lass. After all, yer kin are accusing me of crimes."

She stood up and found her chemise. "Lies." She sat down and pulled on her stockings, because the floor was chilled from the night. "I think Bari believes them, and that is what worries me. At times, I think I see madness in his eyes."

Now that her feet were no longer freezing, her belly rumbled. Gahan grinned and offered her some bread and cheese. The meal was simple, but she enjoyed the moment.

"What is that look for?" he asked. "Ye appear so forlorn."

"I fear reality is going to destroy this fine moment."

He stood and lifted the ends of his belt. His plaid was already pleated, and he secured it around his waist. "I welcome it, lass. It's time Bari's hold over ye was broken."

He was bold and determined, just as he'd been the first time she'd seen him. But instead of being intimidated by it, she rose and lifted his doublet off the chair. She held it up for him, easing it up his shoulders then fastening the buttons. Today, she was his comrade.

"I will wed ye, Gahan Sutherland, and I will be proud to say it to anyone."

Approval showed in his eyes. He cupped her face, rubbing it gently. "That pleases me, lass, more than I can say."

He wasn't a man who praised lightly. He was a Highlander and respected strength. Pride surged through her, because she realized she had defeated Bari in the only way that mattered—by making her own decisions and determining her own fate.

"I love ye, Gahan Sutherland, no matter what the future holds."

She turned and picked up the bodice she'd worn the day before. Pinned to the shoulder was a small length of Matheson plaid. She pulled the pin loose and let the fabric flutter to the floor. There was a soft tearing sound as Gahan tore a strip of his plaid. He offered it to her, and she pinned it in place. For just a moment, his eyes glistened, but it was so brief, she just might have imagined it.

"I love ye, Moira, and I pledge ye me strength and me name for as long as I live."

It was a vow heard in the Highlands for longer than anyone remembered—far longer than the vows spoken in the church. They were the words of the Highlands and the warriors who lived by the code of honor.

Someone knocked on the door, and it opened wide. Gahan offered her one last look before he turned to face what fate had in store for him. She intended to face it at his side.

Nine

"YOU HAVE DISOBEYED ME." KING JAMES IV SAT sternly on his throne, but Gahan was looking him straight in the eye.

"Ye did nae order me to stay away from her, Yer Majesty." Gahan held up his hand in protest, adding, "And if ye had, I would be guilty of disobeying ye, for there is no way I was going to let her spend the night unprotected."

"Do you question the readiness of His Majesty's guards?" Lord Home burst out.

Gahan chuckled and stared at the velvet curtain the man hid behind. There was a soft snort before he came into view.

"Ye do nae yet accept what I tell ye of her kin, Yer Majesty," Gahan explained. "Moira will be me wife, and I will never let harm touch her. Even if it means ye are displeased."

Lord Home's face darkened. "How dare you speak to your king like that?"

"If ye want coddling and empty words of praise, I suggest ye summon Bari and his sister. I am a

Highlander and a Sutherland. Ye'll hear the truth from me lips, no matter what it costs me."

"The vow of the knights of the crusades," the king muttered thoughtfully.

"And the Knights Templar."

The king's eyes brightened. "Is there any proof that the knights of that holy order settled in the Highlands?"

Gahan said, "Highlanders are nae like other men. We do nae accept defeat, and we do nae follow the undeserving. I fought for yer right to sit on that throne, and I'm ready to have ye decide this matter, but I will nae stand aside while me wife is left unprotected."

"She is not your wife," Lord Home argued.

Gahan smiled, but the expression wasn't pleasant. It promised Lord Home hell if the man was foolish enough to try him.

"She's wearing me colors this morning," Gahan informed them. "That's me bond and has been tradition in the Highlands longer than any of us recalls. It insults me for ye to claim I have nae honored her."

"I accept your reason," the king said clearly. "Wearing of your colors is a Highland tradition older than time."

Gahan nodded, hearing the man inside the boy.

A page wearing the royal colors approached from the side entrance. He lowered himself. The king gave him leave to rise, but the young man looked at Lord Home and didn't move until Lord Home had also gestured for him to rise.

The young king didn't miss the slight.

"The Earl of Sutherland is here," the boy said.

The king gestured to the guards at the door. They

pulled the doors open, revealing Lytge and Norris Sutherland. They both gave the king a respectful tug on the corner of their bonnets before walking through the doorway.

"Summon Laird Fraser and his sister," the king commanded. "We shall have an end to this."

⤾

"That has gained attention." Nareen Grant smiled sweetly, but her green eyes were full of mischief as she tapped the pin on Moira's shoulder with a delicate fingertip.

"I believe Gahan intended it to."

A soft tinkle of laughter passed Nareen's lips. "It is sometimes a challenge to understand Highlanders, even when we are both women of the same land."

Moira smiled. "Indeed it is."

"And ye are pleased?"

Moira nodded. "Me half brother sees me as a commodity, and me half sister would be a murderess."

"Most brothers see sisters in that light." Nareen was lost in thought for a moment. "Come, walk with me. Ye cannae appear concerned. That will nae do, nae for the wife of a Highlander."

They began to slowly stroll through the palace hallways. There was splendor everywhere she looked, but none of it pleased her. Behind those gilded doors, her fate was being decided. Time crawled by, tormenting her. Yet there was nothing to do but wait.

⤾

"The accusations Laird Fraser makes are grievous." Lord Home spoke firmly inside the king's receiving room. He aimed a hard look at the Frasers and Sutherlands standing in front of the king.

Lytge cocked his head to the side. "Well, it's good to know I did nae ride all the way down here for naught." He glared at Bari Fraser. "Even if I find it interesting that this man just swore his loyalty to me."

"I was trying to find me sister," Bari argued.

"Ye did nae know yer sister was still living."

"Enough," Lord Home said. "His Majesty will ask the questions."

The earl looked back at the king. For a moment, James looked too young to deal with the formidable men in the room.

The king drew in a deep breath and looked at Lytge. "Why did you imprison Sandra Fraser at Dunrobin?"

"Me sons locked her away until I recovered from the poison she applied to the inside of me cup. Life has a way of being dear when ye've almost felt it slip through yer fingers. I did nae order her hanged because I was feeling soft. It's nae in me to kill women."

"It was because ye knew I was innocent," Sandra protested.

"As innocent as Lucifer," Gahan growled.

"Be silent, bastard," Bari snarled.

The king slapped the arm of his chair. "The next person who speaks without being asked a question shall be removed to the dungeons."

"I brought ye something, Yer Majesty," Lytge said, opening a small bundle. "This is the hair ornament young Sandra there wore at me table. Ye'll see it opens to reveal a well for poison. Everyone knew it was hers, and I believe if ye show it to some of yer other nobles, they will identify it as hers as well."

The king took the small hairpin. It looked like a spring flower, but the center opened, revealing its evil purpose. It was made of gold, with pearls set into it. A jeweler had spent many hours creating it.

"You have given me a good suggestion, Laird Sutherland. I will see if anyone can identify the owner of this." The king handed it to Lord Home.

"Nae many will speak against the Sutherlands," Bari argued.

"I am not asking them to," the king said. "Lord Home, you shall ask only if they know who that has been seen on. Since your sister was at Court often when my father ruled, if it is hers, someone will recall. You will all remain at Court until I call for you again. Laird Fraser, you and your sister are dismissed."

The king gestured to the royal guards to open the doors. Bari and Sandra had no choice but to leave. Gahan tugged on the corner of his own cap, but the king shook his head.

"You'll stay, Gahan Sutherland."

"Yer Majesty," he protested, "I would prefer—"

"I know what you seek," the king said as the doors closed. "But I need to understand the Sutherlands, and that includes you. Your bride is sitting just beyond these doors. My court is secure."

Gahan wasn't pleased, not by far. But the sooner the king was happy, the sooner he might return to the Highlands.

❧

Bari Fraser stopped the moment they were far enough away from the other members of Court.

"Did ye wear that flower at Court?"

Sandra was angry, but she nodded. Bari drew in a deep breath.

"Ye'll go to our mother's family in Italy."

Her eyes brightened. Bari started walking toward their apartments. "I'll give ye gold. Ye must get on a ship leaving today. Cover yer face and hair so no one on the docks sees ye. Wear something common. I'll have to condemn ye in front of the king. Ye'll nae return to Scotland in this life."

"I hear it's warm in Italy, and that they wear silk dresses." She smiled but stopped. Bari turned to look at her. "Yet I will have me vengeance on Gahan Sutherland."

"Time is precious, Sandra."

"So is the knowledge that I will nae leave ye here defeated." She fluttered her eyelashes. "One last little strike to make sure the Sutherlands know they are nae untouchable."

Bari was intrigued. "What are ye thinking?"

Sandra smiled and pointed across the crowded rooms of the Court to where Moira sat. Nareen Grant looked up and stood as another lady called out to her. Leaving Moira alone.

"Love is such a rare thing, Gahan Sutherland might never find it again," Sandra purred. "He shall pay the price for locking me away."

Bari nodded. "A fair exchange."

❧

"My lady." Moira looked up, and a young page lowered himself. He leaned close to keep his words from drifting. "Gahan Sutherland bids you meet him in the garden labyrinth."

The boy was gone the instant he finished speaking. Moira looked for Nareen, but the Earl of Ross's daughter was demanding her attention.

The evening shadows were falling, but the moon was full. Gahan's promise to court her floated through her memory. A moonlit labyrinth was a perfect place to begin.

She moved toward the door and went outside without anyone noticing. The air was warm, and the smell of springtime made her smile. The labyrinth was made of hedges that might be groomed to change the maze. They rose two feet over her head. A shiver rippled over her skin as she entered the labyrinth, but she enjoyed it. The sensation was part of the maze's charm.

"Gahan?" She wasn't sure she should call out. There was likely more than one couple trysting in the moonlit garden. Someone whistled like a hawk, drawing a breathless sound from her. She picked up her skirt and hurried around the next bend.

"Ye always were stupid, Moira," Sandra announced with glee.

Bari caught her, binding her arms from behind. He slapped a hand over her mouth to muffle her. "Make it quick, Sandra," he growled. "We must be gone well before anyone looks for her."

Sandra pouted but put her hand into a hidden slit in her skirt and withdrew a dagger from a strap on her thigh. "Gahan Sutherland will suffer for locking me away in that tower." Sandra raised the dagger high, moonlight flashing on its blade.

Time froze, allowing Moira to feel each beat of her heart. Gahan's face rose in her memory, filling her with regret for the years they were going to be denied. She heard the blade whiz through the air. Sandra smiled, and then her head fell away from her body.

Bari released Moira, and she stumbled away, horrified. Gahan stood before her. She wasn't sure where he'd come from. The tip of his sword was poised at Bari's neck.

"Do not run him through," the king ordered.

His expression was grim as he struggled to obey his king. The blade was wet, and she gasped as she realized he'd decapitated Sandra.

"Easy, lass," Cam muttered as he caught her and held her steady on her feet.

The labyrinth was suddenly full of men, the moonlight casting them all in silver, like the heroes of some myth. Even Sandra's headless body looked surreal.

"Ye cannae mean to let him live," Gahan growled.

"No," the king confirmed to his retainers at his side. "He'll be judged by his peers and executed."

Bari was staring at Sandra's body, his face a mask of grief. The king's words drew Gahan's attention. Bari charged him in that moment, lunging around the sword pointed at him. The moonlight flashed off a small blade clutched in Bari's hand. Gahan roared and swung his sword in a wide arc. Bari's head rolled onto the ground, resting near Sandra's.

No one spoke until the heavy silence was broken

by Lytge Sutherland. "I trust there will be no further doubt as to the guilt of those two."

"Or of the Sutherland loyalty," the king assured him quietly. He drew himself up and began walking back toward the palace. The royal retainers followed him.

Gahan handed off his sword to Cam. Moira's entire body shook, her knees threatening to buckle. Gahan gathered her into his embrace, and she buried her face against his chest.

"How did...how did ye know where I was?"

He kissed her forehead. "Ye are mine, Moira, and I protect what is mine. There was no way I'd let ye out of Sutherland sight, even if it was the king demanding me presence."

He took her hand and led her away from the bodies. She did not look back.

❧

"What do ye mean we are still nae free to depart?" Gahan's voice was raised, but the king only grinned at him.

"There is still a sin to be accounted for."

Gahan ground his teeth, frustration edging his tone. "And what might that be, Yer Majesty?"

"You are guilty of fornication, and I will witness the wedding myself," he declared.

"Well now, lad, if that's the way ye plan to rule, there are going to be a lot of weddings!" Lytge exclaimed with a chuckle.

The king laughed. "In this case, I must witness the nuptials before bestowing the title of Laird Fraser upon your son, as there are no other claims better than his wife's. I hope the Fraser clan will return to being productive and happy with a laird who is worthy of their loyalty."

Everyone waited to see what Gahan would say. He would have to wear the colors of the Fraser, leaving his father's plaid behind. It would be a hard thing for any Highlander, because loyalty was more important than position.

"I ask you to become more than what your father has given you, Gahan Sutherland," the king said. "You shall have to earn the respect of the Frasers, and I do not think it shall be a simple thing."

Gahan spoke at last. "It will be a challenge."

"A son of mine is worthy of any challenge," Lytge declared.

"As such, you shall retain the noble crest of your father," the king decided. "Yet you shall be created a baron in your own right, and that title shall pass to your son."

Gahan locked stares with his father for a long moment. The earl nodded once, granting his blessing.

"I will strive to earn that respect, Yer Majesty."

"I believe they will give it," Moira assured him. "I know I shall."

❧

The moment the priest finished the last blessing, the music began. Dancers filled the floors as platter after platter of food was laid on the tables. Wine and whisky flowed freely, but Moira merely sipped at her glass.

"Do ye nae like the wine?" Gahan asked her.

"It is well."

"Then why are ye nae drinking it?"

She set the goblet aside, and a young lad reached for it to make sure it was not unattended. She slid her hand over her husband's jaw and looked into his dark eyes.

"I have been granted something I thought impossible, and would nae suffer having me wits dulled. I want to know ye are me husband, without the slightest doubt. Ye should set yers aside too."

He handed his own goblet to a lad waiting on him. "I believe I am going to enjoy taking direction from ye, lass."

"Hmm, I can think of a few…suggestions I may have." She leaned forward so he was treated to a view of her cleavage. "But I need to be free of this bodice first."

He grinned arrogantly, and it made her bold again. He pushed his chair back and scooped her up, to the delight of the Court. They cheered him on as he carried her out of the hall.

❧

"That savage is looking at ye again," Abigail Ross complained to Nareen. The Earl of Ross's daughter never liked sharing attention.

"I do nae know the man, lady," Nareen said.

Abigail Ross frowned and glared past Nareen at Saer MacLeod. But he only smiled back at her. The curving of his lips didn't soften his features any. Instead, he looked like a hungry wolf making ready to pounce. Abigail shuddered and made the sign of the cross over herself.

"Ye must have done something to draw his attention." She patted her chest, as though she might be able to calm her racing heart with the gesture. "I simply cannae tolerate something like this. Tell him ye are nae interested, or ye shall be dismissed. I need no gossip clinging to the skirts of me attendants."

Nareen frowned, but Abigail gestured her away. "Go on, I'll nae tolerate even the hint of scandal."

She turned with a grunt, her chin in the air.

"Well, that saves me the trouble of getting around that old bat," Saer muttered as he moved close to her.

Nareen offered him a smile, leaning forward just a bit. "It saves ye naught, for she was never the obstacle between us. There is, in fact, naught between us. I find that very pleasing. I also find me position pleasing, so do nae ruffle the lady's feathers."

"If staring unsettles her, it's little wonder she is unwed. But I am nae here to talk about her." He reached for her hand, but she slapped his before their skin connected.

"Ye have nothing I wish to hear. Good-bye, Laird MacLeod." His nostrils flared. It was a small response, but one she noticed. With a little flare of her skirts, she lowered herself and turned away.

Saer watched her go. Her poise was perfect, her carriage unfaltering as she made her way through the Court. She smiled and nodded, never appearing hurried. Anyone else would have seen nothing to fault her for. But he'd seen the fear in her eyes.

What infuriated him was the fact that the fear did not make her timid. Instead, she used it to fuel her determination. His cock stirred as he detected just a hint of the scent of her skin. It was a savage thing to think and feel, but it was honest. He suspected Nareen Grant might just understand him. It would take a woman of courage to do so.

First, he'd have to gain her attention.

※

Saer MacLeod was already in the stable when Kael Grant appeared. The horizon was just showing a hint of pink, but Saer had his stallion saddled and ready.

Kael was surprised to see that his own stallion was also ready.

"Did I get drunk enough last eve to forget I told ye I'd be leaving at dawn?" Kael asked. He checked the straps and bridle on his horse, then nodded.

Saer swung his leg up and over the back of his horse before responding. "Depends on how ye define the phrase 'told me.'"

"It's a simple enough concept, man."

Saer chuckled, the sound low and dark. "Ye're going after yer kinswoman who proved untrustworthy—the cousin who almost sold off yer sister."

Kael mounted, as did his men. He gathered up the reins and glared at Saer. "It needs doing. I trusted her with me sister."

"Aye, that is the sort of thing ye cannae allow to go unpunished," Saer agreed. "And I'm going with ye." The MacLeod retainers were waiting just a few feet away to follow their laird.

Kael's brow furrowed. "Why?"

"Because yer sister is a woman who respects those who prove themselves. I plan to earn her respect and prove me worth."

Kael growled, but Saer was already riding through the yard. The man wasn't asking to come along; he was declaring his intention to do so. It should have bruised his pride, but Kael found himself amused. His sister Nareen had never conformed to the submissive role her sex was restricted to. Men had offered for her, powerful ones. But she'd turned them down because she would not submit. He doubted Saer MacLeod would be content with anything but full surrender.

It was possible the savage laird from the isles was exactly what his sister needed.

"I did not expect to find you here, Laird Sutherland."

Lytge opened his eyes but made the cross over himself before turning to look at the king. It took a moment to rise from his knees.

"For all our bluster and titles, we are but men, Yer Majesty."

James offered him a pleased look. "We are, indeed. I hope I shall see you again."

The earl looked around the chapel, his face reflecting years of memories. At last he pulled in a deep breath and nodded, as though he'd completed something he'd been working on.

"Nay, Yer Majesty. Each man needs to accept his own mortality." He gave the king a hard look. "Ye'll understand it more in time, but I think ye have begun to see that life is a fleeting thing. I'll nae walk the halls of this palace again."

"Yet you are strong and healthy," the king argued.

"And a man who has seen more than sixty years."

Lytge winked. "I'm nae planning on shaking Saint Peter's hand just yet, mind ye. He's been kind to me, though. Letting me watch me sons grow to men. I'm going north to Sutherland to watch me grandson learn to walk, and hopefully see the birth of another one or two."

He reached out and gripped the king's shoulder. The royal retainers edged closer, but James waved them back.

"Ye are always welcome at Dunrobin." Lytge moved back a step and lowered himself before the young king.

"You are a true nobleman," the king replied.

But the earl grimaced. "I'm a Highlander, lad! From the day me mother pushed me into this world, I've been proud to be a man of the North. Me sons will bury me in me kilt, and if God is kind, He'll let me tumble a buxom wench the night before He takes me away."

The earl rose up and flashed an arrogant grin at the king, then turned and strode from the chapel. There was a spring in his step, and he roared when he reached the doors, "Saddle the horses and wake me son, Gahan! We're heading north to Sutherland, lads! I need to see the Highlands!"

∽⌾∾

"Wake up, lass."

Moira groaned and opened her eyes. Gahan laughed at her. "Come, Wife, ye can sleep at Seabhac."

She smiled, her head clearing as excitement burned the fog away.

"Do I detect enthusiasm for our journey?"

"Indeed ye do, Husband." She left the bed and began pulling on her stockings.

The velvet-draped bed didn't even gain a second glance as she left the chamber. The opulent hallway didn't interest her. Being able to appear beside Gahan was what she craved, and for the first time, there was nothing to stop her from doing it.

The earl was already making ready. Lytge turned to look at them. "About time ye got out of bed!"

Horses shifted and snorted. Norris was already in the saddle, eager to rejoin his wife. The Sutherland banners were in the hands of the standard-bearers who would ride at the front of the columns, but the Fraser retainers appeared with their own flags. They looked toward Gahan, waiting for him to place them. There was strain on their faces as they watched to see what their new laird would be like.

"We'll ride behind me father, lads." Gahan took the stallion they'd readied for him. A length of Fraser plaid was draped over the saddle. Gahan stared at it for a long moment before reaching out to take it. "And it seems I'm wearing the wrong colors. Me thanks for correcting me."

The Frasers sent up a cheer. Moira followed her husband into the palace again to seek a chamber to change in.

"Ye're going to wear it?"

"Pleat yer colors for me, Moira. It is yer place to pass them to me."

He pulled his belt open and caught his Sutherland plaid. He took a moment to fold the cloth carefully before setting it on a table.

She shivered with joy. Tears filled Moira's eyes and made wet paths down her cheeks. Gahan cupped her chin and looked at her in confusion.

"I'm happy," she explained. "So very happy to see these colors going on a man worthy of them."

"Yet ye cry…"

"Women do that," Norris interrupted from the doorway. "Do nae waste any time trying to make sense of it."

Moira looked around Gahan as she helped him into the kilt. She stuck her tongue out at her new brother-in-law.

Norris laughed and held the door open for his brother. He looked at the kilt and sniffed. "I suppose I cannae curse the Fraser name anymore."

Gahan smoothed a hand down the front of his kilt, staring at the colors for a long moment. He finally nodded and looked up. "Nay, ye cannae. Because I am Laird Fraser."

He walked to the door, and the Fraser retainers let out another cheer. The horses jerked against their handlers, but the Frasers didn't quiet down quickly. Gahan turned and offered Moira a hand.

"I think it's time ye showed me Seabhac Tower."

She smiled, gripping his hand and pulling him through the doorway. "I cannae wait."

Read on for excerpts from Mary Wine's Scottish romance
Available now from Sourcebooks Casablanca

To Conquer a Highlander

Highland Hellcat

Highland Heat

The Highlander's Prize

From

To Conquer a Highlander

Scotland 1437, McLeren land

FIRE COULD BE A WELCOME SIGHT TO A MAN WHEN he'd been riding a long time and the sun had set, leaving him surrounded by darkness. But the sight of flames on the horizon could also be the most horrifying thing any laird ever set his eyes on.

Torin McLeren wanted to close his eyes in the hopes that the orange flames illuminating the night might not be there when he opened them again. He could smell the smoke on the night air now but didn't have the luxury of allowing the horror to turn his stomach. He was laird, and protecting his holdings was his duty.

Digging his spurs into his horse, he headed toward the inferno. Wails began to drown out the hissing flames. Laments carried on the night wind as wives and mothers mourned bitterly. The scent of blood rose above the smoke, the flickering orange light illuminating the fallen bodies of his clansmen. He stared at the carnage, stunned by the number of dead and wounded. He might be a Highlander and no stranger to battle, but this was a village, not a piece of land disputed and fought over by nobles. This was McLeren land and had been for more than a century.

A horror straight out of hell surrounded him. Mercy hadn't been present here—he'd seen less carnage after fighting the English. The slaughter was almost too much to believe or accept. His horse balked at his command to ride forward, the stallion rearing up as the heat from the blaze became hot against its hide. Torin cursed and slid from the saddle. Every muscle in his body tightened, rage slowly coming to a boil inside him. Hands reached out to him, grasping fingers seeking him as the only hope of righting the wrong that had been inflicted on them.

His temper burned hotter than the fire consuming the keep in front of him. They suffered raids from time to time, but this was something else entirely. It was war. The number of bodies lying where they had fallen was a wrong that could not be ignored. Nor should it be. These were his people, McLerens who trusted in his leadership and his sword arm for protection.

"*Justice…*"

One single word but it echoed across the fallen bodies of men wearing the same plaid he did. Every retainer left to keep the peace was lying dead, but they had died as Highlanders. The ground was littered with the unmoving forms of their attackers. His gaze settled on one body, the still form leaking dark blood onto his land, the kilt drawing his interest. Lowering his frame onto one knee, Torin fingered the colors of his enemy. The fire lit the scarlet and blue colors of the McBoyd clan. His neighbor and apparently now his enemy.

McBoyds? It didn't make sense. These were common people. Good folk who labored hard to feed their families. Every McLeren retainer stationed there knew and accepted that they might have to fight for their clan, but that did not explain the number of slain villagers. There was no reason for such a slaughter. No excuse he would ever swallow or accept. McLerens did not fear the night, be they common born or not. While he was laird, they would not live in fear.

"There will be justice. I swear it." His voice carried authority, but to those weeping over their lost family, it also gave comfort. Torin stood still only for a moment, his retainers backing him up before he turned and remounted his horse. He felt more at home in the saddle, more confident. His father had raised him to lead the McLerens in good times and bad. He would not disappoint him or a single McLeren watching him now.

"Well now, let us see what the McBoyds have to say for themselves, lads."

Torin turned his stallion into the night without a care for the clouds that kept the moonlight from illuminating the rocky terrain. He was a Highlander, after all. Let the other things in the dark fear him.

From

HIGHLAND HELLCAT

"COME, MY BEAUTY, WE SHALL SEE IF WE CAN IMPRESS anyone tonight with our skill."

Brina patted the mare on the side of the neck, and the animal gave a toss of its silken mane. She smothered a laugh before it betrayed to those around just how much she was looking forward to riding out of her father's castle. She gained the back of the mare, and the animal let out a louder sound of excitement. Brina clasped the animal with her thighs and leaned low over its neck.

"I agree, my beauty. Standing still is very boring."

Brina kept her voice low and gave the mare its freedom. The animal made a path toward the gate, gaining speed rapidly.

Brina allowed her laughter to escape just as she and the mare crossed beneath the heavy iron gate that was still raised.

"Don't be out too long… Dusk is nearly fallen…" the Chattan retainer set to guarding the main entrance to Chattan Castle called after her, but Brina did not even turn her head to acknowledge the man.

Being promised to the church did have some advantages after all. Her undyed robe fluttered out behind her because the garment was simple and lacked any details that might flatter her figure. There were only two small tapes that buttoned toward the back of it in order to keep the fabric from being too cumbersome.

"Faster…"

The mare seemed to understand her and took to the rocky terrain with eagerness. The wind was crisp, almost too chilly for the autumn. Brina leaned down low and smiled as she moved in unison with the horse. The light was rapidly fading, but the approaching night didn't cause her a bit of worry.

She was a bride of Christ, the simple gown that she wore more powerful even than the fact that her father was laird of the Chattan. No one would trifle with her, even after day faded into night.

But that security came with a price, just as all things in life did. She straightened up as the mare neared the thicket, and she spied her father's man waiting on her.

Bran had served as a retainer for many years, and he was old enough to be her sire. He frowned at her as she slid from the back of the mare.

"Ye ride too fast."

Brina rubbed the neck of the horse for a moment, biting back the first words that came to her lips.

"What does it matter; Bran? I am promised to the church, not betrothed like my sisters. No one cares if I ride astride."

If she had been born first or second to Robert Chattan, there would be many who argued against her riding astride, because most midwives agreed that doing so would make a woman barren.

Bran grunted. "It's the speed that ye ride with that most would consider too spirited for a future nun."

Brina failed to mask her smile. "But I shall be a Highland nun, not one of those English ones who are frightened of their own shadows."

Her father's retainer grinned. "Aye, ye are that all right, and I pity those who forget it once ye are at the abbey and training to become the mother superior."

Bran turned and made his way into the thicket. Brina followed him while reaching around to pull her small bow over her head. The wood felt familiar in her grip. It was a satisfying feeling, one for which she might thank her impending future as well. Her sisters had not been taught to use any weapons. They were both promised to powerful men, and the skills of hunting would be something that those Highlanders might find offensive to their pride.

She snorted. Going to the church suited her well indeed, for she had no stomach for the nature of men. She could use the bow as well as any of them.

"At least I know that ye will nae go hungry." Bran studied the way she held the bow, and nodded with approval. "Those other nuns will likely follow ye even more devoutly because ye can put supper on the table along with saying yer prayers."

"I plan to do much more than pray."

From

ℋIGHLAND ℋEAT

1439

SPRING WAS BLOWING ON THE BREEZE.

Deirdre lifted her face and inhaled. Closing her eyes and smiling, she caught a hint of heather in the air.

But that caused a memory to stir from the dark corner of her mind where she had banished it. It rose up, reminding her of a spring two years ago when a man had courted her with pieces of heather and soft words of flattery.

False words.

"Ye have been angry for too long, Deirdre."

Deirdre turned her head slightly and discovered her sister Kaie standing nearby.

"And ye walk too silently; being humble doesn't mean ye need try and act as though ye are nae even here in this life."

Kaie smiled but corrected herself quickly, smoothing her expression until it was once again simply plain. "That is my point exactly, Deirdre. Ye take offense at everything around ye. I am content. That should nae be a reason for ye to snap at me."

Her sister wore the undyed robe of a nun. Her hair was covered now, but Deirdre had watched as it was cut short when Kaie took her novice vows. Her own hair was still long. She had it braided and the tail caught up so that it didn't swing behind her. The convent wouldn't hear any vows from her, not for several more years to come.

"But ye are nae happy living among us, Deirdre, and that is a sad thing, for those living in God's house should be here because they want to be."

"Well, I like it better than living with our father, and since he sent my dowry to the church, it is only fitting that I sleep beneath this roof."

Kaie drew in a stiff breath. "Ye are being too harsh. Father did his duty in arranging a match for us all. It is only fair that he would be cross to discover that ye had taken a lover."

Melor Douglas. The man she'd defied everything to hold, because she believed his words of love.

Deirdre sighed. "True, but ye are very pleased to be here and not with Roan McLeod as his wife. Father arranged that match for ye as well, and yet you defied his choice by asking Roan McLeod to release ye. There are more than a few who would call that disrespectful to our sire."

Her sister paled, and Deirdre instantly felt guilty for ruining her happiness.

"I'm sorry, Kaie. That was unkind of me to say."

Her sister drew in a deep breath. "Ye most likely think me timid, but I was drawn to this convent. Every night when I closed my eyes, I dreamed of it, unlike ye…"

Kaie's eyes had begun to glow with passion as she spoke of her devotion, but she snapped her mouth shut when she realized what she was saying.

Deirdre scoffed at her attempt to soften the truth. "Unlike me and my choice to take Melor Douglas as my lover."

It was harsh but true, and Deirdre preferred to hear it, however blunt it might be.

"He lied to ye. Ye went to him believing ye'd be his wife."

"Ye do nae need to make excuses for me, Kaie. I made my choice, and I will nae increase my sins by adding dishonesty to them. Everyone knows, anyway. It seems all I ever hear about here, how I am unworthy of the veil ye wear so contentedly." Deirdre shrugged. "At least no one shall be able to claim I am intent on hiding my actions behind unspoken words and unanswered questions."

Her sister laughed. A soft, sad little sound that sent heat into Deirdre's cheeks, because Kaie was sweet and she didn't need to be discussing such a scarlet subject.

"Ye have ever been bold, Deirdre. I believe ye should have been born a son for all the courage ye have burning inside ye. For ye are correct, I am content, and there is no place I would rather be but here. Living a simple life. Roan McLeod was a kind soul to allow me to become a bride of Christ instead of his wife. Wedding me would have given him a strong alliance with our clan."

Scottish Lowlands, 1487

"Keep yer face hidden."

Clarrisa jerked back as one of the men escorting her hit the fabric covering the top of the wagon she rode inside of. An imprint of his fist was clearly visible for a moment.

"Best keep back, my dove. These Scots are foul-tempered creatures, to be sure. We've left civilization behind us in England." There was a note of longing in Maud's voice Clarrisa tried to ignore. She couldn't afford to be melancholy. Her uncle's word had been given, so she would be staying in Scotland, no matter her feelings on the matter.

Better to avoid thinking about how she felt; better to try to believe her future would be bright.

"The world is in a dark humor," Clarrisa muttered. Her companion lifted the gold cross hanging from her girdle chain and kissed it. "I fear we need a better plan than waiting for divine help, Maud."

Maud's eyes widened. Faster than a flash, she reached over and tugged one of Clarrisa's long braids. Pain shot across her scalp before the older woman sent to chaperone her released her hair. "You'll mind your tongue, girl. Just because you're royal-blooded doesn't give you cause to be doubting that the good Lord has a hand in where you're heading. You're still bastard-born, so you'll keep to your place."

Clarrisa moved to the other side of the wagon and peeked out again. She knew well who she was. No one ever let her forget, not for as long as she could recall. Still, even legitimate daughters were expected to be obedient, so she truly had no right to be discontented.

So she would hope the future the horses were pulling her toward was a good one.

The night was dark, thick clouds covering the moon's light. The trees looked sinister, and the wind sounded mournful as it rustled the branches. But Clarrisa didn't reach for the cross hanging from her own waist. No, she'd place her faith in her wits and refuse to be frightened. That much was within her power. It gave her a sense of balance and allowed her to smile. Yes, her future would hold good things, because she would be wise enough to keep her demeanor kind. A shrew never prospered.

"Far past time for you to accept your lot with more humbleness," Maud mumbled, sounding almost as uninterested as Clarrisa felt. "You should be grateful for this opportunity to better your lot. Not many bastards are given such opportunities."

Clarrisa didn't respond to Maud's reminder that she was illegitimate. There wasn't any point. Depending on who wore the crown of England, her lineage was a blessing or a curse.

"If you give the Scottish king a son—"

"It will be bastard-born, since I have heard no offer of marriage," Clarrisa insisted.

Maud made a low sound of disapproval and pointed an aged finger at her. "Royal-blooded babes do not have to suffer the same burdens the rest of us do. In spite of the lack of blessing from the church your mother suffered, you are on your way to a bright future. Besides, this is Scotland. He'll wed you quickly if you produce a male child. He simply doesn't have to marry you first, because you are illegitimate. Set your mind to giving him a son, and your future will be bright."

Clarrisa doubted Maud's words. She lifted the edge of the wagon cover again and stared at the man nearest her. His plaid was belted around his waist, with a length of it pulled up and over his right shoulder. The fabric made a good cushion for the sword strapped to his wide back.

Maybe he was a Scotsman, but the sword made him look like any other man she had ever known. They lived for fighting. Power was the only thing they craved. Her blood was nothing more than another way to secure what the king of Scotland hungered for.

Blessing? Not for her, it wouldn't be.

About the Author

Mary Wine is a multi-published author in romantic suspense, fantasy, and Western romance. Her interest in historical reenactment and costuming also inspired her to turn her pen to historical romance with her popular Highlander series. She lives with her husband and sons in Southern California, where the whole family enjoys participating in historical reenactment.